Maggie leaned back against the dark red plastic seat, "Millie, are you still making your own pies?"

Millie put her hands on her hips, "Now, honey, who'd make them if I didn't. I sure am. Want some?"

"You bet, Millie. Got any key lime pie?"

"That I do. Picked them limes this mornin' and squeezed 'em myself. Want some?"

"Sure. But first, we need sandwiches. What's good?"

"I reckon I should tell you it's all good. And it is, pretty much. But, I'd have the fish sandwich myself, with fries. They're always good. And the fish was caught this mornin'."

"Perfect. That's what I'll have."

"Me, too."

Don't miss other

Maggie McGill Mysteries by

Sharon Burch Toner

Maggie's Image

Watch for the next Maggie mystery

To be available in 2010

MAGGIE'S

ART

A Maggie McGill Mystery

SHARON BURCH TONER

ACKNOWLEDGEMENTS

My heartfelt thanks to Patricia Ybarra and Orangeport Studios whose special genius creates cover designs that truly capture the spirit of the Maggie McGill Mysteries.

I also wish to thank marine consultant, Gloria Smith, whose knowledge of sailboats and the sea has been so valuable and taught me, irrevocably, the difference between the helm and a tiller.

Chapter One

"You must help me, Maggie! I'm desperate! I feel so angry! I told him not to take Bitsy to the beach. I mean, Bitsy's not used to the sun. You wouldn't think a dog could get a sunburn, but she does. When she came back her little nose was really pink! George just refuses to pay attention to anything I say. Then, he . . . "

The beach. Hot sun. Waves lapping on the white sand. Pelicans diving for fish. Maggie struggled to bring her attention back to Mrs. Fortescue and her problems with her husband, George. Was the air in her office stuffy? Why was she having trouble focusing on Madeline Fortescue? Forcibly Maggie brought her attention to her client.

" . . . so, I just told him I wouldn't stand for it!" Madeline Frotescue stopped and peered over her sparkling purple glasses waiting for a response. But because she hadn't heard most of what it was that Mrs. Frotescue wouldn't stand for, Maggie was at a loss to know what to reply.

"How did you feel about that?" A therapist's standard response. Glancing at the clock Maggie noted thankfully that the session was nearly over.

As the door closed behind her client, Maggie breathed a sigh of relief that was made even greater when she realized that Mrs.

Frotescue was the last client of the day. Maggie leaned back in her chair and propped her size five feet on an open desk drawer.

What was happening to her? She had struggled all day to maintain her focus with her clients. Today had been one of the worst of her counseling career.

Anyone might find it difficult to stay focused with Mrs. Fortescue. But the others. Her clients needed and deserved better than they had received from her today. Worse yet, today was the culmination of a trend that had begun months ago.

Maggie sighed and put her feet back on the floor. Absentmindedly, she returned her pen to the drawer, locked the client files in her desk, and, gathering her things, left her office. The still bright sunlight hit her with an almost physical force that caused her to screw up her eyes into a fierce squint. A gentle warm sea breeze stirring off the ocean a few blocks away provided only small relief from the sun's persistent warmth. As Maggie walked slowly across the hot parking lot to her car, the heat of the pavement seared through the soles of her shoes causing her to curl her toes in protest.

Last month she had traded her racy old sports car for this new sedate sedan. Sensible. A sensible car. She was a sensible person. A pleasant home. An established career. Good friends. What more could anyone want? She should be excited about her life. She should be happy.

The car was stifling inside, hot as only a car sitting in the sun on a Florida summer day can become. Unbelievably, suffocatingly hot. The heat rose up to meet her as she opened the door. A living thing, it reached out hot cloying arms and, enveloping her, pulled the breath out of her. Quickly she slid into the driver's seat, opened all the windows, started the engine, and put the air-conditioning on high. Her hands tingled at the touch of the hot steering wheel, causing her to guide the car with only her fingertips for the first few minutes. Ugh!

A few blocks down the street, the air-conditioning began to put a cool edge on the unbearable heat. She rolled up the windows, pushed a CD into the player and settled for her drive home, a condominium in an over-fifty complex only blocks from the Gulf of Mexico.

The median of the Tamiami Trail, a wide multi-lane avenue, was lined with palm trees, their tops tossing now as the wind picked up. As she negotiated the afternoon rush hour traffic, Maggie marveled at how quickly this small south Florida town had grown into a city.

A few giant raindrops plopped lazily on the windshield as she pulled into the carport. She jumped from the car and dashed for the covered walkway leading to the elevator. The afternoon rain was late today, but black clouds behind her ominously promised spectacular rain and pyrotechnics soon.

Her neurotic black cat, Tilly, met her at the door. Maggie turned the air-conditioning down a few degrees. Followed by Tilly she changed her work clothes for shorts and a tee shirt and examined herself in the mirrored closet door. Her normally happy face frowned as serious green eyes gazed back at her from under tousled reddish-blond hair. The white shorts and dark blue shirt revealed a petite, just five feet even, middle-aged woman with laugh lines around her eyes and mouth, pale skin that freckled more easily than it tanned, a still trim body. Critically, she examined her tummy and behind. Plumper than she would like. Oh, well.

With a sigh she wandered through the apartment, poured a tall iced tea and collapsed on the sofa to consider her situation. Tilly settled into her lap after a few circles. Outside the sky darkened dramatically. With a loud clap of thunder, the rain began to pound down. Tilly quivered and tucked her head under Maggie's arm.

Is this burn out? Did she need another vacation? Should she consider another line of work? What would it be? She'd worked hard to get where she was. Going back to graduate school in mid-life hadn't been easy, and establishing a practice had been a struggle. At this point it might be too late to start something new.

For the first time she wondered if she should have remarried. Michael Thompson certainly had been eligible and he had professed undying love and affection. A nice man. Maggie had liked him and felt comfortable with him. He was financially comfortable. Life with Michael would have been comfortable. But Maggie hadn't been willing to settle for comfortable. She wanted more. More what she wasn't sure. But more.

Round and round the thoughts raced through her mind. Finally with a sigh she sat her perspiring tea glass on a coaster on the wicker coffee table and, closing her eyes, leaned back into the sofa's soft pillows. Sighing again, she let the tension of the day drain out. Her body seemed to relax in jerky little creaks. Above her head the ceiling fan droned with a gentle pit-pat of the blades circulating slowly. Outside the rain came down steadily, monotonously.

Maggie wandered through a spacious house filled with pleasant furnishings. The house was traditionally designed and furnished. Small groups of people clustered in the corners of the rooms. Some of the people followed her, holding on to her clothing. She could feel them slowing her progress. The people seemed to want something from her. As she walked, she felt herself growing tired and then weak. As she grew weaker, moving became an effort. She must get out of there. Maggie opened the heavy carved entry door only to find iron bars across the entrance. She turned around and for the first time noticed iron bars on all of the windows. Frantically she struggled from room to room, only to find each opening covered with iron bars. Prison! She was in a prison! She felt weak, heavy, unable to move.

Maggie woke with a start, pushing at the sofa pillows that had fallen on her while she slept. Tilly stirred but slept on. Yuck! What a dreadful dream! She sat for moment, still as a statue, halfway in the dream, halfway awake, staring across the room, but seeing nothing.

Finally, she shook herself and said aloud, "Oh dear! Oh dear!" Clearly, a part of her psyche felt imprisoned. Had her life become too traditional? Too pleasant? Too predictable? Too sensible? It fit. It made her problems focusing perfectly understandable. If a part of her felt trapped, then, of course, it would be seeking escape by spacing out. Oh, dear!

Briiing! The shrill ringing of the telephone interrupted her thoughts. Briiing! Briiing!

"All right. All right," Maggie muttered aloud.

Briiing!

"All right. I'm coming."

Still muttering she picked up the phone.

"Hello! Mom! Is that you?" Allie's voice was clear and close.

"Oh, hi, honey," answered Maggie. Then, as she became more alert, Maggie squealed, "Where are you? I thought you were in Europe."

"I am. In fact, I'm calling from my hotel on the Left Bank, in PARIS!" Allie's voice rose with excitement, "You can't believe how perfectly wonderful it is here! Think about anything good you've ever heard about this city and magnify it at least twenty times and you might come close to knowing how marvelous it is!"

Maggie sighed inside herself. Giving a little shake to dispel the dream, she said to her daughter, "Really! It sounds perfect. How come you're in Paris? I thought you were working." Maggie's daughter, Allie, was a photographer who traveled both in the States and, at times, abroad, making photo portraits of children and their animals.

Allie giggled, "I was. But I finished early and decided to have a few days here to reward myself for being so diligent. And am I ever glad I did! I've been doing *le shopping*!" Allie paused, then, with concern in her voice, "Mom, are you all right? You sound down."

"Oh no, I'm fine," Maggie lied. "Just a little tired. You know, the end of a long day and all that. But what about you? What're you doing up so late?" Checking her watch, "It must be near midnight there."

"It is late," Allie said. "Mom, I head back tomorrow. You know, I changed my flight for this stopover and now I have a choice of returning through New York or through Miami . . . "

"Oh, for heaven's sake! Please do come through Miami. I'll meet you at the airport."

"Do you have time to spend with me?"

"I'll have time! Let me know when to meet you. I'll be there. I can't wait to see you. I'm so happy!" Maggie's heart felt light. They chatted for a few more minutes and said good-bye. Maggie danced into the kitchen, suddenly hungry. Humming a little tune, she made a fast dinner, while her mind raced with preparation plans and anticipation.

A slender young woman tugging a large wheeled bag and wearing a tote bag on each shoulder struggled through the heavy glass door exiting customs. Allie! At last! Allie! Maggie ran forward. After a hug she took a tote bag and stood back to give her daughter a maternal inspection. What she saw caused her to smile with love and pride. Allie. Medium height, slender, with shoulder length blonde hair worn simply and brushed to one side. Direct blue eyes looked back at her from under straight dark brows. Allie was a lovely young woman stylishly dressed in dark slacks, flat shoes and a lightweight linen blazer.

Allie returned her appraisal and with dancing eyes said, "I love your hair."

"Thanks. That's a great outfit! Paris?"

"No, California."

"I can't wait to hear all about your trip. How was the flight? Did you meet anyone? Did you shop?"

Walking to the parking garage, they chatted. They piled the luggage into the spacious trunk of Maggie's sensible car and Maggie thought how nice that they didn't have to struggle to fit it in. That's something to be said for this car.

Reading her thoughts, Allie said, "Nice car, Mom. Lots of room. How's mileage?"

"Surprisingly enough, better than with the sports car," Maggie said with a wry grin.

"What? Don't you like it? It really is very pretty."

"Oh, Allie. It's so *sensible!* It isn't nearly as much fun as my old one," Maggie complained.

Allie grinned, "Nothing wrong with sensible. Look how easily we got all this luggage in."

After a silence Maggie exclaimed, "I almost forgot! How's Gabe? Where is he? In a kennel?" Gabe was the Jack Russell Terrier who had adopted Allie last fall during their adventure in California.

Allie chuckled and said, "Gabe's absolutely wonderful. He's staying with Max. You remember Max? Well, he and Gabe have become friends."

"What about you and Max? Are you seeing much of him? How d' you feel about him?"

With a little laugh Allie said, "Yes. I see him fairly often. It's great fun going out with him. He's so spectacularly good-looking. Heads always turn. But, there's something missing between the two of us. I think he must be more in love with himself than he could be with any woman. It's fascinating watching him pass a mirror!"

Maggie grinned at her daughter, "He certainly is something to look at. I suppose it'd take an amazing amount of character for him not to be a little impressed with himself."

Allie was silent for a few minutes, gazing out the car window. She said, "Look at that fellow," gesturing to a stately blue heron perched on a tree limb. "He's just about as elegant as any creature could be, but he seems to manage it without becoming obsessed with himself. That sort of unselfconsciousness is wonderful. He doesn't do anything except be who he is, and he does it perfectly. Being instead of doing. We humans could take a lesson from him!"

Maggie agreed thoughtfully, "Yes, that's so."

Allie's face was turned to the passenger window as they

approached Costa Mira, "Mom, I can't believe that this town has grown so far out into the everglades. When will it ever stop?"

Maggie agreed, "Don't know. But it just seems to keep going."

"You know, each time I'm back here, I have a harder time putting it together in my mind with that little town we moved to . . . how long ago was it?"

"Well, let's see. You were eight when we moved here. It must have been about twenty-four years ago. Not really such a short time."

"Yeah, I guess. Even so, you must admit it has changed a lot. When we first came here there were only two grocery stores and those really weren't supermarkets. There was only one traffic signal in the whole town. I don't remember any fast food restaurants and there were no buildings taller than three stories. Now, just look at it!"

Maggie gazed through the windshield at multi-lane streets, huge intersections, all with traffic lights and left-turn lanes, fast food establishments in every block, the tops of tall condominium buildings lining the beach that could be seen from this busy street, and agreed with her daughter, "Yes, honey, you're right. It has happened very quickly."

At Maggie's home Allie went from room to room, inspecting Maggie's latest decorating additions and changes, exclaiming over new guest room colors and a new bedspread in Maggie's room. Maggie had chosen a light palette for her decor. Soft aqua, lime green and pale yellow against soft, deep white furniture. She stepped out through French doors to the balcony that Maggie had furnished with lounge chairs and a small table, "I love this balcony. The view of the lawn and all those palm trees is just perfect. It calls to me each time I"m here. Very peaceful!"

In the office-guest room Allie stopped at an easel in the corner, its work-in-progress turned toward the wall. "Mom, What's this? You've taken up art? May I look?"

Maggie nodded her permission and Allie turned the painting to the room removing the drape from the easel. She stood in silence examining the medium-sized painting. Brilliant colors playfully defined a stylized cat glaring out from the canvas.

Maggie tried not to fidget while her daughter contemplated her work. It's only for fun she told herself. It really doesn't matter whether anyone else likes it or not. Even so, she did want Allie to approve her work.

Just when the silence had become unbearable, Allie said in a hushed voice, "Mother! This is amazing. I didn't know you were so good. I'm not an expert, but I know a little about art and I think this is quite wonderful! Have you shown it to anyone?"

"No. No, I haven't. Who would I show it to? I'd be too embarrassed. Really, it's just for my own amusement."

Allie raised her eyebrows and said in the slow, quiet voice she used when she was very serious, "That may be, but we need to find someone to look at it."

Maggie started to demur, "Oh no, really I . . . "

Allie interrupted, "Mother, this is not a time to be modest. This painting is very good. I think it might be marketable. We need to get an opinion. We need to find out what to do next."

Maggie sighed and said, "I'm flattered that you like it. But, I did these just for myself, as a way to relax after work. They're sort of funny, really almost cartoons. I can't imagine that anyone would consider them art."

"Them! You mean there're more than this one! How many are there? Oh, please, let me see them!" Allie's quiet voice rose in excitement.

With a look of resignation and without a word Maggie opened the closet door and dove into the corner, leaving only her behind visible, wiggling as she wrestled with the closet's contents. From the depths of the closet came a series of sounds: grunts, scraping and rustling noises, oohs, ughs and squeaks. Finally, Maggie emerged, her hair more tousled than usual, dragging three canvases behind her.

Allie took the paintings from her mother and propped them up on chairs and bureau tops around the room. Then she took Maggie's hand and pulled her to sit down beside her on the bench at the end of the bed. "Just look at them objectively. Imagine you've never seen them before. Look at them as part of a series. Look! Tell me. What d' you see?"

Maggie sat beside her daughter and tried to see what Allie was seeing. Four raucous animal faces stared back at her from the canvases: the nearly finished cat, a dog, a pig and a fish. Maggie looked at first one painting and then another. She saw only her own rather primitive style. She saw only the memories of what she had been experiencing when she painted the pictures. Each one carried a secret story, a story of her deepest thoughts and feelings, coded into the painting, each stoke a memory. "Allie, honey, I appreciate . . . "

Allie squeezed Maggie's hand, "Shh, for just a moment, Mom. Just keep looking. Try to see what I see."

Maggie sat quietly, willing to humor this daughter whom she loved above all else. As she looked from painting to painting, she began to see some of what Allie saw. It almost was as if her focus changed and she saw with new eyes. After a long silence she said slowly, "Well, maybe I do see them differently now. Maybe they have possibilities. But, you know, they're very primitive. A serious art person probably would just laugh."

"More the fool he," Allie said. "But, I don't think we'll find anyone who'll do that. They may be primitive, but that's just it. It gives them their freshness, their uniqueness. It makes them what they are. They're so alive! They're perfect!"

Chapter Two

Maggie fidgeted in her chair. She couldn't remember when she had felt more uncomfortable. M. DuMonchet cleared his throat as he walked around the gallery, rubbing his short dark beard, examining the four paintings on display. In spite of her linen slacks and tailored shirt, Maggie felt as if she were naked. How embarrassing! To have one's most private moments on display in front of a stranger. She could not even look at Allie who sat beside her in a bentwood chair.

The DuMonchet Gallery occupied the corner of a block of elegant boutiques and galleries in the fashionable old section of Costa Mira. Even this old part of town seemed to be losing some of its beach character. Old frame buildings that had presented a casual beach ambiance gradually were being replaced by more substantial masonry edifices that assumed a southern European decor.

Tasteful gilt lettering in the corner of each large window of the gallery stated simply, "DuMonchet, Art". Their knock on the door of the closed gallery had been met by a tall, slender woman with improbably blue-black hair cut asymmetrically very short and close to her head. She was dressed in a flowing black silk caftan. Her make-up was carefully done, even at this early hour. Her incredibly dark black-purple lips made a smile that did not extend to her nearly black eyes. She gave Maggie's proffered hand a limp handshake and with a French accent said, "Ah, yes, Mrs. McGill. How nice to meet you. I am Veronique Duval, Monsieur DuMonchet's assistant. He will be with you in just a moment. Please to come in."

Following her across the threshold, Maggie raised her eyebrows at Allie. Allie whispered, "I'll bet her favorite holiday is Halloween!"

Maggie smothered a giggle and looked around at the gallery. It was a large room with soft gray carpet. The walls were hung with a tasteful selection of landscape paintings. Portable walls, installed diagonally through the center of the room also displayed paintings.

Near the middle of the gallery Veronique turned and with a smile, "Please to have a seat." An assortment of unpaired earrings jangled as Veronique glided across the gallery to summon M. DuMonchet. From their perches on bentwood chairs, Maggie and Allie could hear a muffled conversation in the back room and then M. DuMonchet appeared to view the paintings. The drone of muted conversation continued from the office and Maggie felt relieved that Veronique did not return to the gallery. It was difficult enough showing her work, but showing it to the elegant Veronique would have been much too much.

He hates them. Maggie tried not to look at M. DuMonchet, but after all, it was difficult to know where to look. M. DuMonchet was a short, dapper, rather round man with a small dark Van Dyke beard and shining brown eyes. His carefully combed dark hair showed a touch of gray and was thinning on top. He had greeted her somewhat off-handedly and proceeded with the inspection of her paintings without further conversation.

The gallery was closed at this hour and Maggie was grateful there were no other people there. She sighed and shifted her weight again. What if he is stifling laughter! Maggie sneaked a look under her lashes. Did she see laughter behind the beard? It's all Allie's fault! She had been perfectly happy doing the art stuff just for fun.

Allie had wasted no time. The very evening she first saw the paintings she called a friend in Los Angeles and then another. Finally she had been given M. DuMonchet's name here in Costa Mira.

"Mom, this man is quite well known and respected both here and internationally. His gallery deals not only with local artists, but also with works from abroad, too. His most recent big show was for Felipe Fernandez, a very successful Colombian artist. M.

DuMonchet's opinion is worth something. You'll know after he sees your work whether it has value or not. It's only because my friend in L.A. called him that he agreed to see your stuff. If he should happen to like it and perhaps even show it, it would be a major coup. He's a very big deal!"

Now two days later, this fiasco! Maggie jumped a little and brought her attention back to M. DuMonchet who pulled another bentwood chair across the room to sit down facing Maggie. He took a deep breath and spoke, "Mrs. McGill, do you plan to paint more of these animals?" His French accent was less noticeable than Veronique's.

"Er, I hadn't thought about it. You see, I just paint them for relaxation. Ah . . . I . . . I guess so. I mean, I've had a lot of fun doing it. Yes, I suppose I'll continue with them. I've been thinking about a horse next. I think that could be . . . " Maggie broke off, not quite sure how to proceed. She sat mutely for what seemed a lifetime and then, embarrassed, stood up and extended her hand, "M. DuMonchet, thank you for your time. I hope this hasn't been an imposition for you." She moved toward the cat that had started the whole thing.

M. DuMonchet rose, smiled warmly, and said, "Mrs. McGill, please. Please sit down. I'm interested in exhibiting your work in our gallery. If you would, please, just have a seat for a few moments. I like your work very much. It shows great promise. We could hang the four you have now, but I really think it'd be better to wait until you have a larger body of work completed. If they're of the same caliber as these we'd do a whole show with them."

Maggie stared at him. She was completely speechless.

Allie broke the awkward silence with, "That is an intriguing suggestion, M. DuMonchet. Exactly how many paintings would you need for a complete show?"

"Oh, we'd like at least a dozen. With twelve we would divide the gallery and do a combination show with one other artist. Twenty would be better. With twenty or more, we would devote the entire gallery just to these works." Turning to Maggie he asked, "Do you have any other work completed at this time?"

Maggie still had not quite taken in this surprising turn of events, "I . . . I, er, that is, ah, no. I mean, nothing else. I only started painting last winter." She stopped, was quiet for a moment, and then said, "Are you saying that you think people might actually come to look at these pictures?"

Pascal DuMonchet smiled a real smile at her, "Oh yes. I'm sure of it. In fact, I believe they not only will look, but what is more important, I feel sure they'll buy." Then, becoming more serious, "And you, Mrs. McGill, are you interested in painting more? It would be hard work turning out another eight or more with this same theme. What do you say? Are you interested in doing it?"

Maggie continued to stare at him for a few moments. She still was adjusting to the idea of her cartoons being considered art, "M. DuMonchet, of course I'm interested in doing more paintings. I already have ideas for a few more. What time frame do you have in mind?"

Pascal DuMonchet breathed a sigh and said, "As you know, not much happens here until the winter season. We could do a show early in December, but it's more important, I believe, that the quality of the paintings remains high. If December is too soon, then late January would be good."

Maggie smiled back at him, "Well then, I'll begin work and see what happens."

They talked for a while, discussing schedules and timing. Maggie agreed to give M. DuMonchet thirty days notice before she would have her paintings ready. After warm handshakes Maggie and Allie left the gallery with light hearts and a light step.

In Maggie's sensible car Allie laughed and said, "Hurray, Mom! All right! May I touch your hand! An aspiring artist with a one-woman show! I'm so excited for you!"

Maggie stared at her, speechless. She began to giggle. As the giggles grew, Allie, infected by them, began to laugh also. Convulsed with laughter, Maggie was unable to speak. Finally, wiping her eyes, Maggie croaked, "I can't believe it!"

"Believe it, Mom. You did it!"

Maggie nodded, "But, it happened because of you. If you hadn't insisted we do something about them, they'd still be in my closet."

"However it happened, it did. You officially are an artist. Want to celebrate?"

"Of course. It's nearly lunchtime. Let's try someplace new. How about that place over there? Les Artistes. How appropriate!" Maggie indicated a tiny bistro sitting at the back of a leafy courtyard.

In the center of the courtyard was a high banyan tree whose huge trunk and many supporting roots were a natural freeform sculpture. In its branches were orchids and other air plants. The two women threaded their way past wrought iron benches and hanging pots of geraniums and petunias. The worn bricks underfoot were outlined by borders of moss. A blue and white striped awning shaded glass topped tables and wicker chairs. They were shown to a table in a deeply shaded, leafy corner of the patio. The aroma of espresso filled the air. Even the southern Florida heat hadn't permeated to their table. It was a magical sheltered spot.

Over glasses of iced Pelegrino they toasted first each other and then the success of Maggie's new art career. Maggie leaned back, "When you called from Paris I was having doubts about my life and career. I was afraid I was burned out. This turn of events seems truly serendipitous. The art thing gives some balance to counseling. Doing art is less like doing and more like being. Just what you were saying about the heron."

Allie agreed, "It's very exciting. You can't say that you're in a rut now!" Changing the subject, she asked, "What about La Veronique? She's quite a character!"

Maggie knitted her brow. "She certainly has an unusual appearance. Where d'you suppose she found lipstick that color? It was nearly black!"

Allie shook her head, "Don't know. D'you get the impression she wasn't having a good day?"

"Definitely. She was pretty grumpy. But, at least, she was trying to be professional with us. Were they having an argument in the back room?"

Allie said, "It sure sounded like someone was. There were some heavy vibes there. Didn't you sense it when we went in? Do you think they're lovers?"

Maggie raised her eyebrows and said, "I'd doubt it. But then, I'm often surprised by what people do particularly when it comes to relationships. It's interesting that no one indicated what her connection with the gallery was. An employee? A friend? A partner? I wonder who was she talking to after he came out?"

Allie replied seriously, "Well, if she's a partner, I'd be careful about your business dealings with them. I like M. DuMonchet and he has an excellent reputation for being both successful and reputable, but she doesn't seem so great. Grumpy to say the least!"

Maggie wrinkled her brow as she thought and said, "Yes, I agree. But maybe we just caught her on a bad day. I'll be sure to discuss these things with M. DuMonchet before I sign anything or let him show my work." She was silent for a few moments, then said, "How old do you think Veronique is?"

"Well, that's an interesting question. My guess is late-thirties. What d'you think?"

"Probably. Wh . . . " Maggie's voice trailed off as she looked across the patio. Allie turned, following her gaze. Veronique and a tall, thin man in khaki slacks and a not too clean tee shirt were entering the restaurant. Worn Birkenstocks completed his clothing. A shock of dark hair continued to fall into his eyes in spite of his efforts to brush it back. They were deep in conversation and did not notice Maggie and Allie sitting in the deep shadows.

"Well, I wonder who that is? They definitely didn't look happy. D'you think she saw us?" Allie asked.

Maggie shrugged, "I don't know. I doubt it. They don't seem to go together, do they? I mean, she's so *avant-garde* and he's sort of scruffy. One wonders where he parked the flowered van!" Changing the subject, "Where's that waiter? I could use some food. How about pasta?"

"Mom, you know the way to my heart!"

Maggie couldn't believe how quickly time had flown. Every possible moment in the last six months had been spent at her easel. She found that her counseling work was going more smoothly, but at times it seemed that counseling was almost dreamlike and that her real life was the time spent painting. The work had been arduous, but also completely enjoyable. She now had twenty-four completed canvases ready for M. DuMonchet.

She still found it difficult to believe that the paintings were anything more than her way of relaxing and having fun. What if he didn't like the new ones? What if he'd changed his mind?

With slightly shaking fingers, she dialed the gallery's number. A woman answered, "DuMonchet Art." A French accent. Was it Veronique?

Maggie's voice quavered, "Hello. This is Maggie McGill calling. May I speak with M. DuMonchet, please?"

"Oh yes, Mrs. McGill. How are you? This is Veronique Duval. M. DuMonchet will be glad you called," Veronique's voice was more gracious than Maggie remembered.

"Hello Mrs. McGill. It is good to hear from you," M. DuMonchet's voice was warm and welcoming.

15

Maggie arrived at the gallery the following Monday, her car filled with canvases. Pascal DuMonchet and Veronique helped her unload the car and arrange the paintings around the perimeter of the gallery showroom.

M. DuMonchet expressed surprise and pleasure that she had completed so many, "Oh, Mrs. McGill. They are even better than I had hoped. You know, I do believe your work gets better with each one you do."

"Ah, yes, Mrs. McGill, they are veery interesting," agreed Veronique.

Maggie breathed a small sigh of relief. She still had not become accustomed to the extraordinary turn of events regarding her hobby.

Veronique left the room and M. DuMonchet chatted, telling her how appreciative he was of the work Veronique had done, working with clients. He referred to her as a valuable employee. As he talked, M. DuMonchet led Maggie to his office down the hall that connected the gallery showroom to a back workroom. Opposite DuMonchet's office were two smaller ones. Veronique occupied the one nearer the gallery showroom. The third office was so tiny and neat that it almost seemed unused. Opposite the tiny office and tucked in behind M. DuMonchet's office was a closed door discreetly labeled, in gold script, *Toilette.*

M. DuMonchet's office held a heavy antique mahogany desk facing the door, but he indicated that they sit at a round rosewood table in the corner, "Mrs. McGill, we'll need to conduct just a bit of business before the show. We have a standard contract with our artists that outlines the responsibilities and financial arrangements."

"Oh, and how is that?" Maggie hoped she was being professional and, at the same time, she felt reassured now that Veronique's role had been made clear.

"We, the gallery, agree to exhibit and care for your work while it is here. It will be insured for ninety percent of the listed gallery sales price."

"That's good."

"The artist agrees to provide work as scheduled, but you've already done that, and to take possession of any unsold works after sixty days."

"That's fair."

"Usually with a new artist the gallery commission is forty

percent; however, in your case, since you are local and because I have so much faith in your work, our fee for you will be thirty-eight percent. You're welcome to take this contract to your attorney for review."

Maggie wasn't sure what she should do, "If you'll just give me a moment . . ." She read through the short contract quickly. It seemed straight forward enough. She felt comfortable signing it immediately.

Back in the gallery, as she was shaking hands with M. DuMonchet and Veronique, a man hurried in from the backroom, the tail of his short sleeved shirt coming out around his ample waist, "Hey, Pascal, what'll we do about . . . " He gave M. DuMonchet's name a midwestern accent, but broke off as he noticed Maggie. "Oh, sorry. Didn't mean to interrupt." Maggie thought he resembled a Corn Belt farmer more than anything.

M. DuMonchet's native courtesy asserted itself, "No, No. Do not disturb yourself, Duane. Come in and meet Mrs. McGill. Mrs. McGill, may I present my partner, Duane Simpson."

Maggie shook his hand and murmured, "How nice to meet you, Mr. Simpson." Duane Simpson's florid face flushed a shade redder than his close cropped red hair as he shook her hand and muttered a greeting. Maggie thought he didn't seem to belong with the suave M. DuMonchet and exotic Veronique. Quickly he excused himself and hurried to the back room.

"Hi, baby."

"Hello Mom. What's up?"

"I just wanted to let you know that I've completed twenty-four pictures and that the opening will be at the DuMonchet Gallery the last Saturday in January. Can you come?"

"Opening! Can I come! Of course. I wouldn't miss it for the world."

"Terrific! Let me know your flight info and I'll pick you up. Oh, I'm satisfied about the business arrangements. Veronique is only an employee. By the way, I've had some more recent dealings with her and she actually seems rather nice. I think we misjudged her."

"Could be. Anyway, I'm glad things are working out. See you soon."

"Can't wait!"

Maggie squeezed Allie's hand. "I can't believe it! All these people!"

"Believe it, Mom, it's real. They're all here for you!"

Maggie looked around the crowded gallery. Twenty-four colorful canvases were hung on the gallery walls. Allie had flown in from California the day before. Maggie's friends were in attendance. What was even more amazing were the other people, strangers to Maggie, who seemed to be fascinated by her work.

Veronique Duval, tonight dressed in an incredibly slim floor length black satin gown with a slit to her thigh, circulated through the crowd, chatting and laughing with the patrons. If possible, her jewelry was even more bizarre than ever. Several large unmatched earrings hung from her ears and her long tapered fingers displayed sparkling rings with large stones. Grudgingly, Maggie had to admit that she was doing a terrific job. Her exotic appearance seemed to add to the excitement and glamour of the occasion. M. DuMonchet, himself, dapper in black tie and dinner jacket, also circulated throughout the room, smiling, shaking hands, even, at times, executing a continental bow over a woman's hand. He had confided to Maggie that Duane Simpson normally was a silent partner who managed the business aspects and left the art side of the gallery strictly up to him.

Earlier, before the gallery opened, Veronique had greeted Maggie and Allie graciously. She spoke with a pleasant French accent, "Ah, Maggie, I want to congratulate you. Your work truly is charming. I think we will have a veery successful opening." Turning to Allie, "My dear, you must be proud that your mother is sooo talented."

Maggie and Allie had dressed for the occasion, Maggie, in a soft celadon green silk two-piece floor length dress and Allie, in a long, chocolate brown velvet sheath.

Maggie almost was beginning to believe that her work was good. She stood in the corner the gallery feeling shy and overwhelmed by the attention she was receiving. She could say only, "Thank you. Thank you," to the many compliments her work was receiving.

"Now, my dear, you must tell me where Pascal has had you hidden. I know all his artists. I come to all the shows and your things are so refreshing. Really, quite, quite refreshing." The speaker, a slight, foppishly dressed man wearing, of all things, a long burgundy silk scarf draped around his neck, continued his monologue, not giving Maggie a chance to respond with anything more than a nod and a smile. "Oh, let me introduce myself. Lazlo Leigh." He extended a limp hand. "Truly, Pascal has outdone himself with your opening. *Tres opulent!*" Maggie thought he lacked only a long cigarette holder to be straight out of central casting. The discourse finally was interrupted by a woman across the gallery who motioned to Maggie's companion.

Across the room Allie was talking to a tall slender young woman who looked familiar. Catching her eye, Allie brought the woman over, "Mom, do you remember Sally Guenther? She's Sally Guenther Livingston now. We used to ride horses together."

Greeting Sally, Maggie recalled a tall, gawky teen that never quite seemed to fit her body, that is, until she was on a horse. There all her parts seemed to fit together and she rode beautifully. Time had treated Sally well. Her teen gawkiness had been transformed into a svelte elegance. "Yes, of course I remember. Hello, Sally. It is so good to see you again."

"Hello Mrs. McGill. I live in Arizona now, but I am here visiting my parents and when I saw the notice in the paper I had to come. Your work is wonderful! I had no idea you were an artist!"

"Thank you, Sally. It is surprising to me that my hobby has come to this."

"Mom, Sally's husband is an Arizona rancher and she has a whole ranch of horses!"

Sally laughed, "Well, not a whole ranch full, but we do have a few. We are in the process of turning our cattle ranch into a guest ranch. You both should come out and stay as my guests. Once we complete our renovations, we'd like to have friends stay for a while as guests. It would give us a chance to iron out some of the wrinkles."

"What a generous offer! Thank you. I'd love to some time," Maggie smiled back at her.

"We'd love to have you. And, as I said, it really would help us if you could come." Sally waved her goodbye as a couple approached Maggie with their compliments on her work.

The opening certainly was an occasion. Champagne and catered nibbles, including caviar, were offered in a corner well away from the art. The gallery had framed her paintings in simple frames that complemented them. The lighting perfectly illuminated her work and added an impressive air of importance to her cartoons. Perhaps M.

DuMonchet was correct in his assessment. The tastefully posted prices beside each painting had sent her into a state of shock. Even with the gallery cut, if only a few sold, Maggie would have quite a windfall.

"Truly, my Maggie, they are magnificent," the soft singsong voice said in her ear.

Maggie whirled to look into the soft dark eyes she remembered so vividly. Hadi! "Hadi! Where? How? Oh, I don't care. I am so *glad* to see you!" Impulsively she threw her arms around her friend.

He returned her hug warmly. Tonight Hadi was dressed in white, from his turban to his white sandaled feet. The white clothing emphasized his dark skin, hair and goatee, but it was his eyes that Maggie remembered so well. She always had the feeling that they had a magical, almost X-ray, quality that could see into the depths of her being.

"Hadi, I'm so very glad to see you. How did you know? Where did you go? Where've you been? We wondered and wondered!" The questions tumbled out.

"Ah, my dear Maggie. Do you not remember? We never are separated. We only lose awareness of one another from time to time." Hadi's soft singsong voice was just as she remembered.

He was as enigmatic as ever. But Maggie did not care. She was delighted to see him again. Hadi had been instrumental in helping her and Allie escape their captors during their adventure in California last year (*Maggie's Image)*, but he had disappeared mysteriously when it was over.

There was something special about him that Maggie could not define. Whatever it was, she was excited to see him again. They chatted for a few moments, catching up on Maggie's life and her new career as an artist.

"Hadi, it's been a serendipitous chain of events. You can't imagine how surprised I've been by them. Allie's here somewhere. I know she'll want to see you. And I'd like you to meet M. DuMonchet. He owns the gallery and he's been very helpful." Maggie looked around the gallery. The hour was late and the crowd was beginning to thin. Across the room she could see Allie talking with a young blond man who obviously was entranced by her. But, where was M. DuMonchet? Neither he nor Veronique was to be seen.

Taking Hadi's arm Maggie walked across the room toward Allie. Tonight, with Hadi, the crowd seemed to part magically. Allie, still talking, stopped in mid-sentence. Her eyes widened in surprise, then she beamed her welcome. She bid the bemused young man a hasty good-bye and hurried to meet Maggie and Hadi in the middle of the room.

"Hadi! Oh, Hadi! It's *so* good to see you." They embraced, and Allie continued, "We think about you often."

"And I, I, too, think of you both," Hadi said graciously, holding both Allie's and Maggie's hands. "This is an auspicious occasion, is it not?" His singsong voice was almost musical.

Allie beamed back at him, "Very. Are you surprised that Mom's such a wonderful artist?"

Hadi took a deep breath, "Ah, no. I always have known that each of you is very special. This is only the beginning. There are many marvelous events and achievements to come for each of you."

Maggie looked at Allie with raised eyebrows. What *could* he be talking about? But they had learned to respect his enigmatic pronouncements.

Maggie found speech, "Allie, where're M. DuMonchet and Veronique? I want to introduce them to Hadi?"

"I'm not sure. They were here earlier. Maybe they're in the office. Let's see."

Only a few art patrons remained still examining Maggie's art. The three of them crossed the nearly empty gallery to M. DuMonchet's office. The door was slightly ajar. Cautiously, Maggie tapped on it lightly. At her touch it swung open. At first she could see nothing. The light was dim. Peering into the room, "M. DuMonchet? Oh, Veronique, forgive me. I am looking for M. DuMonchet." She could see that Veronique was sitting in M. DuMonchet's high backed chair, at the desk, with her back to the door. Only the sleek black hair on the top of her head was visible above the back of the chair. Receiving no response, Maggie again called her name, "Veronique? Do you know where we'd find . . . "

She broke off as Hadi put his hand on her arm, "Oh, my dear Maggie, please come with me. I do not think Veronique can speak to us now."

Maggie wrinkled her brow at Hadi, started to protest, but was silenced by the look on his face. "What do you mean? What's happening?"

She turned to look at Allie who had advanced farther into the room. Allie turned toward her mother, "Mom. Why don't you go back and find a chair." Her face was without color as she looked across her mother's head and met Hadi's eyes.

But Maggie was not to be put off. Why were they acting so strangely? She came into the room and started around the desk. Only then did she see the beautifully jeweled hilt of the dagger protruding from Veronique's chest. A small amount of blood made an even shinier circle on the black satin around the hilt. It was the ugliest sight she ever had seen. Maggie backed slowly out of the room, unconsciously finding and gripping Hadi's hand.

Chapter Three

Maggie shifted in the bentwood chair. Lieutenant Anderson strode across the gallery, pulled up another chair and sat in front of her. "Mrs. McGill, tell me again what happened this evening."

For what seemed the hundredth time Maggie related her memories of her one-person show. What a disaster it had become! The police arrived soon after Allie's phone call and had detained the remaining guests, interviewing and then releasing them one at a time until at last only Maggie, Allie and Hadi were left.

"When did you first notice that Miss Duval was not in the room?" Lieutenant Anderson's question came again.

With a tired sigh, Maggie began, "As I told you, I simply do not remember. There were so many people here. Veronique and M. DuMonchet circulated through the crowd. They moved around the room. Often I couldn't see where they were. As the crowd thinned an old friend of mine came in and . . ."

"Old friend? You mean that Indian guy?" Anderson's voice was edged with suspicion.

Maggie bridled, "Sir! I mean my dear old friend, Hadi, with whom I would trust my life!" Her voice became stronger, "Really, Lieutenant Anderson, I certainly want to be as helpful as I can be, but

I'm exhausted. You've asked the very same questions again and again. There's nothing more I or my daughter or Hadi can tell you about the events of the evening. We're all tired. It's time that we were permitted to go home and rest!"

Lieutenant Anderson looked at her with mild surprise and a measure of respect in his eyes, "Very well, Mrs. McGill. You're all free to go. But let me know if you hear from this DuMonchet. And don't leave town until we check things out."

Maggie found it hard to believe that M. DuMonchet had disappeared, "Of course. We wish to be of any assistance possible. It's a dreadful tragedy. Veronique Duval was a lovely and talented person. She didn't deserve this."

M. DuMonchet's disappearance was a mystery. Where could he have gone?

After a restless night, Maggie sipped her morning tea, "Allie, I simply can't believe that M. DuMonchet could have hurt anyone and especially not Veronique."

She pushed her untouched breakfast toast away and turned troubled eyes to her daughter.

Allie sighed, "I know, Mom. I really liked him. And, we must admit that he recognized artistic genius when we saw it!" Allie smiled at her mother, trying to lighten her despair.

"I just wish I'd known him better." Maggie paused, "Well, and Veronique, too. You know, in spite of her rather strange appearance, she was very good at what she did."

Allie agreed, "Yes, she was. Do you realize we're referring to M. DuMonchet in the past tense as if he were the one who died."

Maggie's mouth formed a silent "Oh", "We are, aren't we? Oh, dear. I hope that's not prophetic. It's just that I can't imagine what's happened to him. I mean, why should he disappear like that. It's very mysterious."

"Yes, mysterious. D'you suppose he could've done her in?"

"Allie! I can't believe you said that!" Maggie was indignant.

"Well, you said it was mysterious. I mean, it doesn't look good for him, does it?"

Maggie shook her head slowly, "No, no it doesn't. Where could he have gone? Do you suppose he's in trouble? I mean someone was in the gallery literally with murder in his or her heart. Maybe M. DuMonchet interrupted that person, or something. I simply can't believe he could have done it. M. DuMonchet was, er, is a *gentleman.*" She stressed the word, giving it full importance and indicating a certain level of civilized behavior and *savoir-faire.*

"Yes, he doesn't seem like the sort who'd do something so dreadful. D'you know anything about their relationship?"

Maggie's face became even sadder, "Only that he told me Veronique had worked for him for many years and that he relied on her expertise and judgment for many aspects of running the gallery. He was very complimentary about her. You know, I was growing to like her. I have an idea there were hidden depths under her exotic facade. I think she had a good heart. It makes me sad."

"Well, her appearance was bizarre, but I admit that what I saw of her last night looked as if she was doing a great job. She really knew how to work that crowd. Probably her appearance worked for her in that way. And, I'm sure you noticed, she was quite pleasant to us." Allie paused, then, changing the subject, "Mom, what about Hadi? Isn't it strange his showing up that way? Talk about mystery! He's the most mysterious person I've ever met!"

"Very mysterious, indeed." Maggie said, "You know, everything about him is strange, but as I think about it, one of the strangest things is that, in spite of knowing nothing at all about him, I feel as if I've known him forever and I'd trust him with my life."

"Me, too. He's very dear, isn't he? How fortunate that he showed up last night, just as the excitement began. His being there made what happened a little less frightening. Where is he now?"

Maggie sighed and sipped her now cold tea, "I don't know. I invited him to stay with us last night, but he declined and said he'd be in touch." She sighed again.

"Mom, what's going to happen to your paintings? Were any of them sold?"

"Well, I don't know. With all the excitement I haven't given them a thought. I imagine the gallery is sealed and that nothing much will happen soon."

Just then there was a knock at the door. Lieutenant Anderson entered courteously. Maggie thought he looked more like a dentist than a policeman. His nearly white blond hair was combed back from his equally pale face. Washed out blue eyes gazed down at her, "Just a few more questions, Mrs. McGill." Taking the proffered seat on Maggie's white sofa, "How long have you known DuMonchet and the victim?"

Maggie looked at him with annoyance, "Lieutenant Anderson, it is just as I told you last night. I met them only a few months ago. Ours was a business arrangement and I know nothing about their private lives."

The policeman shifted uncomfortably, "Yes, I know, but we're trying to get a picture of the set up at that gallery. Anything more you can tell us? We can't find any next of kin for Veronique Duval. DuMonchet has disappeared completely."

Maggie softened, "I understand that it must be frustrating, but really, there's nothing more I can tell you. I knew them only slightly and that just for business."

"Now, this Indian guy. How much d'you know about him? Where is he now? What's his name again?"

Maggie's back stiffened and her eyes snapped, "I've told you before that Hadi is a dear and old friend. He has nothing to do with this. He only came to the gallery to congratulate me. I'll not have you suspecting him just because he happens to have an accent and to dress differently! He was a guest like any other person there!"

Anderson stayed for another twenty or so minutes asking the same questions, getting the same answers. Finally, he left with an air of defeated frustration, leaving his hostesses feeling exasperated.

Allie groaned, "Really! That man! What does he think we can tell him? Does he think browbeating us will result in new information? It makes me want to make up a wild story just to get rid of him!"

"It's really annoying."

"Oh, rats!"

"What?"

"We forgot to ask about your paintings."

Pascal DuMonchet squirmed, trying to find a more comfortable position. *Where* was he? And *how* did he get there? Basic questions, but the ones that held the most interest for him at the moment. He had awakened a few hours ago sitting on a most uncomfortable chair with his hands tied behind him and all of him bound securely to the chair. He rolled his head in first one direction and then the other trying to ease a persistent headache. He had first awakened in complete darkness, but now in dim half-light he could make out only a few details of his prison. It seemed to be a sort of shed that was used for storage of miscellaneous agricultural items. There were no windows and the only source of light came from a thin crack under the door. Initially he found himself passing in and out of consciousness, but now he was more awake and wondered what had happened. His last memory was of leaving the showing of Mrs. McGill's work in search of Veronique. He found Veronique in his office, sitting at his desk, her face pale and strained. She seemed to be arguing with someone that he did not see. His last memory was starting to turn to look at that person. He must have been hit on the head. The pain was beginning to localize to one area above and behind his right ear. Not for the first time he wished he had more hair. But why? And who? And where was he? In the distance he could hear occasional faint traffic sounds. Would it help if he called for help? He called out, but found his voice was only a weak croak. The light under the door was fading. Could he have been here for a whole day?

"Mom, let's check out the gallery. We might be able to pick up your paintings or learn something," Allie gazed at Maggie expectantly.

"Okay. At least it's something we can do. I can't believe it's already Monday morning and we've heard nothing. Maybe there'll be news. Who knows? M. DuMonchet may have returned."

Not only was the gallery closed, but it also was encircled by bright yellow tape proclaiming it to be a crime scene. There were a few curious pedestrians, but otherwise, the gallery seemed to be deserted.

"Rats!"

"Yeah, rats! Okay, what now?"

"I always say, when in doubt, try food."

Les Artistes was nearly empty. At an outdoor table under the banyan tree they ordered salads.

"Mrs. McGill, I thought that was you. Do you remember me, Lazlo Leigh?" He still was foppishly dressed, but the dramatic scarf was gone and his mood was more subdued than at Maggie's opening.

"Oh, hello, Mr. Leigh. Have you met my daughter, Allie?"

Allie shook his limp hand and smiled at him, "How do you do?"

Lazlo Leigh murmured his 'how do you do' and stood shifting from one foot to the other, "Nasty business, this. Have you heard anything about Pascal's disappearance?" His volubility had disappeared and he seemed almost vulnerable.

"No, no we haven't. We were just at the gallery hoping to get some information."

"Well, it all is just too bad. I mean, Pascal and Veronique ran quite a good show there. Too bad. Such a tragic thing!" His voice was hushed and his face somber.

"Yes, it is. We're just having some lunch. Would you care to join us?" Maggie finally took pity on Mr. Leigh's discomfort.

As if he were electrified, Lazlo Leigh jumped into the empty chair, "Oh yes, thank you. I mean, I won't eat, but, well, I wanted to chat with you for a moment. Have you heard anything about Pascal's partner, Simpson? Do you think he'll reopen the gallery if, if, well, if Pascal is unable to do so?"

"Goodness, I've no idea, Mr. Leigh. I only met the man once in passing. Let's hope that we don't have to find out," Maggie said firmly.

"Oh, yes, of course. We hope Pascal soon will be back and things will return, er, that is, he will go on as best he is able. Er, I just wanted to say that I truly was impressed by your work and I, er, I just wanted to tell you. That is, well, I have a gallery myself, you know. The Seashell, just a block down from Pascal's. We have an extensive clientele and we represent some impressive artists. If, that is, if things should not go well with Pascal. Well, if that should happen and you want someone to represent your work, I'd be honored to do so."

Finally! Finally Maggie understood what Lazlo Leigh had been trying to say. She drew a deep breath, "Thank you Mr. Leigh. That's an interesting offer. I'm sure your gallery is very nice; however, as I said, I fully expect this matter to be cleared up soon and that M. DuMonchet will be back at his gallery."

Lazlo Leigh chatted for a few more moments, then excused himself and left.

"Whew! Mom, you're certainly in demand. Now, do you have any doubts that your paintings are really good?" Allie looked into Maggie's eyes.

"Well, yes. It does seem as if people like them.

"Well, Anderson. How's the Duval case going?" Harold Anderson's boss, chief of Police, Carter Blake, peered at Lieutenant Anderson over his glasses.

Anderson shifted uncomfortably, "I personally interviewed every person at that gallery on the night of the murder. Everyone there had opportunity, but, so far, we haven't come up with a motive for anyone."

"How about the weapon? Anything there?"

"No. Fancy little thing. Letter opener. Always on DuMonchet's desk according to his partner. Cleaning crew supported that."

"Prints?"

"Nothing. Wiped clean. Like you might expect."

"Looks like the killer just picked up what was handy."

"Yeah."

"It's a tough one, but we've got to have some results soon." Blake, after all, had his own welfare to consider. It wouldn't do for this crime to go unsolved for long. "Do you need more men?"

"Yeah, sure. We can use all the help we can get. We're doing background checks on anyone who seems suspicious. There's one guy I wonder about, this Indian guy. You should see him, wears a turban and everything."

"Check him out. What about the victim? What do you know about her?"

"Not much. She dressed pretty far out. Lived in one of those little old houses on Beach Street not far from the gallery, alone as far as I can make out. Her name's French. They say she talked with an accent, but so far that's about all we know."

"Check with Immigration. Do you know if she was a citizen or if she had a green card. I want to know everything about the woman. Go through her house with a fine tooth comb. Knowing the victim is crucial to finding the killer."

"Okay. Yeah, okay."

"What about this DuMonchet guy? Any luck finding him?"

"No. Nothing yet."

"Well, get on it. He's the most likely suspect. Anything going on between them? No point standing here talking. You'll have to excuse me. I've got an appointment with this DEA guy."

Carter Blake raised his considerable bulk from his chair and reached across his desk to shake hands with the DEA agent, "Come in, Mr. Carrera. Have a seat. Now what can I do for you?"

Arthur Carrera, tall, slender, with close-cut dark hair over a craggy, melancholy face, shook the proffered hand and sat in the leather armchair, "Kind of you to see me. As I'm sure you know, traffic in controlled substances always is a problem in south Florida; however, until recently we've had little reason to focus our attention on Costa Mira. In the last several months there've been indications that there may be an increase in activity here in your area. I just wanted to let you know that we'll be here and to ask for the cooperation of you and your force."

Blake nodded, "Of course. Anything we can do to help, just let us know. Right now we're stretched pretty tight due to a murder investigation, but I'm sure that soon will be cleared up. After that, we'll have extra men to put at your disposal. In the meantime, keep us informed and we'll keep our eyes open."

Billy Osmond kicked the stone sending it skipping down the dusty path. It was the first time ever that he had cut school. Somehow, it wasn't nearly as much fun as he'd thought it would be. The day was over half gone and mostly it had been boring. Why had he let Roy talk him into it? What if his parents found out?

"What's wrong, Billy? You backin' out? Gettin' chicken?" Roy taunted him.

"Nah, not me. I was just wonderin' what we could do to have fun," Billy lied.

"Well, how's about havin' a smoke?" I got some cigs from my old man's pockets last night."

"Yeah, sure. Sounds good," Billy lied again. He didn't want Roy to think he was a wimp.

"Let's go out to that old shack behind the orange grove. Nobody over there."

Pascal DuMonchet woke with a start. Jerking his head up aggravated the ever-present headache. Voices. He thought he heard voices. Hope sprang then sank. What if it was his captor? Well, anything would be welcome if it meant he could get untied and off this chair. His muscles were cramped and aching. He had lost feeling in his feet and legs. The chill of the night had turned into oven-like heat as the sun warmed the shack. Pascal was as miserable as he'd ever been. The voices came nearer. It sounded like kids. Tentatively, he called out, "Help! Help!" His voice was stronger now. It almost seemed to belong to him again. Louder now, "Help! Please help me!"

Billy stopped suddenly, "Roy, what's that? D'you hear that?"

30

"Hear what. I don't hear nothin'."

"Wait, be quiet. Listen."

Faintly, "Help, please help me!"

Roy's face puckered into a fierce frown, "Yeah, I hear it. Wait. Sounds like it's comin' from the shack."

They listened again. The voice was a little louder, "Please, please help me."

"Okay, now. I'll bet it's a spy. We got to be careful. Wonder if he's got a gun?"

"Oh, for pete's sake, Roy, this isn't a game. There's a real person in there. What're we goin' to do?"

"Well, we could call the police." Then remembering that they were truant, "Or, we could just get him out of there."

"Yeah, let's do that."

By now they were within a few feet of the shed. "Hey, mister. You in there?"

Pascal's voice was shaky with relief, "Yes, ah yes. I'm tied up. Can you open the door?" His accent was more pronounced with stress.

"See, it's a foreigner. I told you it was a spy!"

"Who cares? Let's just open the door and let him out."

The ever-practical Roy, "Hey, mister. Promise you won't tell who let you out?"

"Ah, ah yes, of course. I promise. It'll be a secret."

The boys, reassured, examined the door. It was held by a new heavy padlock. How could they possibly get it open?

"Hey, Roy. Look how rusty the hasp is. I'll bet we can break it." Billy picked up a rock and pounded at the hasp. Roy joined him with another rock. For a few minutes the only sounds were pounding and grunts.

Billy paused to catch his breath, "Roy, look over there. What's that?" Lying in the weeds surrounding the shack was a rusty tire iron. Billy picked it up and quickly pried the rusty hasp from the weathered wood.

Light blinded Pascal DuMonchet as the door swung open. He screwed up his eyes trying to see his rescuers. Silhouetted in the bright rectangle he saw two figures. Boys. Two scruffy boys. Probably about ten or eleven years old. The larger of the two had longish stringy hair. Both wore baggy jeans and tee shirts. To Pascal they looked like guardian angels, "Oh, thank you, my young friends.

Do you think you can help me with these ropes?"

Billy squinted into the gloom of the shack. He saw an older man, even older than his dad, tied to a straight unpainted chair. What there was of the man's hair was messed up and falling in his eyes. As he came closer, Billy would see a dark crusted place on the man's head. Blood. The guy had been hurt. At that, Billy's better nature overcame his fear. He rushed into the shack and started to untie the ropes.

"Hey, Billy. Wait a minute. How'd we know who this guy is? I mean, he could be a really bad guy. What if he tries somethin' with us if you untie him."

"Oh, just be quiet, Roy. Can't you see this guy's been hurt? He ain't gonna do nothin' to us. He almost can't keep his head up." Billy worked on.

Roy, taken aback by Billy's sudden show of spunk, fell to helping him and soon Pascal was free.

Refreshed by the cooler air entering through the door Pascal said, "Oh, thank you, my young friends. Thank you." He stood up and immediately fell back on the chair. His feet and legs still were numb and not working very well. "Oh, ouch. Ooh. That hurts!" He bent over, massaging his legs to bring circulation back.

Billy knelt beside him, helping to rub the blood back into the extremities.

When he was able to stand, Pascal again thanked his rescuers. He searched his pockets and finding some money gave each boy a twenty-dollar bill, "If you'll give me your names and addresses, I'd like to send you a larger reward once I get back to my office."

The boys, delighted by their new wealth, nonetheless, mindful of their truancy, refused to give their names to Pascal, "Nah. No thanks. This is plenty. But remember. You promised not to tell anyone."

Pascal shook their hands solemnly and repeated his promise, "Mum's the word, my friends. Thank you again."

The boys ran off toward the sun that soon would set, excited by both the wonderful adventure and their reward, eager to return home, hugging the secret to themselves.

Pascal watched them romp away from him, then surveyed his position. He had no idea where he was. The 360 degree scan revealed a flat, empty landscape, an occasional palm tree, tall grass. Nothing more. What to do? The sun was low in the sky. Soon it would be dark. Pascal was not an outdoorsman at best and this open country brought images of wildlife and reptiles to mind. But the boys had come from somewhere and they had danced off toward the west. It made sense to Pascal to follow them. Slowly he limped off into the setting sun.

Chapter Four

Briiing! Briing! The telephone broke into the languor of the evening. Maggie and Allie had returned from their outing feeling little more enlightened and much more frustrated that nothing much seemed to be happening and that they knew little more than before. They sat on the balcony of the condo, sipping tea and watching the light fade into night. The sun had set in red-gold spendor behind the tall coconut palm trees that covered the wide lawn.

"Hello."

"Hello. Is this Mrs. McGill?"

"Yes. Yes, it is."

"Mrs. McGill, this is Pascal DuMonchet."

"M. DuMonchet!" Maggie's voice rose with excitement, "Where are you? Are you okay?"

"Ah, yes. That is, I am now 'okay.' But I do need some help. Is it possible for you to do me an enormous favor?" Pascal's French accent was more pronounced than she ever had heard it and his voice sounded weak and strained.

"Of course. If there's anything I can do, I'd be happy to do so. What do you need?"

"Well, first of all, I need transportation. I'm at a crossroads at the edge of the everglades. Could you possibly come pick me up? I know it's a long . . . "

Maggie interrupted, "Don't trouble yourself. We'll be there. Tell me exactly where you are. We'll leave immediately."

Pascal squinted at the faded road sign on the corner and gave her his location, "Ah, Mrs. McGill. Ah, could you not tell anyone you've heard from me, please. I don't wish anyone to know yet."

"Oh? Well, yes. I can do that. But could I tell my daughter, Allie?"

"Oh yes, of course, that's all right."

"Good. See you soon."

They found M. DuMonchet huddled against a telephone booth standing stark against the night sky at a crossroads miles from anything any of them would have considered civilization. The night air was chilly and he was shivering. Well back from the road was what once had been a convenience store. Now, boarded up and deserted, it only lent to the desolation of saw grass and empty landscape. Maggie thought it was a miracle that the old phone booth had held an operational telephone.

"Ah, Mrs. McGill. And, Miss McGill. I cannot tell you how good it is to see you."

Maggie believed him. Truly, he did not now bear much resemblance to the suave and gracious man she had known. The lapel of his dinner jacket displayed a long rip. His clothes were dusty and stained and a strand of his hair strayed across his forehead.

"M. DuMonchet. Do get in and tell us what has happened to you. And please call me Maggie." Slowly, seemingly painfully, he lowered himself into the back seat of Maggie's sensible sedan. "Thank you, Maggie. I am so grateful to the two of you. Indeed, it was a great favor to ask, but I could not think whom else to call. And, you must call me Pascal." Turning to Allie, "I thank you, also, Miss McGill."

"Please, Allie," she answered. "We're relieved that you're okay. We've been very worried about you. Everyone's been wondering where you might be."

Maggie turned, started the car, pulled out onto the road and headed west into the dark night.

"Well, I, too, have been wondering that. I tried to call Veronique, but her phone did not answer. Neither did Duane. You're the only ones I could think of that I could trust."

Maggie shot a glance at Allie who shrugged her dubiety. Clearly he didn't know. Should they tell him? Silence fell in the car. Each was wrapped in his or her thoughts.

Allie broke the silence, "But, M. DuMonchet, er Pascal, what happened to you? Where'd you go? What about that wound on your head? Is it serious?"

Pascal sighed and put his hand to his head, "Ah, no. It does not seem to be. It's sore and I had a headache, but that's fading. As to what happened, I can't tell you much. At the show I wanted to speak to Veronique, but didn't see her. I found her in my office, sitting at my desk, talking to someone. I started to turn to see who it was and that was all. The next thing I knew I found myself tied to a chair in a shack in the middle of saw grass and nothing else. I need to get back and sort it all out."

"Oh, what a horrid story. You must be exhausted."

"To tell the truth, I am feeling not so well. It was an arduous time. But a little rest and sorting out will help a lot."

Maggie took a deep breath and with a quick glance at Allie, pulled the car to the side of the road. Flipping on the dome light, she turned to Pascal, "We have sad news for you, Pascal. I am not sure how to tell you, but you need to know what happened."

Pascal made no response, but his face became set and stony.

Allie joined in, "Well, Pascal, what happened is . . . Well, a dreadful thing happened." She glanced at her mother.

"There's no easy way to say it. Veronique is gone. She was found in your office. She had been murdered, stabbed." Maggie reached over the seat and took Pascal's hand, "We're so sorry that it happened and to have to tell you."

Pascal's eyes filled, he gulped, took a deep breath and sighed his shock and grief, "I should have guessed something horrible had happened. She was very upset, arguing with that person. I knew something was wrong. But I didn't want to think of such a thing. Poor Veronique. Poor, poor Veronique!"

They sat for a while then Pascal broke the silence, "Do they know who did it?"

"As far as we know, no. There's an investigation. Costa Mira isn't used to this sort of thing. The police are pretty much baffled. I believe they may suspect you because of your absence."

"Oh dear! That isn't good news. But I do see that I was wise to call you instead of some of the others. I was afraid that it might have been one of them who hit me and tied me up in that awful place. But I knew neither of you could have done so. And, for some reason, I was reluctant to involve the police."

"Probably wise. But what now? What d'you want to do?"

Pascal sighed again, "Ah, you know, I'm not sure. I guess I should go home and get a little rest. Then I can figure out a course of action."

Allie nudged Maggie. Their eyes met. Agreement was instant. "Pascal, we think you should come back to my place. You can rest there and then make decisions. Probably if you go home you'll end up down at the jail with a lot of questions and be even more exhausted."

Pascal hesitated.

"Come with us at least for the rest of tonight. A hot bath and good night's sleep will help with whatever needs to happen tomorrow."

The mention of a hot bath was all Pascal needed. He agreed.

"Mom. Mom, are you awake?" Allie whispered at her mother's quiet form across the king bed in Maggie's bedroom.

"Yes. I am. Have been for quite a while. I wasn't sure whether you were or not."

"Just woke up. What time is it?"

"A little after seven. I haven't heard a thing from Pascal. He must have been exhausted." They had moved Allie's things into Maggie's room last night and made up the guest bed for Pascal. After some hot soup, they sent him to bed.

"Poor guy. He was pitiful last night, don't you think?"

"Yes. Pitiful sums it up. He was spent both physically and emotionally. Let's hope rest has helped him recover. He'll need all his resources to contend with Lieutenant Anderson."

"Ugh! What a jerk! Lieutenant Anderson gives law enforcement a bad name!"

"Oh, I know he's disagreeable, but this town hasn't had such a crime in my memory. He's probably just out of his depth and running scared!"

"I'm sure you're right, Mom, but I think you're being too kind. It's probably an occupational hazard. I still say he's a jerk."

"Speaking of occupations, I scheduled myself out for the next three days, but after that it'll be work for me. How about you? What's your schedule?"

"I'm free for the rest of the week. Then I need to get back to California for a shoot."

"Well, we have a few more days before we have to worry about schedules then. Let's have some breakfast. Maybe Pascal will be up soon."

Pascal was sitting in the living room when they emerged. He had brushed his dusty clothes and wore the formal trousers and pleated shirt that had been part of his opening attire. "Ah, Maggie and Allie. Good morning to you both."

"Good morning, Pascal. How're you feeling?"

"Much better, thank you. And you?"

"Ready for breakfast. How about some coffee?"

"Coffee would be an answer to my prayers."

Maggie was pleasantly surprised that each of them had displayed a robust appetite. Eggs and potatoes were dispatched along with coffee and tea. She held strongly to the belief in the healing benefits of good food lovingly prepared. She sipped her tea, "Well, Pascal, what're your plans?"

"I've been giving it some thought. I think I need to get in touch with Duane Simpson to find out what's happening with the gallery. Do you know anything?"

"Only that it's closed and surrounded by official looking yellow tape. We were hoping to get in to check on Mom's paintings, but no soap!"

"Oh, yes. I suppose it would be like that. I hadn't thought. Perhaps I should contact my attorney. He might be able to help or at least to give us some information. Maybe he can get the gallery's contents released. The buyers will want their paintings." He smiled at Maggie, "By the way, by my count we sold eight. Maybe more. I don't know what Veronique may have sold."

Eight! Maggie could hardly believe it. Eight!

"Mom! How wonderful!"

Maggie nodded, still not quite able to believe it, "Yes. Wonderful. It's hard to take in. Give me some time to get used to the idea. But, right now we have other things to think about." She thought Pascal still looked exhausted and he certainly looked bewildered. "Pascal, I'm not sure, but I believe your attorney, as an officer of the court, will be required to inform the police of your whereabouts. Are you ready for them?"

"Oh, well. I suppose I have no choice about that. Sooner or later I'll have to deal with the authorities. Probably, I'll just have to make a statement and then not leave town." He shruggd and sighed, "Really, my knowledge of these things is mostly from television."

"Speaking of television, let's see if there's any news." Maggie glanced at her watch, opened the doors of the armoire that housed her set, and pointed the remote.

The news was just beginning. The local announcer recapped the news of the murder, "It has just been announced that a warrant has been issued for the arrest of Pascal DuMonchet, prominent art gallery owner and employer of the deceased. Mr. DuMonchet disappeared after the murder and has not been heard from since. A four-state alert has been issued for him. Anyone with information about this man is urged to contact the authorities." An old newspaper photograph of Pascal at an art show was enlarged and on the screen. "In other news, the DEA . . . " Maggie switched the set off.

Pascal gasped, "This is not good. I cannot believe such a thing. I must go at once and clear this up."

Allie looked doubtful, but nodded, "Probably the best. Don't know what else you can do."

Shock distorted Maggie's face, "I'm not sure that's a good idea. Let's think about it before you do anything. For one thing, you still look worn out. For another, d'you have an alibi?"

"Well, yes. That is, I was in that shack for almost two days."

"But, can you prove it? And, Pascal, I'm not sure, but I'd guess that Veronique was killed while you still were nearby. Think a minute. I'm sure that we discovered Veronique not more than twenty or thirty minutes after I last saw her and, for that matter, you. I don't want to be negative about this, but, so far, what I've seen of Lieutenant Anderson doesn't instill confidence in the Costa Mira police force."

"Ah yes, Maggie. You may be correct, but what other choice do I have? If I go home they'll be looking there. I can't stay here. You already have broken the law by keeping me here overnight. I refuse to put you in danger of legal prosecution," Pascal grimaced.

Allie nodded, "Just what I was thinking."

"The most frustrating thing is that if you go to the police, they'll stop the investigation and then whoever did it will get away and you,

Pascal, will be it!"

"Yes, it appears that I am in the soup, no?"

"In the soup. Yes!"

The old tan Chevy was as anonymous as a vehicle can be. No distinguishing markings, just the right amount of dust. Innocuous and anonymous. It stopped twenty yards from the shack. A soft breeze ruffled the tops of the saw grass as the driver walked casually around the shack. He stopped at sight of the open door. Where was he? Old Pascal could not have escaped. He was tied securely. The door had been locked. The driver looked inside, not really expecting to find anything. He found a pile of ropes beside the rickety chair. The hasp, with rusty nails still attached and with its new padlock still intact was on the weathered door. Well, Pascal couldn't have gone far. Probably find him along the highway. And then he would see what was what! How dare he escape! It was his own fault for interrupting the argument with Veronique. And Veronique. How dare she make such a fuss. Really she had been completely unreasonable!

"Allie, what are we to do? We can't let him go to the police. You know what will happen. Poor Pascal," Maggie bent over toward Allie and whispered.

Allie found herself whispering also, "Mom, why are we whispering? He's in the shower. Can't hear a thing!"

Maggie straightened and said out loud, "I know. But what're we going to do?"

"Well, he's right. We could get into real trouble with him here. Not that anyone'd be likely to know about him. I mean, it was pretty late last night when we came in. Too bad we can't ship him out of the country until the whole mess gets cleared up."

"But the airports would be risky."

"Mom, I wasn't serious. We need to let him do what he has to do. We've done enough already."

"But, Allie. He's such a nice man. A real gentleman. I can't bear the thought of his being put in jail or worse. I mean, I *know* he had nothing to do with it. It's just not fair! Oh, I wish Hadi were here. He'd be able to see clearly through this muddle."

"And who is Hadi? I didn't mean to eavesdrop, but I couldn't help hearing that someone would be able to solve this problem," Pascal stood in the doorway, freshly showered and dressed, smiling at them.

"I forgot. You haven't met him. Hadi's an old friend. He surprised us by showing up at the opening. We were looking for you to introduce him to you when we found Veronique. But now, he's disappeared again." Maggie paused, "He can be very mysterious." She stopped again, "We're just trying to find a solution so you won't have to turn yourself in."

With an inclination of his head, "Thank you, Maggie. That's very kind of you. You both have been more than kind to me already. But, as I said, I must not any longer put you in danger."

"I suppose you're right, it's just . . . " Maggie's eyes were wide with thought, "Wait . . . wait a moment. I . . . I might have an idea."

But her idea was interrupted by a knock at her door. It was loud and made each of them jump. Three pale faces with big eyes and open mouths. Maggie put a finger to her lips and motioned Pascal to the guest room. Quickly, she put the coffee cups and breakfast things, un-rinsed, into the dishwasher. Calling out, "Coming, coming," she answered the knock.

"Mrs. McGill. May I come in?"

"Lieutenant Anderson, this is not the best time."

"Oh?" Giving the word significance and looking over her shoulder, across the entry, into the living room.

Maggie cursed herself, "I mean, we slept late and we're just getting started on the day. Is there something I can do for you?"

"I need to ask you a few more questions." But the damage had been done. Anderson's curiosity had been aroused and he sent out searching glances as if to examine the entire apartment.

Maggie sighed, "Well, okay. Come in. I can't imagine what more we can tell you. We've told you absolutely everything we know. We can't tell you more than that."

Anderson's questioning repeated all he had asked before. Unfortunately his manner showed little improvement. Maggie and Allie were becoming even more exasperated than ever.

"Now, Mrs. McGill, about Pascal DuMonchet? Tell me about the last time you saw him."

Maggie drew a deep breath. It seemed as if her mouth formed the lie without her conscious volition, "He was there at the gallery during the show and then he wasn't. We looked for him, but didn't find him." She was aware that Allie was sitting very still. In disapproval? Well, it was done now.

Anderson sighed, "Yes, that's what you told me. Well, if anything more occurs to you, let me know. And if you hear from DuMonchet, notify us immediately."

Amazingly, Anderson seemed to accept her falsehood. Maggie, who was not accustomed to prevarication, almost expected something dreadful to happen, but it didn't. He bid them good-bye with the usual cautions and left.

"Whew!" came simultaneously from Maggie and Allie.

Maggie turned to her daughter, "Oh, Allie. I couldn't turn him in. I just couldn't. I hope you don't think less of me for lying. But I just couldn't do it."

"Don't be silly, Mom. Of course, I don't think less of you. I'm not sure you were wise, but I understand. He sort of gets to one, doesn't he? I suppose you really couldn't have done anything else. But what now?"

"I was getting an idea when he interrupted. Wait. Let's call Pascal in and I'll tell you both at the same time."

They filled Pascal in on the interview with Anderson. He expressed deep gratitude, but concern for their position.

"Pascal, I've had an idea. See what you both think." Maggie drew a deep breath and continued, "My friends, the Whitmores, are on a cruise until the twenty-eighth. They often take me sailing with them. In fact, they've taught me a bit about boats and sailing. Well, they offered me the use of their boat while they're away. I didn't consider using it because I was so busy with the art and it really is too much boat for one person to handle alone. I think they thought I might want to motor it around the bay. But it occurs to me that it would be possible for a person to stay on the boat for a while without anyone taking too much notice. The marina people know me and are accustomed to my coming and going." She turned to Pascal who was beginning to hope there was an alternative to jail, "I could bring you provisions from time to time. You'd have to lie pretty low, you'd be confined, but at least we'd buy some time and you could rest and get your strength back. Probably you'd be there just a few days until this thing is ironed out. What do you think?"

"Ah, Maggie. Thank you for helping me. But what about your friends?"

"I know they wouldn't mind. We have over four weeks before they come back. But I'd expect that long before then, something will have happened and we'll know more or the whole thing might be resolved."

"Not such a bad idea, Mom. But we'd have to very careful transporting him. Do you think it's possible that we are being watched?"

"I'd be surprised. I doubt that we really have aroused any suspicion. I think Lieutenant Anderson just likes to harass us. But, you know, he was suspicious this morning. Pascal'd probably be safer away from here."

"What do you say, Pascal?"

"It sounds as if it might be an answer. I guess I always can turn myself in. It's not an opportunity that will go away. Let's give it a try."

Chapter Five

The thin sliver of a moon low on the western horizon was only dimly reflected in the blue-black of the Gulf's waters. A soft, dark velvet breeze blew off the water, caressing their faces. The three conspirators closed the car's doors softly and, carrying armloads of provisions, made their way to the boat lying in its slip.

"Shh! Be careful. There's a step here," Maggie whispered.

"Watch your step. Here, let me hold the boat. Now just step up and in."

Maggie unlocked the hatch and did a survey of the main cabin. Everything seemed to be in order. She instructed Pascal in the proper use of the tiny stove and the head. They bid him a goodnight and left.

"Hey, who's there?" The voice was loud and the light in her eyes blinded Maggie. Before she could answer, "Oh, it's you, Miz McGill. I thought a heard a noise and . . . "

"Hi Bert. Yes, it's me and this is my daughter, Allie. We just came down to check on the boat. The Whitmores left me the use of it and I wanted to check it out. We thought we might take her out while Allie's here. But, as it turns out, Mr. Whitmore's cousin dropped in unexpectedly and he's going to spend a few days on the boat. So, you don't have to worry. Everything's okay," Maggie paused to catch her breath.

"Oh, I don't worry if it's you, Miz McGill. I know you'd take care of her like she was your own," his gruff voice softened. "You reckon that cousin'll need anything? Should I look in on him?"

"Oh, no. We've brought him all he'll need. Actually, he said he'd not been feeling well and that he just needs a rest," Maggie was amazed at how easily the lies came once one started.

"I think he mostly just wants to be left alone. You know, a little peace and quiet," Allie added. "We'll stop by from time to time."

"Well, okay then. Glad it was you," Bert turned and headed back to his place, a shed-like building built at the edge of the water that held both his small apartment and the marina office.

Safely in the car, Maggie felt her knees tremble and her voice shaky, "Whew! That was close!"

"Yeah. Close. But you were great, Mom. I didn't know you had such creative deception in you."

"Neither did I!"

Neither woman noticed the nondescript tan car sitting innocently among the others in the parking lot.

What were those two women doing at the marina at this hour? Were those the same women as from the gallery? Surely too late for them to have been here socially. Very strange. Well, never mind. There were more important things to do. Had to clear up some loose ends.

Wednesday morning dawned clear and bright, "Well, Anderson. Fill me in on the Duval case. Anything new?" Carter Blake leaned back in his chair and stared at Lieutenant Anderson.

"We've got more on the victim. Turns out she was French. Thirty-eight years old. Came here nineteen years ago. Got a green card. She's been going to citizenship classes. Exam's next month. Worked for DuMonchet for the entire nineteen years. No family here or in France that we could find. Parents are dead. She had a brother. Still trying to find him to notify him of her death. There's no sign that they were close."

"Good work, Anderson. That's more like it. What about DuMonchet? Found him? Any leads?"

"Nah. Nothing. He's French, too. Showed up here about thirty years ago. Got his citizenship right away. Opened that gallery. As far as we know there's no family at all. Nobody's got anything bad to say about him. Looks like he knew lots of people, but no one close. Kept mostly to himself. No sign that there was anything between him and Duval. He hasn't shown up at his house. Papers and mail are piling up."

"So, what d'you think?"

"Dunno, but I'd guess either he did it and he's gone completely or somebody did him."

"That seems logical. Not bad, Anderson. But we need more. The press is giving it to us. What about people at that show? Anything?"

"Nothing. Those McGill women could be hiding something. I didn't think so at first, but yesterday I was over there and I thought something was a little fishy. But then it seemed okay. That Lazlo guy is fruity as they come, but don't think he'd have the guts. He's got one of those art galleries down the street from DuMonchet's. Not as fancy as DuMonchet's but he must be doing okay. Got a waterfront place in Royal Palms. Now DuMonchet's partner, Duane Simpson. That's another story. He's got motive. That gallery was a going thing. Did okay. They both live well. He's got a wife and two grown kids. Got a nice house in Palm Park. He and DuMonchet had a survivorship insurance policy. He'll get the whole thing if something happens to DuMonchet. What's more, he won't talk to me."

"Very interesting. Duane Simpson? Hmmm. Bring him in. Let him sweat a little. Motive's enough for questioning. We can take a long time with questioning. Then stick a tail on him. See what you can learn. If you can find an extra man, it wouldn't hurt to keep a watch on those McGill women."

Anderson brightened. This interview was going much better than the last, "Sure. Okay."

Duane Simpson was not having a good day, "What's this about? Poor Veronique? Well, okay." He acquiesced when he saw the handcuffs come out. "All right. All right. You don't need those. I'll come."

At the police station it was no better. He refused to talk without his attorney. When Eliot Grayson arrived he found Duane Simpson angry and frightened, "Well, Duane, what's all this about?"

"Darned if I know. They just came this morning before I even had a chance to have breakfast and dragged me down here. I was afraid to talk without your being here. I don't have anything to hide, but, you know, murder's serious."

This was a long speech for Duane who normally spoke not more than a few words at a time. Eliot Grayson had known him for many years. When Pascal DuMonchet and Duane had come to him years ago to draw up the papers for their partnership Eliot had thought them an odd pair, but apparently it was a partnership that had worked, Duane supplying the business and accounting skills and Pascal the creative and art knowledge. They had complemented each other well. But, as Duane said, murder is a serious business and Eliot Grayson was afraid he might be out of his league, "Yes, it is. Tell you what, Duane. I'm going to call some people I know on the other coast that deal with criminal cases. You know, I'm a pretty good attorney in my own field, but I could be over my head with this. You just sit tight and don't say a thing. I'll let them know you'll have another attorney coming. That sound okay to you?"

Duane rubbed his chin, "Gosh, Eliot. I don't know. Sounds pretty complicated. And pretty expensive. You sure you can't do it?'

Eliot thought for a moment, "Okay. Let's do this. I'll stay with you right now during the questioning. You look to me before you open your mouth. If they're satisfied and let you go, okay. But, if not, or if it gets more serious, we call in the big guns."

"Sounds good to me."

"Uh, Duane. Heard anything from Pascal?"

"No. Nothing. Can't imagine where he can be."

"Me neither."

The questioning was long and bordered on harassment. Time and again, Eliot warned Anderson against going too far.

In the end, Anderson knew no more, Duane was exhausted and Eliot Grayson had lost respect for the police force that stood between the community and anarchy.

"Well, Simpson, that's all for now. You're free to go, but don't leave town," Anderson's voice was heavy with suspicion and threat.

Duane breathed a sigh of relief, stood up and left the police office. Outside he shook hands with Eliot Grayson, "Eliot, I can't thank you enough. That sure was tough, but you hung in there. Thanks again."

"Mom, I wonder how Pascal is faring. When should we check on him?"

"Oh, I'm sure he's just fine. Might be a little bored by now, but otherwise, I'd bet he's okay. Maybe we'll go over after dinner tonight and check."

"Good. I know. Let's take him a treat. What would a French art dealer enjoy? Food? Books? Music? How about a change of clothes? He's probably pretty tired of that dirty old outfit he was wearing."

"Sure. He seems to be the sort who takes pride in his appearance. Besides that, it can get cold down there by the water. Let's go to Walmart. Bet we could find an outfit there that would suffice and we wouldn't need to break the bank to do it. I don't think either of us has anything that would go round him."

"Great idea." Allie agreed. "I just thought of something. I wonder if he overheard your story to Bert. If not, we should let him know just in case he needs to use it."

"Gosh! You're right. I hadn't thought of that. See what happens when one starts a deception! It just builds and builds. Well, for sure, we need to go over there as soon as we can. Just in case. But, taking him treats is a great idea. Let's go out now and find something."

The night was dark and breezy when Allie and Maggie arrived at the marina arms loaded with a carry-out French dinner for three, a bottle of decent French wine, a Walmart bag filled with clothing and some toilet articles, a box of Belgium chocolates, a new biography of Van Gogh, the latest best seller novel, and several CD's of assorted music. Allie laughed, "Hey Mom, think we over did it?"

Maggie chuckled, "Maybe. I just got carried away!"

They found Pascal comfortably resting in the main cabin. He greeted them warmly, "Ah, Maggie and Allie. How good to see you. What is all this? Ah my, you're too kind! Clothes? Ah, thank you so much. How did you know these old things were just too dirty for words?" He pulled some bills from his pocket, "Here, let me reimburse you."

"Nonsense. They were quite inexpensive. We can talk about that later when all this is over," Maggie's adamant face made him stop.

They made a picnic in the main cabin. Pascal had disappeared into the forward cabin with the Walmart package. He emerged looking quite stylish in the new outfit they had brought. Maggie thought they had done quite a nice job finding things that fit. Elastic waistbands were heaven sent. Only the sleeves of the sweater seemed a bit long. If the situation had been different it would have been a festive occasion. Between them, the two women filled Pascal in on his new identity, "Just remember that you are recovering from something and need peace and quiet. That way, you can remain reclusive."

"Yes, yes. I will. Thank you is inadequate for the gratitude I feel to you both, but I will say it again. Thank you from the bottom of my heart."

They left, promising to return soon. Clouds obscured the moon and the dock walkway was dark. The breeze had strengthened while they were on the boat and now it tousled Maggie's hair. "Could be we're going lose our good weather," Maggie whispered. They reached the parking lot without incident. But once again, they did not notice the tan car parked inconspicuously among the others.

Those same women as last night. What could they be doing here every night. Went in carrying bags of provisions and now, empty handed. Yes. They were the same ones from the gallery. Could it be? Which boat had they visited? Cautiously, out of the car and down the dock. There. There was one with a lighted cabin. But wait, what was that noise? Someone coming? Quick. Duck behind this boat.

"Lucky we noticed the coffee. Don't know how it could have gotten out of the bag. Hope he likes this special roast," Maggie whispered as they hurried down the dock.

"Hope he's still up. He was looking pretty tired," Allie added. "Wait, Mom. I think I see something up there." She reached out and held her mother's arm.

A form stepped out of the shadows. "Ah, my Maggie and Allie. You are doing the 'good works', no?" His singsong accent was never stronger.

"HADI!" Out loud and in unison.

"You gave us a scare!" Whispered.

"Whatever are you doing here at this hour?"

"Where'd you go?"

"Where have you been?"

"How'd you know we'd be here?"

"Ah, many questions, no? Just now, I think it would be better to talk less and to return to your automobile and go home."

"Yes, of course, we will. But first we need to take this coffee down to . . . "

"Tomorrow would be better to bring the coffee. But now I think you must return quickly to your car."

"But . . ."

Even though it made little sense to the two women, they had learned to trust Hadi's advice and they were turning to return to the parking lot when a low voice said, "Not now, if you don't mind." The voice carried a strong threat.

They turned to see a dark form emerge from the shadows. There was just enough light from the curtained boat windows to show a dim gleam on the barrel of a handgun.

The trio involuntarily backed away from the menace.

"Here, stop right now. Where do you think you're going? Come back here. What're you doing down here? What boat were you on?"

"Ah, er, well, we were just sight-seeing. All these beautiful boats," Maggie's talent for deception had deserted her.

"That's right. I'm visiting from the west coast and she's showing me the sights," Even as she said it, Allie knew how lame it sounded.

"You wouldn't try to fool an old fooler, now would you," the voice sneered. He reached over, grabbed Maggie and held the gun to her head, "Now you, missy. You tell me which boat or the old lady gets it."

Allie gulped to steady her voice, "Yes, okay. I'll do it. Just let her go. Come this way." She led them down the dock, hoping to find a way out of the situation. But the man kept a tight hold on Maggie as he followed.

Hadi spoke quietly in his soft singsong voice, "Now, sir. Please do not harm the lady. We will cooperate with you."

For her part, Maggie was not sure whether she was more frightened by the gun or incensed by being called "old lady."

They stopped beside the Whitmore's boat, *More Fun*. Maggie thought the name ironic and even more inane than usual. This was not even close to fun.

Pascal's face was a study of shocked surprise when he opened the hatch, "Maggie? Allie? Marc? What're you doing here? And why do you have that gun? What's happening?"

Pascal knew this man! Amazing!

Marc shoved them in and down the steps into the cabin, "Pascal, you old dog! You've given me quite a chase! But I've found you, at last. However did you escape from that shack?"

"So, it was you. I wondered. But I didn't believe even you could have done anything so dastardly. And Veronique? Your own sister!

How could you?"

"Quiet! That's enough of that! I don't want to hear another word!" Marc's face suffused with blood and he looked capable of anything.

Maggie was grateful that he had shifted his attention away from her. It gave her a chance to catch her breath and clear her mind. For the first time she was able to examine their captor. Marc was tall and thin with a shock of unruly dark hair over a long unshaven face. A dirty tee shirt hung over tattered khaki shorts. She could not see a resemblance to Veronique, yet he seemed familiar. Maggie felt she'd seen him somewhere before.

"Mom, isn't he the guy who was with Veronique at Les Artistes last summer?" Allie whispered in her mother's ear.

That was it. Maggie remembered that they had seemed to be not getting along very well then. Oh, dear. Veronique's brother. Oh, dear. Poor Veronique.

"Here, you. What're you whispering about? No whispering, and no talking either. Stop it right now!" Marc turned back to Pascal and Allie made a face behind his back.

The face lifted Maggie's spirits and turned her fear into considering their situation as a problem to be solved, rather than a hopeless situation.

"And you, old man. Why have you caused me so much trouble? You seem always to turn up at exactly the wrong time. I'd like to hear how you got out of that shack. But later. Now, I need to figure out what to do next. What am I going to do with all of you? I've got to get out of here. I've stayed around too long as it is. Should've left months ago, but Veronique . . . " Marc broke off what had turned into a mumbled monologue. His speech was remarkably unaccented, nearly completely American.

Maggie tried, "Marc. Why don't you just leave us here? We'd promise to stay on the boat until you have a chance to get away. We're trustworthy. You wouldn't have to worry . . . "

He interrupted her with a scornful laugh, "You must think I'm a fool. You'd call the police before I made it out of the parking lot. Besides, if it were that easy, I would've left long ago. No papers, you see. No, I need to find another way out, a way out of this mess and out of this country." Scorn turned to desperation as he spoke. He sat in silence for a while.

"Well, there's no other way. This boat. What is it? A ketch, sloop? How big? Forty, forty-five feet? Any of you know?"

"Forty-six foot sloop," Maggie answered before she thought.

"Nice. Very nice. Should make it across this pond with no trouble. Belize. That'd be a good place to get lost and start over. Okay. That's it. We're going on a cruise, folks." Marc got up and started opening doors and bins, taking a quick inventory of supplies, "Not bad, but I'd be happier if we had a bit more in the way of provisions and fuel. Here, you, come here."

One by one he tied them up securely, gagged them, turned down the lights and left the boat.

The four bodies were lying on the cabin floor, each trussed as nicely as a Thanksgiving turkey. Silence. Then a scuffling noise. In the dim light, Maggie could see Allie squirming and wriggling. Did she think she could free herself from her bonds? Then Maggie saw that Allie was inching toward Hadi who was lying on the floor near her. Hadi, for his part, was doing the same, attempting to get nearer to Allie. Back to back, they were close enough to touch, and each was working on the strong rope that bound the other's hands. Maggie, thinking this was a good idea, started inching her way across the floor toward Pascal. He, in turn, was moving toward her. Maggie, working on Pascal's ropes, broke every nail in the first few seconds. It was slow, hard and painful work. At first it seemed completely futile, but after what seemed forever, Maggie could see that Hadi must be making some progress. It seemed that Allie's hands were working a bit more freely. That was good because Maggie didn't think she and Pascal were making any progress at all.

At last, Allie's hands were free. Quickly she freed herself and the others of their gags, found a knife in the galley and set to work cutting away first at Hadi's bonds. Then they freed Maggie and Pascal.

Amid choruses of "thank you's" and sounds of jubilation the four prisoners started up the steps to the deck. Suddenly the hatch opened and they found themselves much too close to Marc's handgun.

"Just where do you think you're going?" His voice was low and menacing. "I can see that you'll all need some careful watching. Don't annoy me or you'll be sorry." He motioned for them to sit on the benches that lined the cabin, "Now, what am I going to do with you while I get under way?"

In the end, he herded them into the forward cabin and leaned against the door while he attached sliding bolts in three places.

They listened to the sounds of Marc's working with the bolts, then silence. Maggie groped around the cabin until she located the light switch. With the light on, she surveyed her companions and their situation. Three faces turned to her expectantly. "Well, here we are! Now what? I guess we need to find a way out of here," she tested the door just to make sure. It didn't give, even a fraction of an inch.

"Ah, Maggie. It seems we again find ourselves prisoners, no? Do you not remember? Now is a time for assessing the deeper aspects of our situation," Hadi's singsong voice had a strangely calming effect on the other three. Pascal gazed on him with amazement. Allie and Maggie with fondness.

A glance at Pascal's face reminded Maggie of her social duties, "Oh, Pascal. You haven't yet met Hadi. This is Mohammed Hadi El Kabir, an old friend. And Hadi, meet Pascal DuMonchet who owns the art gallery and who is in a bit of trouble right now."

Pascal nodded and smiled his acknowledgment of the introduction. Maggie had to admit that Hadi did seem a bit exotic. A small, dark-skinned man, tonight wearing a blue turban, perched cross-legged on the edge of the bunk. He was less than average in height. His wrists protruding from the sleeves of the loose white shirt were tanned and bony. His shoulders seemed unusually broad for one so thin. He returned Pascal's look with steady, shining, penetrating deep brown eyes set in a thin bony face. A short goatee-style beard and mustache covered his face.

"Ah, Pascal. It is good that we meet finally."

"Yes, good to meet you, Hadi."

Maggie hoped her two friends would like each other, especially since it seemed they all were destined to spend time together.

"Mom, have you noticed that the boat is bouncing around more?"

"Probably because we're in the forward cabin. It always is more bouncy. The wind was coming up as I remember. Could be a bit of weather, but we're fine here in the marina. Perfectly safe. Our real problem is finding a way out of this cabin."

Four sets of eyes wandered around the tiny cabin that really was just an oversized bunk with a narrow walkway around it. Four small rectangular portholes, two on each side of the cabin, bulkhead storage and two sidelights were all they saw. Too bad that the portholes were so small. Not even a small child could get through them. Maggie stood up on the bunk and opened each of the lockers. Allie explored the bins under the bunk. They found a stash of eight life vests, a long coil of rope, another coil of heavy-duty extension cord, an extra twelve-volt dry cell battery. Above the bunk Maggie found an assortment of deck shoes and windbreaker jackets. She and Allie had worn appropriate shoes for their visit to the boat, but both Hadi and Pascal were pleased to don the non-slip shoes. Maggie mumbled to Allie, "Why couldn't we have brought our purses with us from the car? A cell phone could be the answer to our problems!"

Allie nodded her agreement.

They fell silent and still as they noticed movement on the deck, and quiet scrapings and thuds. "Oh, dear! I do believe he's taking the boat out. Oh, dear!" Maggie's eyes were very big.

"But, where would he go?"

"Didn't you hear? He was talking about Belize."

"Belize? That's across the Gulf. Surely not!"

"Well, I hope not."

Marc was working as quietly as he could. He had to get out of here. Quickly he stowed the gear he'd bought in town. Ten extra gallons of diesel under the deck benches. He tossed the extra food and water into the main cabin lockers. Checking the gauges he was relieved to note that the fuel and water tanks were full. Those Whitmore people had left her ready to go. At least one thing was working out okay. But he had to hurry. It'd be light soon. Didn't want to attract any attention.

What was he going to do with those people? Well, once they got out to sea they might come in handy. They'd lose interest in escaping with hundreds of miles of ocean separating them from land. This was a pretty big boat. Be good to have some help. That girl looked like she might be strong enough to handle the ropes. The other three probably were only dead weight. Probably ought to get rid of them. Think about that later.

Marc cast off the ropes and pushed away from the dock. Quietly he started the engine at the slowest possible speed and lowest sound level, eased her into gear and reversed out of the slip into the channel, through the forest of masts and into the bay at last. There was a strong wind out of the west-southwest. Good. Once out of the bay, he'd put up sail, make good time and save fuel. Tacking into the wind was not his favorite thing, but better than no wind at all.

"Maggie, do you hear that? He's started the engine. We're going. *Merde!* Marc can be very headstrong."

Seeing the fear in Pascal's face, Allie asked, "You know him, Pascal? How is that?"

Pascal sighed, "Ah, *oui,* I've known him and Veronique all their lives. I was a friend of their parents in France. He is Veronique's brother, the older of the two children. He was a handsome child, very bright and precocious. He was the center of his parent's love and attention until Veronique was born. The family was delighted with their new little daughter. All, that is, except for Marc. From the first he was jealous of her. It was more than simple sibling rivalry. Something happened to him. I'm not sure what. It seemed as if Marc felt he wasn't good enough or smart enough or even loved. It was as if, through the years, he blamed Veronique and his parents for everything that went wrong in his life. And a lot went wrong from the very beginning. Even as a young child he seemed to be always in trouble."

Pascal continued, "I came here while they still were children and I lost track of them for a while. Then I had news that my friend, Etienne, their father, had died. Genevieve, their mother, was distraught. She contracted a serious illness. I believe she died of a broken heart, but she loved both her children. By that time Marc had gone, traveling the world. She was concerned for Veronique's well being. She wrote, asking me to watch over young Veronique. After her mother's death, I helped Veronique come here and gave her a job at the gallery. She was about twenty then. She was a quick learner and soon she became very good, a real asset. The customers liked her. But then, several months ago, Marc showed up. No explanations. Nothing. He liked to hang around the gallery. Surprisingly, he even made himself useful in the back room. Packed and unpacked the art. All the same, I didn't trust him. I remembered too much. But he was, after all, Veronique's only family." He sighed again, "Oh, poor Veronique. Life was not always so good to her."

"Ah, yes. Life can seem difficult at times, no?" Hadi's eyes held sympathy for the family and for Pascal who was visibly distressed by the memories.

"Poor Veronique," Allie agreed.

Bert, who was, by nature, an early riser, awoke to what he thought was the sound of a diesel engine. Who could be going out so early this morning? Most of the sailboat people didn't start out before sunrise. Probably no one from this marina. Strange. Well, he'd have a look around at first light.

Chapter Six

The thin sliver of golden light on the eastern horizon was giving way to high overcast when Bert walked down the dock. *More Fun*, the Whitmore's boat was gone. She was the one he'd heard early this morning. Strange. Could Mrs. McGill have taken her out? She'd said it was too much boat for her alone. And she was right. *More Fun* was too much boat for any sensible sailor alone. What about that cousin? Could he have taken her out? Bert glanced at the sky. Not a good day to be out of the bay, even for an experienced crew. Maybe they'd just gone for a spin around the bay. Wind had laid early this morning, but she'd be kickin' up a squall before night. Didn't like the looks of it. Should've got up when he heard her this morning. Maybe he should call Mrs. McGill and see what she knew.

"Hello. This is Maggie. I'm sorry I'm not here to take your call, but if you'll leave a message, I'll get right back to you."

"Er, hello. Er, Mrs. McGill. This is Bert, er, at the marina. *More Fun's* gone out. Wondered if you know anything 'bout her? Not the best weather. Er, I just wondered. Er, could you let me know if you know anything 'bout it. Er, thank you." Bert hated those damned contraptions. Always made him feel tongue-tied. Well, hopefully she'd call back soon or the boat'd come back soon.

Strange, the wind had died. Marc cleared the channel and headed west into an unnaturally quiet sea. To the east was a pale glimmer of light, a golden ribbon below the overcast sky. Looked like it would be cloudy today. Okay. Probably bring up some wind later on. In the meantime, the diesel throbbed along healthily. Nice thing about money. Made everything run smoother. Even boats. He sighed with relief. Finally, he was away from that place.

For a moment he forgot about the people below, forgot about the recent past. Marc stared unseeing into the glassy, dark morning sea as it gradually lightened. He could start over in a new place. This time it would be different. This time he'd make it work. He'd stay on the up and up. Maybe get himself a place over there if he liked it. With what he'd get from the boat, he'd be on easy street. An image of himself, strolling along a colorful waterfront in spotlessly white clothing and a Panama hat, natives bowing deferentially, floated through his mind. He'd be the mysterious cultured Frenchman. He'd even bring back his French accent. Maybe he'd take up art, a sort of Gauguin. Visions of art shows, gallery openings brought his thoughts to Veronique and Pascal. Veronique! Really, she'd asked for trouble! With a violent jerk of his head he got up and wandered around the deck, fantasies gone, memories too present.

The sound of the boat slicing through the quiet sea made the silence in the forward cabin even more noticeable. Maggie had spent a restless time fretting about their situation, reviewing their actions and wondering if there was some way they could have avoided the present situation. The others were either napping or, like Maggie, lost in their own thoughts. Maggie smiled down at Allie, who had curled up next to Maggie for a nap. She stirred and sat up, "Hi Mom. It's beginning to get light. How far out do you suppose we are?"

"It's hard to figure without the instruments, but I'd imagine several miles. He's had the engine going all morning," Maggie sounded as despairing as she felt. How could she have let this happen?

"Ah, Maggie. You sound downhearted. You must not worry yourself. This situation is in perfect order and everything is happening just as it needs to."

Maggie looked across the bunk to Hadi who was sitting cross-legged with what appeared to be perfect comfort. She had learned to trust his guidance, but really! This was not the way she wanted things to happen. "Hadi, thank you for your reassurance, but this certainly isn't my idea of a perfect situation!" She knew she sounded snappish, but she was not feeling philosophical.

Pascal observed the interchange without comment, but his face mirrored his bewilderment and concern.

Hadi turned to him, "Ah, M. DuMonchet, . . . "

"Please, please call me Pascal. This is not a time or place for formalities."

"Just as you say. Well, Pascal, how do feel about the situation?"

"Pretty low, actually. I feel that I'm responsible for you all being here in this danger. I can't tell you how sorry I am to have involved you in this," he dropped his eyes and contemplated his hands.

Maggie, realizing that her funk had helped to create his feelings of guilt, was, in turn, feeling badly, "Oh, Pascal. Please don't let yourself think that. I was thinking the very same things about myself. This is something that has just happened and we mustn't let ourselves despair. No one is to blame unless, of course, it's Marc. Even he, I suppose, could put the blame for his actions on the circumstances of his life. Oh, dear. It's becoming very complicated."

"Ah, Maggie. The psychology. It is always complicated. No?" Hadi smiled gently at her.

She felt warmed by his smile, "Well, yes, Hadi. Often it is. I guess it's different when it happens to you. It makes it harder to be objective and discern patterns. But you know, this is a pretty scary situation. I can't see a way out of it."

Again the gentle smile, "But, Maggie. Do you not remember? The way will be made clear to us when the time is right if we just listen. For now, we need to save our strength and remain calm."

Allie entered the conversation, "Yes, I remember, Hadi. But this time it does seem to be extraordinarily difficult. This man is quite unreasonable and, so far, unpredictable."

Pascal, who'd been looking bewildered, interjected, "I realize you all know each other, but I'm having trouble keeping up with what you are saying. Could you please fill me in."

Eyes met across the cabin. It was Allie who told the events of their adventure in California and of Hadi's almost metempiric guidance through them, "Really, Hadi. You were quite amazing! I'll never forget it."

Again the gentle smile, "Nor I, Miss Allie. You were an

important part of the escape, too," and looking at Maggie, "as were your mother and the others. Each of us had a part to play. And so it will be now. We have no need to fret." Seeing the looks on the three faces turned toward him, Hadi continued, "But we must pay attention and stay alert. You are correct that the situation is serious. Even so, we must remember that when it is the will of Allah, we will be guided out of this desert to a true oasis."

Pascal looked even more puzzled, "Oh, I see." But the question was in his voice.

Seeing his bewilderment, Hadi said, "Ah, Pascal. You have questions, yes? Allow me to tell you a story. I am named Hadi. Hadi is a Sufi. It is said that when one is lost in the desert and if one is fortunate, he will meet Hadi. It is necessary that one follow Hadi without question or hesitation. For a long time they may wander through the desert and perhaps the person may spy a shining oasis in a different direction than Hadi is leading him. One then may hesitate and doubt and say to Hadi, 'Hadi, there is an oasis over there.' The person may then leave Hadi and head toward the oasis. The doubt causes Hadi to disappear and the person, upon reaching the area where he saw the oasis, finds it was but a mirage. Soon the person perishes. But perhaps if he had followed Hadi over the next sand dune the real oasis would have been there. The lesson is to follow Hadi in perfect faith and without question. It is good to follow the path of Allah the same way." Hadi's eyes remained fixed on Pascal.

Pascal nodded. His voice was a bit surer when he said, "I see."

Hadi gazed into his eyes for a few moments, "Yes, yes. Maybe. Yes. I think you are just beginning to see. Good." He turned to Maggie and Allie, "We are on a boat on the sea, but, for us, it is like a desert. Each of us can quiet his or her mind and listen for the will of Allah. Or God. Or whatever you wish to call it. But you must realize that I am not the only one who can hear. Each of us can hear. We have but to clear our minds of interference. That is our work at this moment." So saying, he closed his eyes and was quiet.

The others looked at one another with a look that was equivalent to a shrug.

Carter Blake leaned back in his chair, "So, Anderson. What d'you have to report about the Duval case? Anything new? Found DuMonchet yet?" Blake removed his glasses and laid them on the desk between them.

Lieutenant Anderson fidgeted in his chair, "Er, no. That is, we still haven't found DuMonchet. We think there was another person working at the DuMonchet gallery, a man. But we can't find out much about him. No name. I'm going to talk to Duane Simpson again. He may have some information about this guy. As far as we can tell, he wasn't on the books as an employee, but seemed to hang around a lot." He cleared his throat, "I plan to talk to the McGill women again. I haven't gotten anything out of them yet, but I'll bet they know more than they're saying."

Blake nodded, "Yes. Okay. But first let's find out more about the fellow at the gallery. That might prove useful. What about those McGill women? Anything?"

"Er, no. That is, we're so shorthanded. I finally got someone over there last night. It's been quiet so far."

"Oh. Well, keep me informed. Talk to you tomorrow."

Duane Simpson was spending the morning in his office at home, attempting to do what gallery business he could from there. The doorbell interrupted his train of thought. When his wife, Adele, ushered Lieutenant Anderson in, Simpson found it hard to be gracious, "Oh, hello, Anderson. What d'you want?"

"Well, Mr. Simpson, I just wanted to ask you a few more questions."

"I don't think I'd better say anything without my attorney. You understand. He told me not to."

"Well, that may be, but I just want to ask for information about the gallery. You can talk to me about that."

"Maybe, but I'm paying him a lot of money and I'd better follow his advice." So saying, Duane clamped his mouth shut.

Anderson was reminded of a snapping turtle he'd had as a kid, "Call him then and let's get on with it." Anderson plopped down into a chair and folded his arms.

Duane stared at him for a moment, sighed, and picked up the telephone.

Eliot Grayson entered Duane's study rapidly and with a curt nod to Anderson, turned to Duane, "Well, Duane? What's going on?"

"Don't know, Eliot. Anderson just walked in here this morning and wanted to ask more questions. I thought it'd be better if you were here."

"Quite right. Quite right." Turning to Anderson, "What's this about? My client told you everything he knew at the station."

"We need some information about a man who spent a lot of time at the gallery. That's all. Nothing to get upset about."

"And . . . ?"

"We're interested in knowing more about him. Who he was. Why was he there? That sort of thing."

Duane frowned, "You must mean Marc. Marc showed up several months ago. He just hung around. Sometimes he'd help out a little in the back room. You know, moving stuff around, packing and unpacking stuff. But he wasn't an employee. I think maybe he was some relation of Veronique. They spoke French together. But no one ever said who he was or what he did. He was just there sometimes." Duane glanced at Grayson, "That's all I know about him."

Grayson nodded his approval.

But Anderson lowered his pale brows, "You mean this guy was around a lot in the business where you're a partner and you didn't know anything about him except that maybe he was related to an employee?" His voice was filled with scorn and derision.

Grayson stood, starting to put himself between his client and Anderson, "I don't like your tone, Anderson. Keep a civil tongue in your head."

Duane looking to Grayson answered, "That's just what I mean. I told you. I'm not involved in the running of the gallery. I do the business part of it. Marc was not an employee. So, I had no reason to know more about him. He helped out a little. He was connected to Veronique in some way. That's all I know and that's all I needed to know!"

Anderson's tone mellowed, "Okay. Okay. I see. What's his last name? Can you give me a good description of him? We need to find him. He might know something that would help us clear this matter up."

"Well, I never heard his last name. Could be Duval, or not, if he's related to Veronique. Marc's a pretty good-looking guy, I guess. Tall, over six feet. Lots of dark hair, but he doesn't keep it combed very well. Dark eyes. He's thin, not much in the way of muscles, if you know what I mean. I never saw him dressed up. He always looked a little seedy, sort of scruffy. Sometimes he dressed really bad. I mean, holes in his clothes, or dirty. And sandals. He wore sandals a lot."

Anderson was jotting frantically in a small spiral bound notebook, "Good. That's good. Where'd he live? Did he have a job? What about a car? What kind?"

"Can't help you much there. Don't know where he lived. Don't know if he had a job. If he did, it must have had strange hours. He'd show up at the gallery at different times. No way to predict when he'd be there. I saw Veronique walk him to his car once. Let's see," Duane furrowed his brow, "I think it was tan or beige or something. Older. Maybe ten, twelve, or more years old. Could've been a Chevy or Ford. Can't be sure. But it was dirty. I remember thinking that car sure didn't go with Veronique."

Anderson put his notebook back in his coat pocket and sighed, "Well, that wasn't much, but thanks anyway. You've been a help." With a nod at Eliot Grayson, "Mr. Grayson." He left the room.

Eliot Grayson stood to leave, "Good, Duane. You did very well."

For his part, Duane heaved a big sigh and shook his hand.

"Sit down, Mr. Carrera. Sit down. Can I get you anything? Coffee? A drink?" Carter Blake motioned to the DEA agent.

"No, thank you. Nothing. Thank you for seeing me." Arthur Carrera folded his tall, lanky body into the chair opposite Blake's desk, "I want to talk about a person who may be involved in your murder investigation. Marc Duval. Know anything about him? Know his whereabouts?"

Blake leaned back in his chair and regarded Carrera silently. Melancholy dark eyes looked at him across the desk. Blake thought this could be a break for them. They hadn't even been able to ascertain for sure that Duval was the guy's last name. Obviously DEA had more information than they did. How to get it out of them? "Well, sir. No. That is, we have him under investigation, but right now we're not sure where he is. What is your interest in him?"

"I told you at our last meeting that we were investigating increased activity in controlled substances in this area. We suspect that Duval may be a part of that. As you know, he's a French national and in this country illegally. The INS is after him, too. But we want to find him first. We want information from him before he's deported. I was hoping you'd be able to help us find him."

"Well, we've got an APB out on him and we'll certainly let you know if he shows up."

"Good. But, tell your men to take all precautions. He can be dangerous."

"Yeah, er, yes. I will."

The standard handshake and he was gone.

Blake sat for a moment, then picking up the phone, "Hello, Anderson? Blake here. Get an APB out on one Marc Duval, French national, here illegally. And, Anderson. Do it yesterday!"

Chapter Seven

Sounds of locks being released brought the inmates awake. The door swung open and Marc stood before them, "I guess you can come out now. You're not going anywhere. The only way off this boat is very damp. Behave yourselves and this won't be so bad. You might even enjoy it. A cruise. You're just out for a cruise." His speech was more accented than they had heard before.

Pascal found his tongue first, "Ah, Marc. You must turn around and take us back. Whatever has happened, it will go better with you if you go back and face up to it. Do you not see? This is madness. Kidnapping! That is what it is!"

"Quiet, old man! You just be quiet!" Marc's voice rose to a shout. "All my life people have told me what to do. No more. No more. I do not want to hear it! I do not! Silence your tongue or you will find yourself someplace you do not want to be." He calmed his rage and, taking a deep breath, turned to the others, "Now. If you all can conduct yourselves well, you are free to go. If you are hungry, there is food in the galley. Remember the rules of the boat. Clean up after yourselves and don't make trouble. If you do, you will regret it, believe me." He indicated the small gun he wore in a shoulder holster. "By the way, in case you should want to call for help, don't even try." He pulled a tiny piece of electronic apparatus from his pocket, "The radio is off and off limits. Understand?"

Marc turned to Allie, "You know anything about sailing?"

She hesitated, "Not much. I've been a guest on friends' boats, but I really don't know anything."

"Well, we could be in for a blow. The sea is growing. I don't like the look of it. We'll be okay, but I may need some help," he glanced through a porthole at the ever-darkening sky.

Marc surveyed his "crew." As sailors, he considered them a sorry lot. Just another piece of his luck! Why couldn't he have kidnapped some real seamen? Pascal was useless, he knew. The old woman wouldn't be any help. She'd probably have hysterics if it got rough. As for that weird guy, couldn't count on him for anything. He probably didn't even understand English, or French, for that matter. That left the good-looking one. If he weren't escaping, if things were different, he'd turn on the charm with her. A small unpleasant smile crossed his face.

Maggie wondered what had brought the smile to Marc's face. Only after he mentioned the weather did she glance through a porthole and notice that, indeed, the sea was getting rougher. The smooth glassy sea of a few hours ago was still glassy, but long, heavy swells rolled under the glassiness. She grabbed a handhold as the boat rode down a particularly deep swell. Whatever happened weather-wise, it was good to be out of the cabin. Maggie made her way to the deck. What she saw was not reassuring. The sky had darkened to a uniform dull gray. And the wind was freshening. As she watched, whitecaps began to form on the swells. A "blow" seemed an understatement. Maggie never had been out in weather that looked so threatening. The Whitmores always headed for port at the first suggestion of bad weather. But this looked even worse than bad.

Pascal sighed. Marc had not changed. He had been just this willful and angry as a young boy. It was obvious that talking to him would do no good. But what could help them now? They were in his power. *Ah, merde!* What a dreadful situation! And now. Now the weather was not good. He peered cautiously through a porthole. What he saw was not comforting. Angry dark gray swells were his only view. Pascal would be the first to admit that he was not a good sailor. No. He was a land person.

"Ah, M. Pascal. It does look as if we will have some exciting weather. No?" The soft singsong voice seemed to be almost in his ear.

Pascal started and turned to see Hadi sitting across the cabin, "Yes, indeed. It does not look good."

"But, monsieur, do you not think that the weather just is, having nothing to do with either good or bad?" Hadi smiled gently at Pascal.

"I hadn't thought of it that way. To me, to be on the sea in such weather is, indeed, bad. I do not like it at all."

"But, that is just it, *mon ami*. That is just it. It is what you think of it that makes it seem good or bad. Of itself, the sea or the weather or the two together just are. It is only our judgment that deems them one or the other." Hadi paused, but seeing Pascal's skepticism, he continued, "For the fish the sea is home and the best of all possible worlds, no?" He peered across at Pascal.

"Yes, of course. But I am not a fish."

"Precisely."

"Precisely."

There was a short silence as the two men gazed at one another across the little cabin. The corner of Pascal's mouth twitched. Hadi's eyes danced. Then with grins they both burst out laughing.

"Ah, Hadi. Thank you. I wasn't sure I'd ever laugh again. We must discuss this again more thoroughly."

"Without doubt. We will, without doubt."

Hadi had just gotten the last word out when Maggie came down into the cabin, "The weather doesn't look good. I'm not an expert, but I think this could get intense. Pascal. Hadi. You must be hungry. Please have some food. If it gets as rough as I fear, eating may become difficult." So saying she indicated food in the fridge and lockers.

"Mom, do you think we should . . . ?" Allie's voice broke off as she saw the food. "Just what I was thinking. It's going to get rougher if I'm not mistaken and this may be the last time for food for a while. I was just topside. *He* thinks I know a little about sailing. And *he* thinks I'm going to help him! Well! Just let him think what he wants. I'd push him overboard if I had a chance! The brute!"

"Ah, Miss Allie. What has happened? It is not like you to be so fierce. I do not believe you actually would push him over," Hadi grinned at her.

"Well, maybe not. But the thought did cross my mind. He just wants to use my strong back. That's a switch, isn't it? What do you think of our Captain Queeg? Quite a tyrant, isn't he? Pascal, I hope you're not feeling badly because he was so rude to you."

"Ah, no, Allie. Not now. I'm sorry that he is as he is. I don't take it personally. I've known him for a long time. It is nothing new. But it makes me sad. It is hard to believe that he is the son of my friends. They were very good people. And it's a dangerous thing for all of us. He can be unpredictable."

"Yes, sad and dangerous. The question is, what're we going to do now. Here we are. Not where we want to be. We need to get ourselves out of this. I don't think talking to Marc is going to get us anywhere. What can we do?" Allie's look challenged the other three to come up with a solution.

"Ah, my Allie. Do you still not know that we must wait on the will of Allah?"

"Oh, yes, Hadi. I do understand. But Allah needs to get his act together. We're in for a bumpy ride and we need to find a way out of this sooner rather than later!"

Hadi took a deep breath and with a downward motion of his hands exhaled, "Ah, yes. The action. Always we want the action. But do you not remember? Allah holds us in the palm of his hand and cares for us always. He will arrange the events perfectly."

Allie's look was a mixture of love and exasperation that sent the others into paroxysms of laughter. Just then Marc entered the cabin, "What's going on down here? You all are in very good humor for what looks like a rough sail! Let me in on the joke. I could use a laugh, myself."

Still laughing, they could only shake their heads at him.

"Well, maybe you think it's funny, but I'll let you know it's not. Are you laughing at me? If so, you'll regret it!"

As Marc's anger and voice rose, the others controlled their mirth. Maggie croaked, "Oh, no Marc. We're not laughing at you or at the storm. We're laughing at Allie. Please don't be upset."

Mollified, Marc gestured at Allie, "Well, get yourself topside and help me with the sheets." He turned and went up the companionway.

"Aye, aye, sir!" Allie said behind his back with a mock salute as she marched Nazi style behind him.

The situation on deck was worsening. The wind was steady and strong out of the southwest. Sea and sky were a uniform deep gray so that it was difficult to say just where the horizon was. But the sea was strengthening with eight to ten foot swells. Angry whitecaps rushed to slam against the boat that now seemed pitifully small. The *More Fun* was headed into the swells, pounding against each one gamely. Marc, at the helm, shouted at Allie, "Let's change to the storm jib and reef the main. We'll tack as long as possible, then go to the motor." Allie and Marc worked as a team to bring the sails down and tie everything down securely. She had to admit, as much as she resented him, that Marc was an excellent sailor, and she thought to herself that they could be thankful for that.

"Er, Chief. Looks like the McGill women have taken off," Anderson fidgeted.

"What do you mean, 'taken off'?" Carter Blake's voice rose.

"Er, you know you said to put someone on them. Well, last night was the first time I had anyone. He was out there from nine o'clock on. But McGill's car wasn't there all night. It didn't come back today and no one went in or out of the condo. I sent him to knock on the door. No answer. They're gone."

Blake's face had gotten darker and darker as Anderson talked, "Damn it! Those women don't fit in as murderers. What the hell's going on?" He collected himself and more calmly, "Well, get someone out there to talk to the neighbors and put an APB out for the car."

"Okay. Right now."

Maggie clutched at any handhold as she groped her way around the cabin, putting away any loose objects and double-checking to be sure that all doors were securely fastened. The *More Fun* was pitching and rolling violently and keeping her feet under her was not easy. Pascal sitting on a banquette in the main cabin, was looking quite green.

"Pascal, are you okay? You're looking a bit pale."

"Ah, Maggie. In truth, I have felt better," he muttered between clenched teeth.

"I am so sorry. I'd recommend fresh air, but it's not too nice up there right now. Hang on." She smiled her encouragement. Turning, Maggie found Hadi's eyes following her.

"Maggie, my hat is off to you. You shine especially brightly in a crisis, no?" Hadi's singsong voice held admiration.

She smiled at him, "Well, Hadi. If that is so, it may be because

69

you've taught me well. Somehow, even though part of me finds this terrifying, there's another part of me that refuses to be too upset. Strange, isn't it?"

Hadi smiled warmly, "My dear Maggie, maybe not so strange. Maybe only that you are coming to yourself."

Bert peered at the sky. Didn't like the look of it. And where was the *More Fun?* If Mrs. McGill had her out something was wrong. He knew Mrs. M. was too savvy to stay out, even in the bay, with weather like this brewing. Something was wrong. Bert had worried about it all day. What should he do. Finally, he picked up the phone, called the Coast Guard and then, with misgivings, called the police.

"We've had a spot of luck," Anderson grinned across the desk at Carter Blake.

"About time. What sort of luck?"

"This afternoon the caretaker down at the marina, Bert Gossett, reported a boat missing. When our guys got down there, guess what they found?" Anderson peered triumphantly at Blake.

Blake shrugged.

"The McGill car, sitting right there in the marina parking lot, pretty as you please."

"And . . . ?"

"Well, that's it. The car was just sitting there."

"We need to find those women. Hear?"

"Yeah, okay. We'll keep looking."

"Talk to this Gossett. Talk to boat owners. Find out if anyone saw anything. Get on it!"

"Okay. Okay."

Bert was beginning to wish he'd never called the police. But he didn't know what else he could've done. He'd tried everything. It didn't do to mess around with a storm like this one. First the squad car came by and they asked a bunch of questions. Now this Anderson fellow was being downright rude. "I told you. I don't know what happened. Miz McGill was here the other night. With her daughter. They brought some stuff to the cousin that was stayin' on the *More Fun."*

"Cousin? What cousin? Their cousin?"

"No. I told you. A cousin of the Whitmores. I never saw him.

He was gettin' over something. Needed rest and quiet."

"The Whitmores?"

Bert spoke slowly and deliberately, "I told you. The Whitmores own the *More Fun*. Miz McGill is their friend and they let her use the boat." It seemed like this guy Anderson wasn't too bright or something. He just couldn't get it right. How many times had he told Anderson the very same thing?

"So you think the McGill women went out on the boat?"

Bert didn't like the policeman's tone, "I don't know. I think it could be that *Mrs.* McGill took her out, especially, if her car's here. But I don't know what to think. *Mrs.* McGill's too smart to go out in weather like this and the boat's not in the bay. The Coast Guard looked. I don't know, but I don't like it. I sure don't like any of it." He shook his head and stared at the floor.

Anderson leaned back on his heels, "No. No, Bert. I don't like it either."

Outside the afternoon sky had darkened to an almost midnight black.

"Well, I don't know. It looks like that art guy did it. Imagine that. She was a pretty woman in a strange sort of way. Don't know how anyone could have killed her," Billy Osmond's father said from behind his newspaper.

Billy was having a guilt attack. The television news had just reported on the hunt for Pascal DuMonchet. Both Pascal's and Veronique's photos had been broadcast. Billy was pretty sure that was the guy they'd let out of the shed. A murderer? But, if he was a murderer, why had he been tied up in there. It didn't make sense. He felt he ought to tell someone. But that was a scary thing. His parents would be real upset. Probably ground him for a year!

"Billy, what's wrong? You sick? You didn't eat much dinner and it was your favorite."

His mother's concern just added to his guilt. She wouldn't be so nice if she knew the truth.

"Billy?"

"Nah. Dunno," he mumbled.

Billy's mom sat down beside him, "Look, Bill," she always called him Bill when she was serious, "if something's bothering you, you need to tell me. Whatever it is, we'll work it out."

He looked into her eyes. Nice eyes. Caring eyes. But worried eyes right now. Billy looked away, "Nah, Mom. It's okay. I . . . I . . ." He faltered, unable to go on. He turned his head, but not before his mother had seen the two big tears escape under closed lids.

Even though he was growing up and probably wouldn't welcome it, Billy's mother instinctively reached out and put her arms around him. For a moment they sat just so. Then with a quiver and a sigh, Billy straightened and wiped his eyes with the back of his hand. "Okay. Okay. I guess I gotta tell. Please don't be mad at me." He sneaked a look and continued, "Well, the other day . . . er, that is, well . . . "

"It's okay, Bill. Just let it out."

Billy gazed at his mother, then, with a rush before he could take it back, "TheotherdayIcutschoolandwentoutinthewoodswithRoy."

Only years of communication with her son made this admission coherent to Billy's mother. "Oh, you cut school?"

"Yeah, that's right. But I'm sorry. I'll never do it again. It wasn't even fun."

"Well, that certainly wasn't a good thing to do, but I'm glad you told me. Actually, I was going to talk to you because Mrs. Roberts called me to ask about you. So I guess I already knew. I'm really, really glad that you told me yourself. D'you understand why?"

"Yeah, I guess. It's kinda like you want to trust me?"

"Exactly."

Billy felt so relieved that he nearly forgot to tell her the rest of the story. Then, "Well, that's not all . . . " And he told her everything the two boys had done that day. "Then, there's that guy on the TV. You know, Mom, I can't see how he could've done it. He was *old*. And he was tied up. Had been for a long time. He couldn't even walk at first. He was real weak. And he was nice. Real nice."

"Oh, Billy. This is scary. You could have been hurt." Impulsively, she took his hand, but relinquished it when he pulled away.

"Nah, it wasn't like that at all. He was okay."

"Even so, I think we're going to have to talk to the police. They're looking for the man and you have information that might help them."

"Aw, Mom!"

The eight-foot swells of the morning had grown to over fourteen feet, still rolling in from the southwest. The *More Fun* continued to crash through them gallantly. Everyone, with the possible exception of Pascal who refused to look outside, knew that the swells were only harbingers of a bigger storm somewhere.

Marc, Allie, Maggie and Hadi scrambled over the wet deck, tying down everything they could, closing the hatches and making the boat as seaworthy as possible for the storm they knew was coming.

Once things were battened down, Maggie gave it one last try, "Marc, this is going to be a really bad storm. It already is, but you know, we all know, that it can only get worse. If we turn around now and run, we might be able to outrun the worst of it. We could go in at some sheltered place other than Costa Mira. You could go your way. We wouldn't try to stop you. Then by the time we found civilization, you'd be gone. We'd all be safe. Won't you think about it?"

Marc, who had gained respect for this "old woman" during the hard work on deck, was quiet for a few moments. Maggie thought he really was considering heading back to Florida.

"No way, old woman. No way." His voice was quiet, but firm, "This is my chance to get away and make a new start. I can't go back. The only thing that makes sense to me is going ahead. This boat is a nice toy, but you know what? It's also a serious boat. It is capable of making it right across the Gulf to where I want to go. If I turn back now, there'll never be another chance. And you people get to come along for the ride." He turned his back on Maggie and busied himself with some ropes.

Maggie grabbed a line and hung on as a particularly huge wave broke over the boat. Soaked to the skin, she turned and went down into the main cabin. "He won't listen to reason. He refuses to turn back. Oh dear! I'm not sure what upsets me more, being captured by Marc or this storm."

"It is exciting, no?"

"It is exciting, yes!" Maggie said to Hadi. "More than exciting. It's very scary."

Allie stood in the middle of the cabin, feet well apart, hands on hips, rocking with the motion of the boat, reaching out from time to time for a handhold, "Well, what'd we propose to do about it? Now, Hadi, please don't tell me to wait on the will of Allah. I think the time for waiting is past. We need to do something to help ourselves." Allie was vehement, "Look at Mom. She's drenched and cold. Look at us all. Exhausted, frightened, miserable!"

"Ah, Miss Allie. You are correct that each of us has had happier times. Yet, to act before Allah has shown us a way, could not benefit us. I know it is hard to wait. But I think we will not wait much longer."

Anderson burst into the office, "Piece of luck, Chief! A real piece of luck!"

Carter Blake leaned forward, "Now, calm down. What're you talking about?"

"Well, a little over an hour ago, this woman brings her kid in. Seems he cut school Monday. He and a buddy were way out on the other side of the Thompson grade, happened on a shack. There was a guy tied up in there and guess who it was!" Anderson was triumphant.

Carter raised his eyebrows in question.

"DuMonchet. It was DuMonchet. Kid saw him on TV. Told his mom. Kid said DuMonchet was tied up, to a chair. Said he'd been there a while. They untied him, but he couldn't walk. Was real weak. Isn't that great?"

Blake's mood didn't match Lieutenant Anderson's, "Yeah. Just great."

"What? You're not happy? Why not? Now we've got a start on finding him."

"Why not? I'll tell you why not. If he was tied up like that for long enough to incapacitate him, chances are he's not our murderer. That means we have to start at square one. That means more pressure from the press. That means even more headaches! That's why not!"

"Oh, hadn't thought about that."

"Yeah! Okay, tell you what. You put the pressure on. See if you can find this brother of hers, this Marc Duval. He may be our next best bet."

"Okay."

The last sail was down finally. It had taken all of them except Pascal to get it down and tied. Pascal came on deck to help, but was sent back down by Maggie and Allie when they saw how ill he was.

Maggie had no fingernails left. She was wetter than she'd ever been in her whole life. The salt water stung her eyes. The rain blown in by the storm pelted her skin. Just keeping her feet on the heaving, slippery deck took all her attention and energy. Maggie made sure each of them was wearing a life vest. There wasn't time to be afraid for herself. But the mother in her feared for Allie's safety. Marc had made Allie his de facto first mate. She was on deck scrambling over ropes and doing all possible to help him hold the boat on course and out of trouble.

Allie was working hard, helping Marc keep the boat headed into the wind. To be hit from the side by one of the monster waves would be a disaster for the boat. They had started the diesel engine and it continued to chug away, coughing when a wave lifted the screw out of the water, but taking hold again when it settled down into the sea.

Maggie muttered under her breath as she and Hadi worked together. She muttered her anger toward Marc and toward herself. She muttered her desire never to see the sea again, but most of all, she muttered prayers for their safety.

Hadi worked silently and seemingly effortlessly. It was amazing. In all their adventures, Maggie never had seen him tired or discouraged. She must ask him how he did it.

The waves now were unbelievably huge. Maggie had not known the sea could be so violent. They rode down the crest of a huge wave, dropping with a thud at the bottom. From there, if one looked up and up, one saw nothing but sea towering above them. Violent, angry sea. But the boat would climb up the wall of the next wave to the crest where the view was not much better. An eternity of angry swells disappearing into the blackness of the sky. *More Fun* crashed through the oncoming seas and it seemed as if each wave would engulf and bury them.

"Oh, dear!"

Marc hung on the wheel. He had ordered each of them tied to the boat. He needed everyone's help to keep them going. Of course, Pascal, that old man, was no help. Pascal had been very important in his gallery. But now, in the real world, he was useless. The old woman had been right. This was one of the worst storms he'd ever seen. They were in a tight spot and their survival hung on the performance of that diesel engine and their ability to stay with it and keep her headed into the wind. He had lucked out after all. That girl was stronger than she looked and no stranger to a boat. Well, with a little bit of luck, they'd make it.

An especially heavy wave hit just then. One moment everything was going okay. Diving into one swell after another. Over and over.

The same thing, and yet, each wave was a little different from the last. Each had its own character. Each demanded attention and concentration. Then with a wham the big one broke over the bow. There was a loud cracking noise. Marc jerked his head up just in time to see that the main sheet had broken loose and the boom had begun to swing wildly. He started to jump for it when it swung back with incredible speed and struck him in the head.

Allie head the cracking sound. It was as if a rifle had gone off next to her ear. She saw the boom catch Marc in the head and fling him like a child's rag doll against the lines. He lay there for a moment, pinned against them by the wind and water and then with the next lurch of the boat he slid slowly into the sea. Allie screamed, "Maaarc!!!"

Chapter Eight

From the other side of the boat both Maggie and Hadi watched in horror. The boat, with no one holding her on course, lurched and began to turn sideways to the swells. Allie, who was nearest, threw herself toward the helm and using all her strength, pulled on it, attempting to right the boat. It gave a sickening sideways wallow and water poured over the decks. The boom now was swinging wildly back and forth with every movement of the boat.

Maggie started to crawl toward the spot where Marc had disappeared. It was useless, Maggie thought, but she had to make a try at finding him. Hadi caught her arm and motioned toward the boom. He was right. That boom had to be tied down. They could lose it and the mast. It could rip the boat apart. It had to be stabilized! How to do it? Just then the hatch opened and Pascal staggered out. He looked even more terrified when he saw the boom, but headed toward it, slipping and sliding along the deck. Maggie grabbed a line, tied it around Pascal's waist and secured it to the nearest cleat. The three of them threw themselves across the boom while it continued to swing madly to and fro. One moment they were suspended above the wild sea and the next they had swung across the boat and were suspended above the sea on the other side. It was no use. Even their combined weight had no effect. As the boom crossed above the cabin, Maggie dropped off. On the next swing, both Hadi and Pascal dropped down beside her.

She was giving up hope when she saw the line in Hadi's brown hands. The clever man had caught a loop over the boom. The three of them, still struggling to stay on the boat, worked as one to belay the line around a cleat and then another. With the leverage they were able to stop the wild swinging of the boom. Frantically, they attached more lines and worked to tie it down to first one cleat and then another. It was long and exhausting work, but finally, they had stabilized the boom.

Allie, clinging to the helm, tilted her head in a "well-done." She had been able to right the boat and turn it back into the wind.

Then they made their way to the spot on the deck where Marc had disappeared. Daylight was fading and they could just make out the spot. A line was drawn taut down into the water. Could it be? Was he still there? Not possible. Again, the three worked as one, pulling and heaving the line in. And there, dangling in his harness was Marc. Grunting and straining, they pulled him up and onto the deck. It was impossible to determine his condition. There was no way he could have survived. Even so, they dragged him to the cabin and down the steps.

Maggie and Hadi left him with Pascal and scrambled back onto the deck to help Allie. It was a long and exhausting night. Maggie had never experienced such blackness. They steered the boat more by feel than by any other sense. Finally, just before dawn, the rain stopped and it seemed that the waves were not quite so violent.

The sea still was heavy when there was a gradual lightening of the sky. Maggie, Allie and Hadi huddled at the helm, taking turns holding it on course. Conversation was impossible with the roar of the sea and wind. But at least the waves no longer broke over the boat and there was less danger of being swept overboard. As soon as she was able, Allie turned the boat so that they were going with the seas and wind. But, even so, the going continued to be rough.

With daylight they checked the damage to the boat. The jib had come loose sometime during the night and was gone. Some of the edges of the sails were hanging down. Lines hung loose here and there. A few stanchions had pulled loose from the deck, but, amazingly, there seemed to be no major damage. The diesel continued to chug along, plowing them through the heavy sea.

"Maggie and Miss Allie, please go below and rest. I will steer the boat for a while," Hadi smiled at them.

They protested and he assured them that he was not tired and should an emergency occur he would call for them. Gratefully they made their way down to the main cabin. Maggie thought she was too tired to sleep, but a chance to get off her feet and relax was appealing. She had almost forgotten about Marc. They were surprised to find Pascal sitting on a banquette next to Marc. A white bandage encircled Marc's head.

Whispering, "Pascal! We forgot! Is he . . . ?"

Pascal smiled, "Yes. He is alive, but just barely. He has not regained consciousness, but he breathes!"

"But how? I mean, he was in the water for a long time. What happened?" Allie was asking the questions. Maggie suddenly felt too tired even to form words.

"Ah well. You see, last night when we brought him down, I was sure he was gone. But even so, I tried mouth-to-mouth resuscitation. Just when I was ready to give up, he coughed and spit up half the ocean and then he breathed. And here we are. But he needs medical care."

"I'm sure he does. We must get all of us back as soon as possible."

"Ah, yes. The storm. It is better now, no?"

"It is much quieter now. I think the worst is over. And you, Pascal, how are you feeling?"

"You know, I am feeling okay, much better than before, thank you."

"You found your sea legs?"

"Yes, that, and more. I had a sort of waking-up, a sort of realization. I don't know how to describe it. But, you know, I've never been a sailor. I never liked the ocean. Then last night suddenly I was back with my parents and my little sister, Yvette. I had forgotten about it, but one summer my family took a vacation, our first after the war, to the seaside. I was very young, no more than five or so. Yvette must have been about three years old. It was a grand time. We rented a small sailboat for a sail along the coast. A sudden storm came up, wind, rain and big waves. Even though we could see the shore, the little boat was in trouble. My father did everything he could. A big wave came over the boat and little Yvette was swept into the sea. We were panicked. My father jumped in after her and was able to save her. After what seemed to me to be forever, we were rescued. We all were safe, but we'd been terrified. Somehow when the memory came back, something in me changed and I felt strong again. My fear had gone. It was then that I came up on deck to help."

He pulled his shoulders up in a Gallic shrug.

"Well, it's good that you did. You made the difference in saving the boom. We couldn't have done it without you." Maggie had found her tongue, "Thank you, Pascal."

"Well, yes. You are welcome. But I should thank you both, and Hadi, too. We should thank ourselves, don't you think?"

"Yes, of course. You're right."

Pascal said, "I think we owe a special thanks to Allie." He turned to her and continued, "Allie, without your stepping in last night after Marc went overboard, this boat surely would have been lost. I don't think any of us could have done what you did. Thank you from the bottom of my heart."

Maggie looked with love and pride at her damp and disheveled daughter, "Oh, yes, honey. Thank you for being here and for being so strong and smart. We'd been in a pretty fix without you."

Allie demurred, "I just did what I could and we were lucky that it worked out." She turned to Maggie, "Mom, do you know anything about the engine fuel? We ran full throttle all night. I don't know what the capacity is or if there're spare tanks. Do you?"

Maggie wrinkled her brow, "I'm trying to remember. You know how it is when you're a guest. You don't pay much attention to details like that. I know Marc went out for more supplies . . . " Her voice trailed off and they heard the diesel sputter and cough, then catch and continue chugging, "Yikes! What was that? Well, let's look into it."

Allie ran up the companionway, opened the hatch and called out to Hadi, "What happened?"

Hadi waved and called, "The engine. She ran out of fuel. I switched to the auxiliary tank. Everything is working just as it should."

Allie turned back into the cabin, "It's okay now, but if the weather continues to calm down, probably we should put up some sails. The wind is out of the west right now. It should blow us straight back home."

"I wonder where we are? Do we have compasses and stuff? There's no way of knowing where that storm blew us."

"Let's check. Marc messed up the radio. I wonder if he still has the radio part in his pocket. Pascal, would you check his pockets. See if you can find it."

Pascal searched through Marc's pockets, but found nothing.

"It would've been a miracle, wouldn't it?" Ruefully, "Probably we'd have been totally frustrated trying to put it back together."

"Well, I think it'd be helpful if we knew where we are. After all, that's an important part of getting to where we want to be." Maggie furrowed her brow, "It wouldn't be possible, I suppose, that we could've been blown far enough south to be south of Florida? It that were the case, then we'd want to go west, or north, not east. What do you think?"

Pascal shrugged again, "You know that I'm not a sailor. I have no idea."

Allie looked equally puzzled, "I hadn't even thought of that, Mom. That would change things. We sure wouldn't want to head across the Atlantic!"

"How was Marc navigating? I think this boat has all sorts of equipment. Let's look." Maggie approached the chart table, "Pay dirt! I just hope we can figure out what is what and how to work it!"

"Let's see, Mom." Allie was standing just beside Maggie. Together they pressed first one button and then another. But still, nothing happened.

"Look, Allie, this says GPS. That's for navigation. Any idea how it works?"

"None. Let's experiment." They pressed yet more buttons. But still, nothing happened.

"What do you suppose we're doing wrong? Is there a master control somewhere?" They searched. Opening a cabinet, Maggie found more equipment.

She pressed a button and deep, male voice filled the cabin, "Oh, the shark . . . "

Maggie shuddered, "Well, at least we have music! Why couldn't it have been GPS?" She turned off the music, "I don't want to hear about sharks!"

Allie went up on deck. Hadi still sat at the helm. The sky was dark, but growing brighter in the west. "Hadi, do you have any idea where we are? We're concerned about navigating back to Florida. Is it possible we could have been blown so far to the south that we'd miss Florida by heading east?"

Hadi smiled gently, "Ah, Miss Allie, please to not distress yourself. Do you not know that Allah always guides us home? We have but to listen. The sea. She is quieter, no?"

Allie looked out at the still dark sea. The swells were broader and not so high and the wind was not as strong, "It is quieter, yes.

But this could be serious. The instruments don't seem to be working, or at least, we don't know how to make them work."

Hadi stretched his arms one at a time, "Would you like me to look at the instruments? I have some knowledge of such things."

Was there any end to this man's expertise? Allie hoped she didn't show the surprise she felt, "Oh, yes. Would you please." So saying, she moved to the helm and Hadi stood, stretched again and went below.

Maggie still was at the chart table, staring at the instruments. She turned as Hadi came down the steps.

"Ah, my Maggie, we have a puzzle, no?"

"We have a puzzle, yes. Nothing seems to work."

"I will look at it. Perhaps I can lend some help." Hadi walked confidently to the instrument panel, pushed switches and turned dials. A voice filled the cabin, "This is U.S. marine weather forecast for the Gulf of Mexico shipping interests . . . "

"Oh, Hadi. How wonderful! The radio works! How did you do it?"

"It is no great talent, my Maggie. No great talent. It is just that I have had some experience making things work. But it receives only. We would need the part that Marc had to be able to transmit." Hadi continued to stare at the chart table, his lips pursed, humming softly to himself, "Ah, here we are, the GPS. That should be some help." Again, he turned knobs and adjusted dials. Green lit letters appeared on the front of it. It lived!

"Oh, Hadi! That is wonderful! I do think you must be a genius!'

He smiled at her gently, turned back to the equipment and continued humming. From time to time he muttered softly, "Ah, yes . . . let's see . . . what about . . ." Finally he straightened, stretched, and said, "Ah now, my Maggie. Now, I think Allah has provided direction for us." So saying, he climbed back on deck where he gave Allie directions for the proper heading. "You see, Miss Allie, all is in order. I believe we still are in the Gulf of Mexico. This course should lead us back home. Allah continues to guide us. We never have to fear. All information is here for us. We have only to listen."

"But, how, Hadi? How were you able to do it?"

"I had only to listen to the small Allah voice inside and all was clear. The Allah voice told me what dials to turn and what to do. The truth, Miss Allie, is that I never have before seen that sort of equipment, but I knew that I would be helped. It is as simple as that. It always is." His liquid brown eyes glowed softly as he gazed into Allie's blue ones with such love and acceptance that at that moment she knew with every fiber of her being that, indeed, she was held in God's hand and cared for forever.

Allie smiled back, the certainty lightened her fatigue, giving her new energy and confidence, "Oh, Hadi, at this moment I have no doubts. I do know that we are cared for. Just look at what we came through. That, in itself, was like a miracle." She fell quiet, but then turned and more quietly said, "But it's hard to remember sometimes. It can be hard to remember."

"Ah, yes, my Allie. It can be hard. But, you have had this experience and the knowledge of this experience never will leave you. Never. Even if you should forget, the knowledge will be inside you."

By midday the sun was out and the sea was much quieter. As the storm clouds disappeared over the eastern horizon, the cold northwest wind of the morning became a brisk breeze from the north. The *More Fun*, sails set, plowed through the glistening sea toward the east and hopefully, the Florida peninsula. Hadi and Allie set the helm on course. Now that the seas were calm, they could use the autopilot. All could relax below while Maggie passed hot chocolate and sandwiches.

Hadi paused before eating and boomed, *"Enchallah!"*

Maggie and Allie joined in, *"Enchallah,"* then giggled at Pascal's puzzled look.

Maggie grinned across at him, "'*Enchallah*' is a thank you to Allah for our food." She paused for a bit and then asked, "Pascal, how's Marc? Any change?"

Pascal shook his head, "No. No, I'm afraid not. He continues to breathe, but that is all. He hasn't regained consciousness. I wish we could get him to a doctor."

Allie nodded, "Any idea, Hadi, how long it's going to take for us to get back?"

"No, Miss Allie, I don't know. It is in the hands of Allah as all things always are. We will arrive when the time is right." Hadi moved across the cabin to where Marc lay. He bent over the prostrate form, holding Marc's hand in both of his, "But you are right. He does need medical attention."

Pascal sighed, "We risked much to get him back on board and it seems like a miracle that he's survived. We just need another small miracle to get us back in time. Right, Hadi?"

Hadi smiled at his friend, "A miracle? But is not life itself a miracle? Each breath is a gift for every living thing. We do not often have the opportunity to know this truth. A miracle. Yes. Miracles happen every moment. Another small one would be good, no?"

"Ah, *oui*, Hadi. One more small one, we could use."

The afternoon sea had calmed to two to three foot waves and the boat rode easily on the gentle swells. The sun had warmed and the sailors found they were shedding jackets and sweaters. Unfortunately, the north wind of the morning had switched around to the northeast and had quieted to a slight variable breeze.

Allie kicked off her shoes and, with her hands behind her head, stretched back on the deck watching the sun sink slowly toward the horizon, "Hadi, what do you make of this weather? What happened to our wind?"

"Ah, Miss Allie. The wind, she now is docile, no? She is like a wild horse that has spent its energy and now rests, calm and serene."

"But, what a contrast! Twenty-four hours ago this sea was raging and now we're becalmed. I don't get it." They sat in silence gazing out across the calm sea. "But, you know, it's beautiful. I mean, here we are becalmed in the middle of the ocean. Except for our type of boat, it could be any time since the beginning of time. It feels . . . almost primitive."

Maggie turned her face to the sun, "You know, if only we could forget why we're here, this could be almost pleasant. I mean, here we are on a beautiful yacht, on an amazingly blue ocean, warm sun. It could be perfection."

Hadi smiled at her, "Ah, my Maggie, but is it not truly so? It is just what it is, whatever the circumstances. Can we not enjoy this moment for what it is?"

Pascal knitted his brow in thought, "But Hadi, we can't ignore the facts. The facts are that we were brought here against our will; we suffered through a devastating storm; our boat has been damaged; we have a severely injured crewmember; and, right now, we're becalmed and not entirely sure where we are! We can't ignore reality."

"Ah, my friend. What you say is true. It is important to

acknowledge the details of one's situation. But they do not constitute all of reality. In fact, those details are extraneous to the true reality of who we are and what our condition is. Can't we acknowledge those details of the situation and still enjoy the perfection of this moment? Indeed, one's life is made of a string of moments, strung together, each moment a sparkling jewel that then dissolves and is gone. The only thing we have is the ever present instant, the now."

As they watched, an object slowly drifted their way, floating first up, then down, then sideways in the way of things drifting on the sea, but always coming toward the boat. Squinting, they tried to make out just what it was. Not drift wood, but what. "Oh, dear me!" from Maggie, "I can't believe it! A plastic bag!" She looked eagerly across the placid water. "Nothing. Do you think it means we're near land?"

Hadi's face was solemn and sad, "Ah, no, my Maggie. I do not think so. Trash like this has been seen in the middle of the largest oceans in the world. Modern man is very clever and has found a way to make his presence known even here."

Maggie's brow furrowed in a fierce frown, "I'd heard that, but I couldn't imagine it. I do love the gadgets and conveniences we have now, but the consequences can be horrid. Sometimes I pray that God will forgive us our cleverness. Cleverness is far from wisdom."

Their reverie was interrupted by a loud clicking very near the boat. "Look, Mom, Hadi, Pascal! Look!" Sleek silver bodies sliced through the water. Smiling faces seemed to encourage them.

"Aren't we lucky! They're so beautiful!"

The dolphins stayed with them for over an hour, frolicking and clicking around the boat. Then, as silently as they had arrived, they disappeared.

"Wow, what a treat! I wouldn't have missed that for the world. Now, Hadi, I understand what you were saying. It's true that we had that precious time with the dolphins and I'll never forget it."

"There are stories, you know, about dolphins rescuing floundering swimmers and mariners. I don't suppose they . . . " Maggie's voice trailed off.

"Who knows, but at least they brightened our day. Wonder when the wind will pick up?" Allie looked questioningly at the others.

Maggie leaned back against a life preserver and looked up at the sails hanging limply above her head, "We're certainly not getting anywhere this way. I vote for starting the engine. What do you think, Hadi?"

Hadi turned to smile at her, "It would seem that all is in harmony for us to return to the land, no? Let us do it."

Allie nodded, "I hate to use all our fuel, but I don't see any other choice." She leaned down and turned the key to start the engine. The starter whined for a disturbingly long time, then the engine coughed and came to life.

Maggie rose and moved toward the helm, "Whew! For a minute I was afraid it wouldn't start. Allie, how much fuel do we have left?"

"I'm not sure, Mom. The gauges both say full, but we know that can't be. I'm afraid the storm must have damaged them in some way."

"I guess we have no choice but to use the engine now and hope there's enough or that the wind picks up and takes us home."

"Come in, Mr. Carrera. What can I do for you?" Carter Blake extended his hand over the desk.

Arthur Carrera shook it and sat down across from Blake, "Well, Mr. Blake. I've come to talk about your murder case and our drug investigation. I'd like to get into that gallery to take a look around. Wonder if you could arrange that?"

Carter Blake rubbed his chin, "Let's see, I'm going to have another look around over there before we release it. I don't see why you and your men couldn't go with me. But, may I ask, what do you expect to find?"

"Of course, we aren't sure. But we know that Duval was hanging around there, and knowing his record . . . "

"Okay. If there is some drug involvement, it is something we should know and it would provide an additional possible motive. When do you want in?"

"As soon as possible. Today? How about later this morning, say ten-thirty?"

"Sure. No problem. I'll make the arrangements."

"See you there."

The yellow police tape still surrounded the gallery. The morning sun breaking through retreating storm clouds did little to dispel the lost and lonely look of the place. In fact, it almost looked dingy. The storm had left debris, huge palm fronds and a few battered coconuts, piled up against the heavy glass door, along the sidewalk and planting beds. Carter Blake parked behind the two dark sedans from which the DEA men were exiting. He shook hands with Arthur Carrera, then shook his head, "I can't imagine what you expect to find. We went over everything with a fine tooth comb."

"I'm not sure either, but our investigation seems to be leading us to Duval. Maybe his sister was in it with him. Maybe we'll find something that'll help us find him."

Blake opened the door himself and led the men into the dark chill of the gallery. Maggie's cheerful, bright-eyed animals seemed to mock the solemnity of the occasion. The caterer's tables remained in the corner, *foie gras* and caviar congealed in silver serving dishes. There was a faint aroma of stale champagne.

Carrera looked around the room and shook his head, "Interesting stuff, art. Wonder where all the ideas come from."

"Beats me. Little old lady named McGill did these. But she's disappeared, too, apparently."

"Really! Well, guess we'd better get started."

"Okay, the place is yours. Do what you want, but try to finish up today. I need to release the hold on this place and let the owner back in." Carter Blake stood back with arms folded across his chest.

"All right men. You heard him. Get started. And I mean go over everything. You know what to do."

Two of the half dozen men began searching the showroom. They lifted paintings off the walls, removed electrical wall plates, and even pulled the pale gray carpet up around the perimeter of the room. In the offices of Pascal and Veronique two other men began an exploration of every small space. Duane Simpson's tiny office was so small and neat that there was little to search. Even so, every inch was covered.

The two remaining men disappeared into the tall, sky-lit backroom. The backroom was about the same size as the showroom and the perimeter of the room was lined with racks designed to hold pieces of art vertically. In these were individual paintings, most still wrapped in their brown paper, that were to be the gallery's next exhibit. At the very rear on either side of the large freight door were unopened crates of art still labeled and plastered with unbroken customs seals. The center of the room held two large wooden worktables.

The chilled silence of the gallery was broken only by murmured communications between the men as they worked. Carrera, with

Blake following, drifted from one site to another, with an occasional word of encouragement or direction.

Two hours later Blake was feeling hungry, grumpy and tired. He tried a cracker from the caterer's table, but it was soft and stale. Just as he was ready to suggest that they break for lunch, there was a muted cry of excitement from the back room. He and Carrera hurried back there. All six men were ripping the dust covers off the framed art and opening crates and boxes. One of them held up a small heavy plastic bag of what looked to be sugar, "They're in every frame and every box that was shipped in from South America! There's no telling how much is here. But there's a lot!"

Carrera heaved a sigh of satisfaction, "Well, there's the connection. Pretty slick. The drugs are here. Duval, we know, was in it up to his neck. I wonder if the sister and DuMonchet were in it also."

"If DuMonchet was, he must have run into trouble with someone. You know that he was found tied up in a shack out on the edge of the glades? Kids found him. But he's disappeared again."

Carrera raised his brows, "Hadn't heard that. If he's in trouble with the drug people, it's bad news for him. He'd be better off facing a murder charge."

"Yeah. Right."

"This find confirms our suspicions about Duval. He's a pretty slippery character. If DuMonchet wasn't in on it and found out, that could explain his being kidnapped. Might even be a motive for murder." Carrera gave Carter Blake a sidelong glance.

"Yeah. Could be. But, his own sister?"

"Believe me. Duval's no angel. He's got a rap sheet longer than your arm. No murders that we know of. But I wouldn't put it past him!"

Blake sighed, "He sure has pulled a disappearing act, like he jumped in the ocean and swam away."

"What about the partner? What's his name? Simpson? Think he knows anything about this?"

"Don't know. We talked to him about the murder, of course. Didn't get much."

"I think I'd like a few words with that guy."

Chapter Nine

Maggie stepped down into the cabin, "Pascal, how's the patient doing?" she asked, indicating Marc's immobile form.

"Oh, Maggie. I do not know. He just lies there. He has not moved since we brought him down last night. I don't think this is good, but I'm no doctor."

'I don't think it's good either. But, at least he's continuing to breathe. I guess we can be thankful for that. He's caused us a lot of trouble and grief, but I can't wish him ill now. You know, he looks so innocent and peaceful lying there. It's hard to remember that he threatened us with a gun."

Pascal sighed his agreement, "Yes. It always has been so with Marc. He has caused many people trouble and pain. But, I remember the boy and I remember his family. I, too, cannot wish him anything but to recover." Pascal sat in silent thought, then, "And you, Maggie. How are you getting along with our adventure? Are you not tired?"

Maggie echoed his sigh, "Yes, Pascal. I'm tired, so tired that I dare not think about it, so tired that I'm not sure I'd know how to rest."

"But you should, you know. I want my primary artist star to have the energy to paint many more exciting paintings," Pascal smiled at her.

"That seems so long ago and so far away. Do you think we'll ever get back and be able to pick up the pieces again?"

"But, of course. That is life."

"I know you said that some of the paintings had sold, but I really haven't had time to take it in. What will it mean? Really, it's an amazing thing."

"It seems so to you, I know. The paintings are extraordinary. That they were recognized as such is not extraordinary. It is what I would have expected. You truly are an excellent artist, Maggie. You need to accept that."

Maggie sighed again, "Yes. I guess so. But at this moment it still doesn't seem real."

The silence between them was broken only by the chugging of the diesel.

"Right now, the only realities seem to be that engine and the sea. No?"

"Yes."

"Hello. Mr. Grayson? This is Duane Simpson."

"Hello, Duane. How are you doing?"

"Okay. But, you know, I need to get into the gallery. There are things there I need to attend to. Anyway they'd let me in?"

"Don't know, Duane. Let me look into it. I'll get back to you."

"Well, Anderson. Any news about the Duval case?" Carter Blake leaned forward over his desk, frowning up at Lieutenant Anderson.

"Gee, chief. Not much. Finding those drugs was a real break, but nothing new since then," Anderson squirmed a little and wished he could sit down.

Blake ignored his discomfort and said, "Simpson's lawyer wants to know if we can release the gallery so he can get in and do some paper work. What'd you think? Have you got things cleaned up down there?"

"Yeah, I guess so. The DEA guys and us've been through it with a fine tooth comb. They did their own fingerprinting again." He shrugged and said, "You'd think they'd trust our prints. Only thing we found was the drugs. We printed more fingerprints than you'd believe. You know, that party and everything."

"What was the final take on the drugs?"

"Last I heard they'd found over a hundred kilos, all attached to the frames of that stuff coming in from abroad."

"But nothing new about the murder?"

"Not really. We're still looking for her brother. But no luck, yet. We keep looking for DuMonchet and those McGill women. It's like they went up in a puff of smoke!"

"Yeah, smoke. Give the gallery one more walk through just to be sure and we'll let Simpson in. Can you do it today? I need to let Grayson know."

"No problem. I'll go over there right now. Should be clear by three o'clock."

"Well, okay then. I'll let Simpson in. Wonder what's so important to him?"

"I'd like to speak to Arthur Carrera. Carter Blake calling."

"He's in the field. Can someone else help you?"

"Just tell him I called and that we plan to release the gallery at three o'clock this afternoon."

"Okay."

The *More Fun* cut through the now placid ocean cleanly as its diesel engine purred along. Pascal came out on deck, "I am happy that we're under way. I fear for Marc. He seems to be even paler and I think his breathing may be more shallow. It'll be good to get him some medical attention."

"Yes," Maggie agreed, "no matter what he's done, he deserves a chance to recover and speak for himself."

"Ah yes, that is true. We must not act as judge and jury for this man. That is not our duty or our right," Hadi said.

Allie frowned, "Well, I don't want to seem judgmental, but he certainly caused us a great deal of trauma and danger. We can be sure of that. It was, after all, our real experience and it's been darned hard!"

Hadi's face was solemn as he looked at Allie, "It is so, Miss Allie. Yes, that is so. He served as the instrument to bring us to this place in our lives. We certainly did not choose to be here under these circumstances. But, as we have discussed, has it all been negative?"

Allie, who had learned to love and trust this strange little man, bit back the retort that was on the tip of her tongue. The effort forced her face into a fierce frown that was met by uproarious laughter.

"Oh, honey. We do love you!" Maggie gasped when she was able.

The two men nodded and Hadi said, "Cannot it be that we profit from adversity? Might it be that our adversaries teach us and help us to grow?"

The other sailors gave guarded encouragement and he continued, "If that is so, then perhaps Marc has been a great teacher to us. There are times when even the most negative events may, indeed, bring positive outcomes. Your Bible gives examples. After all, there would not have been an Easter if there had not been a Judas. Remember Joseph. When he was sold into slavery did he not say that while they meant it for evil, God meant it for good. So may it be with our situation. Marc acted from his own need and it has caused us some trouble. We certainly would not have chosen the things that have happened as a result, but perhaps we will profit from his actions."

The *More Fun* continued through the quiet sea in a thoughtful silence.

Even though the police had gone and the yellow tape had been removed from the entrance, curious passers-by stared as Duane Simpson let himself into the silent gallery. He closed the door behind him and inspected first the front showroom and then the offices and the back storeroom. What a mess! The caterer's things still were spread out on the back table. The offices showed evidence of the search, but the workroom stood nearly bare. Strange. Where was the art for the upcoming show? The entire gallery had a feeling of . . . of having been violated.

Maggie's raucous paintings had a forlorn look. Duane was surprised and pleased to see many "Sold" signs on them. He reminded himself that he knew very little about art and he was grateful that Pascal did. Wonder where old Pascal had got to.

His reverie was broken by a tapping on the heavy glass front door. Two men in dark suits waited outside. Looked like police. Oh, well. So much for getting anything done. He opened the door a crack, "Yes?"

"Duane Simpson?"

"Yes."

The suited men pulled out their identification for Duane's

inspection.

"DEA?"

"Yes, sir. We'd like you to come down to our office. We need to talk to you about some things."

"I've already told the police everything I know. There's really nothing more I can add."

The DEA agent answered firmly, "I understand, sir, but there're still some things we'd like to go over."

"I'll have to call my lawyer."

"You do that, sir."

Arthur Carrera shook Duane's hand, "Thank you for coming in, Mr. Simpson." Turning to Eliot Grayson, "And thank you, Mr. Grayson. We'll try not to keep you over long. I apologize for taking your time, but there are some new developments and I'd like to go over them with your client."

Duane sighed and leaned forward in his chair, "Let's get on with it, then. What do you want to know?"

"Mr. Simpson, you are a full partner in the DuMonchet gallery? Is that right."

"Yes, a full partner."

"Exactly what is your contribution to the partnership?"

"My contribution? Er, well, I run the business. That is, I take care of the business parts and Pascal tends to the art end of it."

"Okay. What are your duties exactly?"

"Duties? Er, I keep the books. Make sure the bills are paid. Tend to all business affairs, taxes, permits, contracts, legalities. You know, business."

"And your partner, DuMonchet? What does he do in the business?"

"Well, Pascal deals with the artists. I mean, he finds them. He chooses the art. He deals with marketing, shows, you know, that kind of stuff."

"I see. The gallery imports art from other countries. Who arranges that?"

"Pascal. Er, Pascal finds the artist and arranges that it is shipped in to us."

"But, who actually arranges the shipping and sees that it clears customs?"

Duane took a deep breath, "I do that part." He glanced at Eliot

Grayson, "You see, Pascal isn't so great with business details. He's like an artist himself. So, I do that part."

Eliot Grayson broke in, "Mr. Carrera, where are you going with this questioning? What does any of this have to do with the murder?"

"We're not sure. The DEA is not investigating the murder. We'll leave that to the police. But we're very interested in the over one hundred kilos of high quality cocaine that were discovered in the art shipments stored in the backroom."

Duane caught his breath, "What? I don't believe it!"

"Believe it. That is just what we found."

"But how? When? Where?" Duane shrugged his disbelief at Grayson.

"Over a hundred kilos, attached in the framing of every piece brought in from South America. We found it all in your storeroom. And we want to know what you know about it?"

"I? I know nothing. This is the first I've heard of it." Again Duane's look beseeched his attorney's help.

"Mr. Simpson, can you give us names and addresses of your contacts in Latin America? We'd like to do some investigation on the other end of this."

"Er, yes, I suppose so."

"Mr. Carrera, do you suspect my client of involvement in drug smuggling?"

"Well, Mr. Grayson, it's like this. The drugs were found in the storeroom of a business in which your client is a full partner. By his own admission he's involved with the shipment of those pictures from South America to here. What would you think?"

Eliot Grayson cleared his throat, "That's not hard evidence and you know it. Are you prepared to arrest my client?"

"Not at this time."

"My client has stated he has no knowledge of the drugs and I'm advising him to say nothing further unless you get a warrant for his arrest."

Arthur Carrera sat back in his chair, "Now, Mr. Grayson. You know we must check out every possibility."

"Yes, I guess so, but now you've done it. Is that all? You wouldn't want to harass Mr. Simpson. He's a respectable citizen and he's been cooperative by giving you all the information he has."

Carrera nodded, "There is the matter of the pieces of art that held the drugs. We have impounded them as evidence. I can give you a receipt for what we took."

Duane gulped at this, "That art is for our next show. We need it to stay in business."

Carrera sighed, "I understand; however, that is just the way it is." He paused and then said, "Okay. You can go, Mr. Simpson. But stay in town. And, er, let's keep this drug involvement just between us, okay?"

Duane agreed, "Sure. It certainly wouldn't do the gallery any good for that kind of news to get out."

The sun sent long slanting rays of golden light down the quiet Costa Mira streets as Duane Simpson let himself into the gallery. Now he understood the disorder and feeling of violation he'd found there. What a day! Duane wasn't fooled by that guy Carrera's polite interrogation. It frightened him far more than Anderson's discourtesy ever had. Murder was serious and so were drugs!

Deep in thought, Arthur Carrera stared out into the now placid Gulf of Mexico with unseeing eyes. As he sat in his car in the parking lot of the beachside park, worrying the problems of the puzzle, under his breath he hummed a tune that had been stuck in his mind for over a day.

Again and again he went over the details of the investigation of what he considered his case and how it appeared to be the dovetailing with the murder of Veronique Duval. He had not known her, but her photos showed an exotic looking woman who, he was sure, had not deserved to die as she had. It was possible, of course, that DuMonchet was the culprit, but Carrera really did not believe so. As for Duane Simpson, time would tell. He was more inclined to believe that the brother had done it. Nothing he had heard about Marc Duval led him to think kindly of the man. But how had he disappeared so completely? And DuMonchet, too? Another disappearance. What had Blake said? That artist woman disappeared? Carrera didn't like it. Way too many disappearances!

Of course, it was possible that DuMonchet was in the drug smuggling up to his ears. Maybe he'd taken off with his proceeds up to now, afraid the drugs would be discovered in the murder investigation. Maybe he and Duval were partners. Stranger things had happened. But that didn't mesh with his being tied up out in the glades. Carrera sighed. Could this drug operation be only here in

Costa Mira? Could it be connected in some way with the operations on the east coast? It seemed to him that when it came to drugs, there was a sort of spider web of interconnections. Too often he had pulled one thread of the web, made arrests, and then discovered that the web had mended and was operating as usual. It could be very discouraging. But, whatever the situation here, he had this thread to work on.

"Dum-de-dum . . . " That tune would not leave him alone. What was it? Where had he heard it? Probably the radio, a popular song of some sort. "Dum-dum-de-dum." The darn thing kept on. Pretty tune. An oldie. Did it have words? What were they?

He took in a sharp breath as the sun fell out of sight. Yes. There it was. The green flash. It wasn't often that he got to this coast and had an opportunity to see the sun set into the ocean. The green flash seemed like a prize that he had won a few times in his life. But it never ceased to be special. He wondered if there was a scientific explanation for it. If so, he hoped not to know it ever. He liked the mystery and magic of it.

Carrera stared out across the sea with its brilliantly changing colors with unseeing eyes, "Dum-de-dum. Tra-la-la." The elusive melody floated in and out of his consciousness.

"Sailing. Sailing. Over the bounding main. Dum-de-dum. Sailing away. Sailing away."

With a start Carrera's head jerked up, he straightened in the seat and hit his forehead with the palm of his hand. Of course. That was it. Duval hadn't left by any form of transport they'd checked. That was where he had gone. Must have. He had gone to sea. But how? When? Carrera stared into space, considering the possibilities. What about the missing women? What if Duval and the women had gone out together? Did the women go willingly? If so, how were they involved? If not, why had they been taken. If they had gone out, how had they fared in the storm? Where did they get a boat? Did the McGill woman own one? Could they have survived in the weather? Was the Coast Guard out looking for the boat? Way too many questions? Need to find some answers. But it all made a sort of sense. He reached down, started the car and headed Blake's office.

"Blake? Do you have a minute?" Carrera caught Carter Blake just as he was leaving his office.

Carter Blake's eyebrows shot up. He sighed and motioned the

chair across his desk, "Sure. What can I do for you?"

Carrera shook his head at the offer of a seat and spoke hurriedly, "Well, I've got a hunch. Tell me. Any reports of boats in distress? Any news from the Coast Guard?"

"No. Nothing in distress that I know of, although with that storm . . . But, wait a minute. There was a report of a missing boat. When was it? Oh, yes. Thursday. A big one from the marina. The caretaker reported it. Probably some kids took it out for a lark. Could have got caught in the storm. Don't know. You could check with the Coast Guard. They should know."

"Okay. Will do. Thanks."

"No problem. What's up?"

Carrera shrugged, "Oh, it's just a hunch. I'll let you know if it pans out."

The Coast Guard verified that a boat had been reported missing from the city marina. But details were sketchy. Carrera finally found himself at the marina well after dark. There he found Bert Gossett. "It's like this, Mr. Carrera. The *More Fun* was there. That cousin of theirs was stayin' on her. Quiet guy. Never saw him. But he didn't cause no trouble. Then one mornin', the mornin' of the big storm, I heard her goin' out. Only I didn't know it was her. But I heard the engine. Real quiet, but I heard her. Should've got up. But it was early, before light. Didn't really think it was a boat from this marina. Later I thought maybe Miz McGill took her out, just in the bay, you know. But she didn't come back." Bert looked at the ground and shook his head, "Nope. She didn't come back. Don't like it. That was a big blow we had. Don't like it at all."

"It certainly was a big storm. Tell me, Bert, Mrs. McGill? Who is that?"

"Oh, Miz Maggie McGill. She's a friend of the Whitmore's. *More Fun's* their boat. They loaned it to her while they're away."

"Maggie McGill." Carrera knew he'd heard that name recently. But where? When? Wait. He had an image of vivid colors and animal faces--the gallery. The artist's name was McGill. And she was missing. It fit. Maybe they all were on the boat. At least he hoped they still were. "Well, Bert. Thanks for your help."

At Carrera's insistence, the Coast Guard doubled its search efforts for the *More Fun*. He would put a DEA helicopter in the air over the Gulf of Mexico at first light tomorrow. But the Gulf is a large body of water and that part of the search would have to be discontinued with nightfall.

Maggie always expected to hear a hiss when the setting sun hit the sea. They watched with fascination as the fiery ball touched the water, flattened and sent a golden ribbon all the way to the boat. The four sailors gave a collective gasp as the last sliver of the golden sun dropped into the water, followed by a brilliant green flash. The *More Fun* chugged along through a glassy calm sea that turned first golden, then pink and finally a deep rose fading to dark blue and black.

Pascal was the first to speak, "All my life I've heard people speak of the green flash, but I never was sure whether it was a real thing or some sort of mystical myth. Now I've seen it with my own eyes. How beautiful. How mysterious."

Hadi's eyes glowed, "Beautiful, yes. Mysterious, yes. A myth? Can it not be that a myth might be true?"

Maggie thought for a moment, "I wonder? Do you mean that fairy tales are true?"

"Perhaps, my Maggie. What do you think?"

Maggie frowned in concentration and said slowly, "Maybe that the essence of the fairy tale is true even if the details seem to be fantasy."

"It is as I have said. You are, indeed, beginning to see."

Allie frowned, "But Hadi, it is just as we discussed before. Facts are facts and fantasy is fantasy. We can't get around it."

"Yes, Allie, and just as before, it always is important to acknowledge facts, but facts are not all there is to truth. Have you not heard it said that logic is the *beginning* of wisdom? In the case of fables and fairy tales, it is not that the facts are true, but more that the ideas are true. Can you accept that?"

"Yes, maybe. I guess I need to think about it." Changing the subject, Allie asked, "What about the engine? Shall we leave it running all night? What about watches tonight? Shall we take turns?"

Maggie said, "I think taking turns is the only thing to do."

Pascal agreed, "I can take the first watch. There are four of us. Two or three hours each should cover it, don't you think?"

Maggie's watch was nearing its end. She drew her jacket around her more tightly against the chill of the night and sat quietly at the helm as the *More Fun* continued through the still, dark sea. She was beginning to appreciate the charms of going to sea. The time alone at the helm was one of the most peace-filled ones of her life. Even though she still felt tired, it was good to have this quiet time to go over the events of the last few days. Into the empty darkness she whispered a prayer of thanksgiving for their delivery from the dangers they'd faced and one of supplication for their safe return to their homes.

Was it her imagination or did she feel the stirring of a breeze? Yes, she thought it was. Not enough yet for the sails, but definitely more air movement than that created by the movement of the boat. As she gazed across the black sea it seemed as if she saw a faint lightening of the eastern horizon. Sunrise already? Surely not. It was only a little after five. At this time of year the sun didn't come up until after seven. But Maggie had to admit she'd little experience being at sea at night. Who knew what mysterious lights one might see? Hadn't she read somewhere of a reference to a false dawn? Or maybe it was one of Hadi's false oases. She grinned into the night at the thought.

"Good morning, Maggie." Her reverie was interrupted by Pascal who came up from below.

"Good morning, Pascal. You're up early."

"I couldn't sleep more. Thought I'd keep you company. How's it going?"

"Just fine. Completely uneventful, except . . . Tell me, Pascal, do you see anything to the east?"

"To the east?" He gazed out across the black sea, "Hmm, I'm not sure. Just stars and ocean. Should I be seeing more?"

"No. No, I guess not. For a moment I thought . . . oh, it's nothing. But I do think there's a breeze starting. Can you feel it?"

"Yes, I believe I do. It's hard with the boat moving, but I do think I do. That is good news, no?"

"Good news, yes. Let's hope it gets strong enough to do us some good."

"Yes. Let's." They sat is silence for a while. It was a comfortable silence, the silence that can be shared by good friends. "Maggie, have you thought about what comes after this horrible mess is over?"

"Er, no. That is, it's hard for me to imagine being back in the same old routine. I guess things actually will settle down again. But what do you mean?"

"I've been thinking about you. You're a very talented artist, you know. Even though we can't know what Veronique may have sold, I know what I sold and I'd guess she did equally well. If so, we'll have left fewer than ten of your original twenty-four paintings. That would mean that it was an extremely successful show, especially for a new artist. Do you have any idea what that might mean to you?"

"Oh, Pascal. Do you really think so? I mean, that would be a true miracle, wouldn't it?"

"No, Maggie. Not a miracle. It's something far more marvelous. It is the result of your talent and hard work and, if I may say so, our marketing skills. You should have a nice sum of money coming."

"I'm trying to do the arithmetic. It's hard to believe the amount I'm coming up with. Why, it would take months of counseling to come up with that. Amazing."

"Yes, the money is good. Do you have plans for the money? Travel? A new car?" He glanced her way.

Maggie just shook her head.

"It's fun thinking about it. But more important, I think, is what decisions you make about your life."

"My life? Oh, you mean, should I continue to paint?"

Pascal turned a startled face to her, "Continue to paint? Maggie. I certainly hope there's no question that you'll continue to paint. I was just hoping you'd have more time to devote to your art."

It was Maggie's turn to be surprised, "Are you talking about my changing my occupation?"

"It's a decision only you could make."

"I'd never given it a thought." But her thoughts turned to her feelings of burnout a few months ago, "That is, I'd never considered it possible. You know, I worked very hard to become a therapist, and I'm a fairly good one."

"I'm sure you are, Maggie. I'm sure you're a good therapist, but you are also a notable artist. I think you don't realize how inspired and unique your work is."

"That is for sure, Pascal. I think of art as a hobby. It's amazing to me that people would want to buy my work, especially at the prices you put on it at the show. I'd have been thrilled if someone had offered me five dollars for one, or even taken one as a gift, for that matter." Maggie paused for a moment and continued, "But I must admit that painting became quite a release for me, I mean, personally. I'd become pretty burned out by the counseling and art was a wonderful escape. Painting made it possible for me to continue as a therapist."

"You needed something that made it possible to continue in your occupation?"

"Yes, I guess. Oh, I'm feeling confused now. I think I just need . . . " Maggie and Pascal both froze as the diesel coughed and sputtered and then stopped.

"Oh dear!"

"Merde!"

The boat rolled gently in the quiet sea. Silence became palpable. The only sound was of the waves lapping gently against the hull. Maggie and Pascal looked at each helplessly. Just then Hadi climbed out of the cabin, followed closely by Allie who was rubbing the sleep from her eyes.

"What happened? Why did the engine stop?"

"We don't know."

"It just did."

The next half hour was spent trying everything they could think of to get it going again. But, without success. Finally, the four dejected sailors slumped staring at each other.

"We've come through so much. I just can't believe we can be stopped now," Allie looked at Hadi as if challenging him to say something positive.

Hadi shrugged and said nothing.

Maggie broke the silence, "Probably it just ran out of gas."

Nods of agreement followed by more silence.

Maggie's gaze lifted to the prow of the boat, "I think it's getting light."

They watched as the eastern sky became faintly grey and then tinged with pink. Brilliant colors spread across the sky. Finally, the sun rose, bright red and gold. With the sunrise came a breath of air. The small air movement turned to a gentle breeze from the east.

"Quick. Quick. Raise the sails!" The team they had become worked quickly to raise the sails. Allie took the helm and started a tack, always moving toward the sun. Spirits rose.

Maggie went below to brew coffee and tea. She checked Marc who, as well as she was able to determine, remained much the same. Saying a little prayer for his recovery, she started a makeshift breakfast. Maggie continued to be a firm believer in the therapeutic effects of food that was prepared with loving hands. Her work was interrupted by a shout from the deck. She scrambled up into the light.

"Mom! Look! Land!"

Maggie squinted off into the sun and, sure enough, she saw just a thin line on the horizon. "Beautiful," she breathed. The jubilant sailors hugged one another and sat to watch as the thin line slowly grew into a shoreline. Indeed they had found land. But where? What land? Through binoculars she was able to make out feathery tops of trees. Palms. "What do you think, Hadi? Where are we?"

Hadi nodded, "It would seem, indeed, that Allah has delivered us to an oasis, a true oasis."

Allie asked, "But which oasis? Do you mean Florida?"

"I do, Allie. But it will be some time before we arrive. My Maggie, were you not preparing food for us?"

"Oh, yes, I was." Maggie hurried below and brought up a tray laden with hot mugs and snacks.

With a hearty *"Enchallah"* all round and munching happily they watched the shore come ever closer.

Maggie peered through the binoculars, "Pascal, do you think, is it possible, do you think we are coming back to Costa Mira?" She handed the binoculars to him.

"It doesn't seem possible, but I do think I am recognizing buildings. Look down there to the right. Is that the entrance to the bay?"

"Yes, yes it is. I know it. Quick, Allie turn down that way."

And so, in a slow and stately way, they sailed into the Costa Mira bay and toward the marina. They lowered all but their tiniest sail. Carefully Allie maneuvered the *More Fun* as near to the marina as she dared. She knew well the dangers of trying to dock such a large boat without a motor to adjust the speed and provide a brake. So, she kept the *More Fun* in tight circles out from the marina.

Bert Gossett, who had been walking the docks, saw them coming. Clever old salt, Bert, realized that they needed help docking. He jumped into his dingy with its ten horsepower motor and went out to help them. With the help of the sailors, he tied the dingy to the side of the *More Fun* and, like a tugboat, towed her toward the slip. As gently as placing a baby in its crib he eased her into the slip.

"Land sakes! Miz McGill, I just 'bout gave you up for lost. Thank God you made it back." Bert scurried around, grabbing lines and securing them, "What happened? There's been no end of trouble, people lookin' for you. Police. Others. How's the *More Fun?* She don't look too bad." It was a long speech for him. He paused, looking from one happy sailor to another, his smile going from ear to ear.

Maggie grinned at Bert, "Bert, you don't know how happy we are to see you. I'll tell you everything soon, but first we need an ambulance. We have an injured man below." They hurried into Bert's office and called the ambulance.

Chapter Ten

"Now what?" Allie asked. The ambulance had taken the still unconscious Marc to the hospital where his condition was listed as guarded. The four weary sailors had piled into Maggie's sensible car and were still together in Maggie's condo.

As if on cue, there was a knock at the door. Maggie raised questioning eyebrows and opened the door. Lieutenant Anderson was accompanied by a tall, slender man with close-cut dark hair. "Mrs. McGill, this is Arthur Carrera from the DEA. We'd like a word with you."

Maggie's sigh was resigned, "Yes. I've been expecting you, Lieutenant. Do come in." She ushered them into the living room.

Anderson stared at all four of them, but particularly at Pascal DuMonchet, "Are you DuMonchet?"

Pascal returned his look with a weary, "Yes, I am."

Anderson cleared his throat with a suspicious, "Harrumph!"

Maggie motioned the two men to chairs, "I know you must want some information from us, but really, we just returned from something of an ordeal and we're very tired."

Arthur Carrera shook Maggie's hand, "I'm happy to meet you,

Mrs. McGill. I understand that you've had quite a time of it and I know you'll welcome a rest. I have no role in the murder investigation, but it seems that the case I am working on may be connected to the murder. So the Costa Mira police and I are cooperating in our respective investigations. We need to get what information we can from you."

Somewhat mollified, Maggie assented, "Thank you. I'm not sure that we can tell you very much beyond the details of our kidnapping and the trip."

Arthur Carrera folded his lanky body into one of Maggie's easy chairs and began, "First, tell us about the kidnapping. How did that occur?"

Together the four recounted the kidnapping and the events of their sailing trip. Carrera interrupted only to ask for clarification of one point or another.

Carrera nodded his head, "And Marc Duval? Tell us about him."

"What do you want to know? We've told you how he kidnapped us and threatened us. What else is there?"

"Mr. DuMonchet, Marc was working at your gallery. What do you know about him?"

"That he is Veronique's brother. I had known him and his family years ago in France."

"Was he on your payroll?"

"Oh, no. He was not an employee. It would be too much to say that he worked at the gallery. Marc was sometimes there and sometimes would help with the heavy work in the backroom."

"Didn't it strike you strange that he would work without being paid?"

Pascal's face told of his discomfort, "Perhaps. I did offer to hire him, but he always refused. I thought perhaps there were some irregularities with Immigration. But, for old times' sake, I didn't pursue it. I gave him small amounts of cash from time to time when he had been especially helpful. I hoped he was turning over a new leaf."

"But you never suspected him of doing something illegal?"

Pascal discomfort turned to confusion, "I knew Marc as a child. I remembered things about him from then. I guess I knew he was capable of breaking the law. I certainly wouldn't have trusted him with money. I'm not sure what you want from me."

"Do you know anything about his dealing with drugs?"

"Drugs? No. I mean, I suppose he could have. But I didn't notice . . . Why do you ask?"

"I am sorry to tell you, Mr. DuMonchet, that your gallery has been used as a transfer point in a major drug smuggling operation."

"What? My gallery? You must be mistaken. I would have known. I don't believe it!' Pascal started to rise, but collapsed back into the sofa where he'd been sitting. His face was white with shock.

"So, you deny any knowledge of this?"

Numb with dismay, Pascal could only nod his head.

"At this moment, I'm inclined to believe you." Carrera gave the facts about the discovery of the drugs in the art at the gallery. "So, you see, we need to get any information about Marc that we can. Did he say anything about his situation? Did he mention any associates? Any plans?"

Maggie looked at Pascal and shook her head, "No. Not much. He did tell me he wanted to go to the other side of the Gulf, Belize I think, to start a new life, that he felt trapped and that was his only chance. But he never said why or what had happened to him. To tell the truth, I thought it was because he had killed his sister and this was his only way to escape."

Allie agreed, "He seemed pretty desperate. I mean, that storm was really scary. We were so lucky to survive it. He had to be desperate to head into it."

"But he never admitted to the murder?"

The four looked at one another. "No. He never mentioned it."

Hadi interrupted, "And how is Marc? Has he regained consciousness?"

Carrera shook his head, "Not yet. The doctors are not giving much information."

Anderson had not taken his eyes from Pascal during the interview, "And you, Missur DuMonchet? Why did you disappear after the murder?"

Pascal sighed and again told his story of entering his office, of seeing Veronique in his chair, and of waking up in the shed, "It all seems so long ago. It is like a dream."

Anderson bristled, "Did you kill Veronique Duval?"

"Of course not. She was a friend, no, almost like a daughter, and a valuable employee. I shall miss her greatly."

Again, "Harrumph!"

Allie intervened, "We have cooperated and told you everything we know. Are you charging any of us with anything? Should we have an attorney present?"

Anderson grunted.

Carrera smiled, "No. There are no charges from the DEA. We are very interested in what you have to tell us. We had hoped you would be able to fill in some missing pieces. For my part, so far, I have heard nothing that would cause me to detain any of you." He turned to Anderson.

Anderson frowned, "Well, er, that is. No. Not now. But don't leave town!"

The DEA agent spoke again, "There is just one other thing. It would be helpful if we could keep this discovery of the drugs quiet for a while. Do you understand?"

He looked around the room. All heads gave a silent nod.

"You see, if, indeed, you, Mr. DuMonchet, are not involved, then someone most certainly is, and we do not want to alert that person that we are on to his operation."

Again silent assent.

Carrera stood and shook hands all round. "Thank you all for your help. We'll let you get that rest now."

Anderson followed him to the door and they were gone.

"Well, that was intense!"

"Yes, my Allie, it was. But it needed to occur. *N'est pas?*" Hadi gave her an encouraging smile.

Allie nodded her agreement.

Pascal frowned, "It seems clear to me that I am the object of their suspicion. I understand that. It does not look good for me. After all, Veronique was my employee. I knew both her and Marc for many years. The murder and the drug smuggling," at this Pascal shook his head in disbelief, "occurred in my gallery. I am surprised that they did not arrest me straight away. I am so sorry to have involved you all in this."

"But, Pascal, my friend, you would not have harmed Veronique. We also know, because we know you, that you were not involved in the drug smuggling."

"Thank you, Hadi. All the same, the facts do not look good."

"Do you remember the story of the true oasis, my friend?"

"Yes, of course."

"So now, your journey becomes one of crossing the desert of suspicion. But, it is the same. Always we look for the true oasis."

Allie gave Hadi a fond look, "But Hadi, Pascal is correct. *We* know he did nothing wrong. Still, it doesn't look good. Pascal, do you have an attorney? It might be good to get his help."

"Yes. I'll call Duane. He can advise me."

"Duane? Is he an attorney?"

"No. Duane is my partner in the gallery. He'll know what attorney to get."

Allie's face told her doubt. "But Duane is connected to the galley. He could be a suspect. I think you need to be very careful, Pascal. I think you need to trust no one right now."

Maggie's face told a similar story. "I'm afraid she has a point, Pascal. And so do you. Everything that has happened seems to be connected with your art gallery. Until we are sure that Marc was the only one involved, I think you need to be especially careful. It is possible that Veronique was involved in the smuggling. It is even possible that Duane was involved. Be careful until you know."

"I cannot believe that either Veronique or Duane had anything to do with murder or drug dealing. I simply cannot believe that. But, I will take your advice and I will be cautious." With a smile to Hadi, "I will seek the true oasis." After a thoughtful silence, "Thank you, my friends, for your help and support during the last few days. We've had amazing experiences. I have learned much from each of you. But, most of all, thank you for your trust in me. It means more than I can say."

"You don't need to thank us, Pascal. Because we've come to know you during our adventures, we know you couldn't be involved in those things."

"All the same, thank you. And now, I think I must go home and get to work," he rose and started toward the door.

"Ah, yes, my friends, it is time for me to go also," Hadi rose and followed Pascal.

"Wait. Just wait a moment." Allie quickly blocked their path. "It doesn't seem right that you just go off. And you, Hadi, you come and go so mysteriously. I don't like it. Where are you going? When will you come back?"

Hadi stopped and took her hands, "Ah, Miss Allie. I go somewhere else. Do you not remember that we always are together? Do you not know you will find me when you need me? It is a matter of trust. Do you not remember?" He turned to Maggie, "And you, my Maggie. Do you remember?"

"Yes, Hadi. I remember. But it is hard to say good-bye."

He released Allie's hand to take Maggie's, "Then do not. We never are separated in thought. There is no need for farewell."

Allie sighed loudly and smiled, "I guess sometimes we must just accept what is."

They embraced all around and then Hadi was out the door.

"Pascal, we have no control over Hadi. He comes and goes mysteriously always. But you. We will not allow you to disappear from our lives. You must give us daily reports. And let us help you in anyway we can," Allie said.

"Oh, yes. I will. I promise."

"By the way, how are you going to get home now?"

"Oh, no problem. I'll find a taxi."

"Nonsense! We'll take you."

In front of his house, Maggie said, "Pascal. We will expect you to come to dinner tomorrow night."

"Oh, yes. Thank you very much. I'll be there."

Pascal's key turned the lock and he entered his house. It seemed as if he'd been away for years, not just a few days. As always, Pascal's house greeted him with a feeling of peace and repose. He'd bought it years ago when the gallery had just begun to be successful and property values were much lower. It was a seventy-five-year-old craftsman style frame bungalow, a block and a half from the beach. Although not large, it was larger than he needed. The wide porch that stretched across the front of the house was mirrored in the wide living room. He gathered the scattered newspapers, took the stack of accumulated mail from the porch's mailbox, and entered with a sigh.

He had furnished the graceful living room with deep comfortable furniture. Pascal plopped into his favorite easy chair and started to go through the mail. When he realized that he really wasn't reading anything, he set it aside.

A shower. That would be heavenly. After a long shower and a shave, he felt more like his old self. Time to get down to business.

"Hello Duane. This is Pascal."

"Pascal! Oh, thank goodness. I've been so worried about you. Where are you? How are you?"

Pascal chuckled, "There, there, my friend. One thing at a time. I'm home. Just got here. It's a long story. But I'd like to hear yours first. I know a lot has happened. Can you fill me in? Or better yet, maybe we could meet for dinner."

"Why don't you come over here? Adele's out of town. Went to visit her mother. She left a meatloaf. I was just going to have some."

"Perfect. See you soon."

The two unlikely friends related their respective stories over Adele's meatloaf. The evening with Duane left Pascal unable to accept that he might have had anything to do with the drug smuggling.

"Well, Duane. It seems obvious that Marc Duval must have used our art shipments as conduits for the drug smuggling," Pascal leaned back in the easy chair in front of Duane's fireplace and took another sip of coffee.

Duane sighed his agreement, "I feel foolish that I never even suspected what was going on."

Pascal shook his head, "You feel foolish? No, my friend, it is I who feels foolish. After all, I knew Marc from along ago. I knew how unprincipled he could be." Now Pascal sighed and lifted his shoulders in a Gallic shrug, "I hoped he had reformed. I wanted to give him a chance."

"What's his condition? Has he come out of it? Has anyone talked to him?"

"No. At the last report he still was in a coma. They aren't giving out much information, but I think it is very serious. He took quite a blow to the head."

"Pascal, do you think anyone else was involved? Did Veronique know what he was doing?"

Pascal rubbed his hand across his face, "I cannot believe Veronique knew about it. They never were close. She would not have deceived me. She was better than that. I know it."

"Yeah. I'd have a hard time thinking she was in on it. But what about somebody else? Any ideas?"

"I've been wondering about it. There had to be some organization to it. I don't think he could have done the whole thing himself. Marc wasn't that organized. He would have had to have contacts in South America. There had to be someone distributing the drugs in this country."

"Good point."

"I'd imagine that part of it was handled through some big outfit on the East Coast. Carrera said the activity over here was fairly new."

"Makes sense. What about us? Do they suspect us?"

"Oh, Duane. I don't know. If they had any strong suspicions, I don't think we'd be having dinner here. But, it was our gallery. They have to be keeping an eye on us."

"D'you think so? Hell, Pascal. I hate that!"

"I'm not so fond of it myself."

"Then there's the murder. At first they thought you did it. Do you know they had a warrant out for your arrest?" Duane shook his head.

"Yes. Yes, I do."

"Well, looks like they've changed their minds about that."

"I hope so."

"Do you think he killed his own sister?" Duane's question was filled with outrage.

"It is horrible to consider, but it looks as if he did." A pause, "Ah, Duane, what about Veronique? I mean, you know, the arrangements. What has been done?"

Duane sighed, "Well, you were gone. There was no one to make arrangements. So, I just told them to do a cremation. I didn't know what to do. I tried to think about what you would do."

Pascal gazed at his old friend in silence, "Thank you, Duane. That really is the best. Where are her ashes? I'd like to have a small memorial service for her. She didn't have many close friends, but there were some, and there are many who will remember her from the gallery."

Duane wrinkled his brow, "I'm not sure, Pascal. But, I imagine they would be at the place where they did it."

"Yes, of course. Well, I'll contact them and then we can make the other arrangements later. I guess there is no big hurry at this point."

They talked on into the night. Finally, Pascal took his leave. "Thank you for dinner, my friend. And thank you for believing in me."

"Dammit, Pascal. I can say the same to you. It's good that you're back." Duane's ruddy face turned even rosier. He averted his eyes and changed the subject, "We need to get down to the gallery tomorrow and get it open again. We've got a business to run."

Pascal took his hand, "True. I'll see you there."

Ginny Randall straightened her starched nurse's cap and walked down the hall to the coma's room. She knew she should think of him as a name, but it was hard when he just lay there. She wondered about him. Not a bad looking guy in a scruffy sort of way. Wonder what he did that there was such a fuss about him. Marc's pale face had not changed since her last check on him. She adjusted the IVs and checked his vital signs. Everything was just the same. Well, fellow, you're lucky to be alive, I guess.

Wait! Did his eyelid flicker? Maybe. "Hello, Mr. Duval. Hello. Are you waking up?" No. Nothing. She must have imagined it. Even so, she made a small entry in his chart just to indicate that she had made an effort to talk to him.

After their guests had left, Maggie and Allie gave simultaneous huge sighs and plopped down on Maggie's comfy sofa. "Well, I guess we need to get our lives in order. What day is it?"

"Friday? Or maybe Saturday?"

After checking the newspaper, "Oh my! It is Saturday! Can it possibly have been a full week since the opening? I can't believe it! I have some fences to mend with my counseling clients. Rats!"

"And I need to call California to put things right there. I also need to change my air reservations. When do you suppose they'll let me leave here?"

"Don't know. I can't imagine that they'd need you here any longer, but let's find out."

"Okay. But I'm not going until I'm sure that you are safe. Mom, I know we need to attend to our businesses, but let's also attend to our bodies. We just had a pretty intense adventure. How about letting things ride until Monday. We could use a day off, don't you think?"

"Yes, I do. And I agree. Let's do only the most necessary stuff and then take a breather. But remember that Pascal is coming for dinner tomorrow night."

"Okay, but what about food right now? Are you hungry?"

Maggie paused a moment as if to think, "I am! In fact, I'm starved! It's been a while since we had a real meal!"

"Right."

Maggie wrinkled her nose, "I'm not sure what's here."

"Oh, let's not try to cook. I know! Is that Vietnamese restaurant still here? Let's order in."

"It is. How about chicken noodle soup?"

"Perfect. Oh, and some of those little rolls in the thin wrap."

Pascal couldn't believe state of the gallery. His beautiful gallery. What a mess! Maggie's paintings still hung on the walls. He was gratified to see even more sold signs than he had remembered. The caterer's tables were gone, but the aroma of stale champagne and old caviar remained, as did the crumbs and crumpled napkins. The air was heavy and cold. He was prepared for the empty backroom, but not for his office with the chalked silhouette and dark stain on his chair. Poor Veronique! He wandered around the gallery aimlessly picking up a piece of litter here or there, but unable to make any real progress.

"Hey, Pascal! You in there?" Duane's voice sounded from the backroom.

"Yes. Yes, I'm here."

"Sure is a big mess. Those cops really screwed up the housekeeping."

"It is a mess and I just can't seem to make any progress with it."

'Yeah. Me too. The only thing I did was let the caterers in to get their stuff."

The two men stared helplessly at one another. After a pause Duane said, "Well, at least let's do what we can with those pictures," he gestured towards Maggie's paintings.

"Yes, we should. But, I don't seem to be able to stay in my office. It feels too, too . . . I don't know. I just am having a difficult time with it."

"Yeah, I know. The cops are through with it. Let's get a cleaning crew in here. In the meantime, we can use my office. Nothing happened in there."

"Yes. That sounds good."

"I do wish Hadi hadn't just disappeared. I'd have liked him to come to dinner tonight," Maggie pouted while pushing the shopping cart through the market.

"Yeah, me too. But you know how he is."

"I do, Allie, but all the same . . . "

"We just have to go on and trust that he is doing what he needs to do."

Maggie looked at her daughter, "I'm surprised to hear you say that."

"I guess I am too, but that's the way I feel. What are you going to serve tonight?"

"Let's just see what looks good."

"We all are so happy to be safely on dry land that anything will be amazing."

"I know that Pascal feels that way, too. But, still, I'd like it to be something good."

"Pascal, come in. What would you like to drink? A cocktail, wine?"

"Oh, wine would be nice if you have any open."

Over wine and tapenade, Maggie asked, "Have you heard anything about Marc?"

"He is just the same. They are hoping he will come out of the coma soon."

"Oh, I do too. But what will happen to him when he does?"

"Well, the charges are serious. I mean, they seem to think he killed Veronique. I've known him all his life and he certainly has done some dreadful things, but I can't believe he'd do that. It is easy for me to believe that he'd smuggle drugs. In spite of his being fairly bright, I'm not sure he has the drive to organize a smuggling operation."

Allie frowned, "But if he didn't do it, then there is someone else who must have done it. Who could it be?"

"That, of course, is the question. I've wracked my brain and I can't think of anyone. Oh, it is such a disagreeable business!" Then, changing the subject, "Maggie, I am concerned about the state of the boat. You know, it did sustain some damage. I feel responsible. Can we arrange for repairs?"

Maggie nodded her agreement, "Yes, I, also have been thinking about it. I'll call Bert tomorrow and ask his advice about what needs to be done. He'll know. But, just for tonight, let's talk about other things. We deserve to have a pleasant evening."

"You are right about that. I was at the gallery this morning and I have good news for you, Maggie. There are seventeen paintings with sold signs on them. That is much better than I had thought or even hoped. As soon as we can, we'll deliver them and you will have a healthy check coming."

Maggie paused, Pelegrino in midair. "Seventeen? Oh, my. Are you sure? I'm amazed."

"I'm not, Mom. I knew they were good and this proves it. Let's celebrate!"

"Well, yes. I guess we should. How about dinner?"

After a late night, Pascal slept in and arrived at the gallery at ten to find a cleaning crew at work. Duane met him at his office door, "Hi Pascal. Thought it wouldn't hurt to get some help with this mess. Looks like they're making progress." Indeed, a flurry of activity was returning the gallery to its proper state. "Shall we start them on your office next?"

"Yes, yes, that would be a good idea. The police are done with it?"

"That's what they said. Anyway, it's our place and we need to get things back to normal."

Pascal wondered if it ever would feel normal again, but he appreciated Duane's trying for it. He spent the rest of the morning contacting the new owners of Maggie's paintings and arranging for the paintings to be picked up or delivered. "And, of course, Duane, there will be checks coming in now for those paintings."

"Good thing, too. I suppose the cops will return the ones they took, but until they do, we don't have much inventory to display. When d'you want to reopen?"

Pascal ran a hand over his face, "I'm not sure. Maybe in a week. What do you think?"

"I think we ought to as soon as we can. Don't want people to forget about us, you know."

"Yes, of course. I mean, no, of course not."

Chapter Eleven

Marc's eyelids flickered. Where was he? He couldn't place his surroundings. Would it help if he opened his eyes? Almost too much effort. Slowly he cracked one eye open. Again, where was he? Both eyes now. Soft green walls, a framed picture. A hotel? No. Hospital. That was it, a hospital. But what was he doing here? Should he ring for a nurse?

Just then the door opened, "Well, hello, Mr. Duval. Did you decide to wake up?" Ginny Randall entered. She took his pulse and checked the instruments behind his bed. "Dr. Johnson will be happy to see you. Would you like a drink of water?"

Arthur Carrera and Lt. Anderson met each other in the hospital elevator. They were informed that Marc Duval was sleeping, that he had come out of the coma for a few minutes and seemed confused, but lucid. Anderson frowned at the nurse, "What do you think? Will he wake up soon? We need to talk to him."

Ginny Randall reminded herself that this man was just doing his job, "Sir, I have no way of knowing. I just know that the doctor left orders to watch him carefully and not to let anything or any*one* disturb him."

"Well, we need to talk to him as soon as possible."

"You'll have to clear that with the doctor, sir. He left orders that Mr. Duval is not to be disturbed."

Anderson turned his head and muttered, "Crap!"

Arthur Carrera turned to the nurse, "When could we speak to the doctor? It really is important that we be able to interview Mr. Duval. He may have information vital to an investigation we are conducting."

"He said he'd stop by later this afternoon. You are welcome to wait in the waiting room. I'll let him know you are here."

"Yes, please do that. Come on, Anderson. Let's take a walk."

Pascal DuMonchet hurried to the hospital as soon as he heard that Marc had regained consciousness. He arrived soon after Carrera and Anderson had left for the waiting room. Pascal explained that he was an old friend of the Duval family and the closest Marc had to a relative here in the States.

Once again, Ginny Randall explained that no one could see Marc until the doctor gave his permission. She gave Pascal all the information she had about Marc's condition. Just as he was leaving Dr. Johnson walked in.

"Mr. DuMonchet? If you would wait here for a moment I'll check on Mr. Duval." Obediently, Pascal stood at the nurses' station. When Dr. Johnson returned, he said, "Mr. Duval has had quite a trauma. I understand you have known him for a while?"

"I've known Marc all his life. I am a friend of his family."

"And does he have family here?"

"He just lost his only close relative, his sister. Other than that, only distant cousins in France. I doubt if they would even know him now."

"So, basically you are as close to family as he has here?"

"Yes, that is so."

"I also understand that there are legal issues with him?"

"Yes, he is suspected of some crimes."

"Well, before I talk to those police, I'll tell you what I know. Mr. Duval has had a bad concussion complicated by time spent in the water. Frankly, given what I know about the story, I'm surprised he's still alive. When I first saw him, I had little hope that we could do anything to help him. He must have a truly strong constitution. Even so, his condition remains serious and I am reluctant to permit anything that could cause him stress. Do you think seeing you would be helpful to him or not?"

"I'm not sure, Doctor. He knows me, has known me all his life. But I cannot say that we are very close. Yet, he must know that I wish him no harm. Perhaps it would be comforting to him, as sick as he is, to see an old friend."

"Yes, perhaps. Well, let's do this. Let's give him another day or so and see what develops. If he seems to improve, then I'll send for you and let you have a short visit with him. I plan to send the police packing at least until I think he is out of the woods."

"Thank you, Doctor. I will wait for your call."

"What a pleasant evening we had last night, Mom. Your dinner was great. I think Pascal enjoyed himself. He had seconds of everything," Allie said between bites of egg and toast and sips of tea.

"Yes, it was a nice time. Pascal did seem to like the dinner. What's more, it was a relaxing evening. No problems, just a quiet dinner. What a treat to be off the boat and out of danger!"

"And your paintings! Did he say when you'd get your money?"

Maggie smiled at her daughter, "You are so good with business, Allie. No. He didn't say except that it would be as soon as they get the money from the buyers. I imagine that might take some time." She shook her head. "It is hard to believe that those little, well, almost cartoons, will bring in so much money. Amazing! Do you know that Pascal suggested that I quit counseling and do art full time?" She raised questioning eyebrows and sipped her own tea.

"You certainly are good enough to do that. But, Mom, which do you like best? What makes you happiest? That is what you should do. Life is much too short to spend time and energy doing things you don't like."

"I know. Remember when you called from Paris. I had had a dreadful day and was sure I was completely burned out with counseling. Since then the counseling has been going better, but I think that is because I've been so focused on painting."

"Sounds like painting is the thing, then."

"Maybe. But, counseling has been my security. It's the thing I know I can do that will support me. I worked very hard to get to this point. It would not be easy to walk away from it. Then, there's the question of making a contribution. I've always felt that counseling was sort of doing my part to make the world a little better."

"But, Mom, don't you think art can do that as well? Where would the world be without the arts?"

"Oh yes, I guess that's so. Still, it's not an easy transition for me. And who knows? I might burn out on the painting also."

"That is a danger with any occupation. I'd say that you've proven that either one could provide a decent income. Any certainly either is an honorable and contributing occupation. What a great place to be, Mom. You can choose solely on what brings you joy."

"Scary!"

"I know. If you came to yourself for counseling about this issue, what would you tell yourself?"

Maggie made a face at her daughter, "Oh, you got me! Okay. I'll have to think about it." Changing the subject, "What shall we do with the rest of the day? We could go shopping, go to the beach, go for a walk at a bird sanctuary, a movie. Any ideas?"

"Quite a selection! I've had about as much ocean as I want for a while. How about the Corkscrew Bird Sanctuary? My legs could use some stretching and that's a very peaceful place."

"Bird sanctuary it is. Let's go."

Marc opened his eyes again. Yes. He definitely was in a hospital. He wasn't sure that he hadn't dreamed it. But why? And how did he get here. The last thing he remembered was that opening at Pascal's. He had come into the gallery through the back door and into Veronique's office. The art show had a good crowd and Veronique was doing her usual thing. Funny how that little girl he remembered had turned out. From there the memories were dim. It seemed that he and Veronique had had an argument, but he wasn't sure. Had he been unconscious since the opening? What day is it? How long had he been here? Questions continued to plague him. When could he get out? He had things to do. He wanted to pick up his money and just get out of town. If he could find a way, get out of the country.

The long boardwalk was raised above the swamp and its denizens and meandered through the bird sanctuary. Allie spotted lizards and snakes and even alligators that all seemed oblivious to the passage of humans. On this weekday morning there were no other visitors and they and the reptiles had the boardwalk to themselves. They walked mostly in silence, each engrossed in her own thoughts.

The sanctuary was very quiet except for the occasional birdcall. The boardwalk ended at a large clearing, a sort of open swampy area. The trees were white with large water birds, mostly egrets. "You know, I'm as fond of nature as most people, maybe even more so, but I have a hard time with swamps and the things that live here," Maggie whispered.

"Well, yes. Me, too. Very crawly!"

"Definitely crawly."

"But the birds are beautiful."

"Yes, they are. Interesting that they evolved from reptiles. Interesting that we like one and not the other."

"I suppose there's a moral there somewhere."

"Probably so, but I can't think of it right now."

Suppressed giggles. "Let's go and find sustenance."

"Perfect."

"What would you two ladies like?" The waitress pulled a pencil from her platinum bouffant hair and a green order pad from her pocket. Peering at Maggie, she exclaimed, "Well, land sakes, honey! I almost didn't recognize you. You sure are a sight for sore eyes! How are you? Where you been so long?"

"Hi Millie. I'm fine, thanks. I'm still around. Been working hard, I guess. I don't get out this way often enough. Maggie smiled up at Millie, "And how are you, Mille? How's life been treating you?"

Millie rolled her eyes, "Well, just fine. I'm still here, still kickin'!"

"Glad to hear it. Allie and I were just at the Bird Sanctuary and we're starving."

Millie turned to look at Allie, "Well, Miss Allie, how you've grown up! You still riding horses? It sure is good to see you."

Allie smiled up at her, "Hi, Millie. It's good to see you, too. Don't ride as much as I'd like. I live in California now and I'm here visiting Mom."

Maggie leaned back against the dark red plastic seat, "Millie, are you still making your own pies?"

Millie put her hands on her hips, "Now, honey, who'd make them if I didn't. I sure am. Want some?"

"You bet, Millie. Got any key lime pie?"

"That I do. Picked them limes this mornin' and squeezed 'em

myself. Want some?"

"Sure. But first, we need sandwiches. What's good?"

Remembering that Millie's place served the best pie in the county, they had stopped at the little white frame building set back from the road in a grove of orange trees. A faded white board sign announced **Millie's Orange Juice Stand**. It was one of the few remaining pieces of the rapidly vanishing old Florida they had loved when they first moved here over twenty years ago.

As Millie placed fish sandwiches, buried in mountains of fries, key lime pie, and two thick mugs of Earl Gray on the glossy wooden table top, she peered at Allie, "Honey, I'm not sure I would've known you. You sure grew up pretty!"

Allie smiled at her, "Thank you, Millie. It's good of you to say so. It's a treat to see you after all these years."

"You, too, sweetie. Say, you two like music?"

Maggie and Allie nodded.

"Well, we've started something new here. On Friday nights we have a fish fry. All you can eat for twelve bucks. Pretty good deal! Especially good when we can get grouper." Millie grinned, "Anyway, when the weather's good we have a band. They're pretty good, nothing too loud, just golden oldies. There's a dance floor out back. You two should come and try it. It's lots of fun. This time of year we get a good crowd. There's an open mike if you'd like to sing!"

"Thanks for letting us know, Millie. It sounds great." Allie turned to Maggie, "Let's see today is Monday. Do we have plans for Friday?"

Maggie said, "Not sure. But let's keep it in mind. It sounds like a very relaxing way to spend Friday evening."

"Good. I don't think you'd be sorry." Millie glanced at diners at another table who were signaling her, "Gotta go. It's been real good t'see you."

Maggie and Allie smiled their thanks and picked up forks and dug in. The fish and fries exceeded expectations. The crust of the thick slabs of fish was light and crunchy and the interior, white and moist. The fries, cut with their skins still on, were so hot they steamed with each bite. The crust on the pie was crisp and flaky and the pale yellow filling was creamy, rich, sweet and tart. Yummy!

Between bites, Maggie said, "Don't know her secret, but this is as good as it gets!"

With a mouthful of pie, Allie said, "I love this flaky crust. Why do some people make it with crumbs?"

"Don't know, honey. Guess it's easier. Not everyone can make a pie crust like Millie's."

"Well, this is the best!'

Over their lunch, Maggie and Allie discussed their recent adventures. "Even though I'm not fond of crawly things, I must admit that the sanctuary was peaceful. It helped to clear my mind a bit."

Allie raised her eyebrows in question.

"Well, yes. I think I'm coming up with a plan. For my occupation, I mean. Tell me what you think. What if I drastically cut down on my counseling business, maybe two days a week only. I would have to pare down my clients, but I probably could refer them out to some therapists I know. It would mean making different arrangements with my office, but I might find someone to share it. Then I'd have more time and energy for art. I probably could live on what I'd make two days a week of counseling, er, that is, exist if I had to. If they sold twelve or more paintings, I'd have a nice cushion from the art show. I could get by on that and the reduced counseling for a year if necessary. So, it gives me some options."

Allie replaced her mug, "That is a very sensible solution. I think you will gain clarity by doing it. You'll get to try both paths for a while. Although, I imagine you'll come to some definite conclusion pretty quickly. Pascal will be thrilled."

"Yes, I think he will be happy. Truly, I don't see how I could possibly turn my back on art after having such an amazing success the first time out. And it is great fun doing it. I think part of my concern is that although my cartoons were successful, I might not come up with another theme or idea when I'm through with them."

"Well, Mom, that is just the creative process, a sort of artist's dilemma. To do art means taking a creative leap and trusting that there will be something there when you do."

"I guess you should know, Allie. After all, it can't have been easy getting your photography business going."

"That's so. But, I can't imagine doing anything else. I really love it."

They left Millie's with a whole pie in a pink cardboard box. Maggie smiled at Millie and said, "It's just for later."

As they went out the screen door, Millie called out, "Y'all come back now, y'hear!"

Maggie's phone messages contained a "thank you" from Pascal.

Allie said, "Mom, I want to treat us to a dinner out tonight. Where would you like to go?"

"What a nice idea! We have many choices. Do you have any preferences?"

They ended up at a waterfront restaurant specializing in seafood. It was a casually elegant places with bamboo and rattan furniture, but with snowy white tablecloths and stemmed glasses. The restaurant overlooked one of Mira Costa's many yacht basins. As the light faded, they watched boats, large and small, come in and dock. Some docked right at the restaurant and the sailors came in for drinks and dinner.

Allie leaned back in her chair, "I wasn't sure I'd be hungry after that enormous lunch, but we both managed to finish off quite a meal. Dessert?"

"Oh my, no. I'll have to eat only salads for a while as it is."

"After that boat episode, I don't think we need to worry. Speaking of boats, what have you heard from Bert?"

"Oh, Allie, that Bert is the best! He has started working on the boat himself. Said he couldn't find anything seriously wrong. But, he thinks it may need some new sails."

"That is just amazing. You are right, he's a real gem. Maybe we should go down tomorrow and take a look ourselves,"

"Great idea. Right now, let's walk around this area and see how the other half lives."

"Perfect."

As they were rising to leave, a voice behind her caused Maggie to stop, "Oh hello, Maggie McGill."

Maggie turned to see Madeline Fortescue gazing at her over purple glasses.

"Hello Madeline. How are you?"

"Well, Maggie. I am okay. That is, I'm as okay as I can be. I've missed our sessions."

"Yes. I have also. But, you see, I've had some urgent business that took me out of town. I just got back and I haven't been able to see anyone for a while."

Madeline Fortescue frowned, "Oh, I see. Well, I hope you will be back in your office soon. I have many things to talk to you about."

Suppressing a sigh, "Yes. I'm sure you do. I will give you a call as soon as I am back in the office." Turning to Allie, she said, "Have you met my daughter, Allie?"

"How do you do."

Allie smiled her greeting, "Nice to meet you."

"Good to see you, Madeline." Maggie eased herself and Allie out the door.

Chapter Twelve

"G'morning, Mom. Did you sleep well?"

Maggie looked up from the newspaper as her daughter walked in, "Very well, thanks. You?"

"Oh yes. Like a log. Is there tea?"

As Maggie poured hot water for tea, Allie said, "Yikes, Mom! Who was that woman at the restaurant last night?"

"That, my dear, was Madeline Fortescue, a client. And, I'm feeling guilty that I haven't been able to see her. I must put my life back together soon."

Allie frowned, "Yes, I see. But, Mom. She was pretty weird! I don't envy you having to deal with her!"

"Yes, I guess so. Not my favorite client, by far. But still, I can't just drop her cold."

Just then the telephone interrupted. "Hello?"

"Hello, Maggie. Pascal speaking."

"Yes, Pascal. How nice to hear from you!"

"How are you? Are you feeling well?"

"Oh, yes. And you?"

"Very well, thank you. I'm calling to let you know that I have a check for you."

"Oh, thank you so much. That was quick. Shall I come down

and pick it up?"

"That would be good. Why don't you and Allie come at noon and we'll have some lunch."

"We'd love to. Thank you."

Cool ocean breezes tempered the warm sun as Maggie and Allie entered the DuMonchet Gallery. Pascal hurried from the rear, a huge smile on his face. "Good news, Maggie. I just delivered the last of the sold paintings and collected the last check. So my check to you will be larger than I had anticipated. We actually sold two more than I thought."

When he mentioned the amount, Maggie could hardly believe her ears. "Oh, my! That is more than I could have imagined! How marvelous."

"Yes, it is. And, of course, since the gallery shares your good fortune, I see it as being marvelous, also. But, of course, Maggie, it is not unexpected."

That, Maggie thought, is as close as Pascal ever will come to "I told you so."

They walked to a nearby restaurant, an old Costa Mira establishment. The second floor dining room overlooked the ocean that seemed especially beautiful today. "Isn't it great to be able to enjoy the beauty of the ocean from this vantage point and not have to worry about it?" Allie commented.

Nodding their agreement, they studied the menu. Pascal, who obviously was a frequent diner here, made suggestions. He ordered for them, somewhat amazed that Maggie did not want wine. "It must be that the Frenchman still is strong in me. I do enjoy wine with my meals."

"It is a very civilized custom, Pascal, but not one I've ever been able to acquire. Perhaps someday . . . " she said, almost apologetically.

"Not to worry, Maggie. It really is just fine, but a bit unusual!"

"Pascal, what do you know about Marc? How is he?"

"Well, Allie, I talked to the doctor yesterday. He said that Marc had regained consciousness briefly and that they were continuing to watch him closely. The doctor thought that perhaps it would be comforting to Marc for me to visit. But, he wanted to wait a day or so. I am just waiting for a call from Dr. Johnson." He paused and then added, "I hope my visit will comfort him and not just irritate him."

"Yes, it is hard to know with Marc. But perhaps this close call will bring him to his senses."

"One would hope so."

Pascal smiled at Maggie, "And you, Maggie. Have you thought any more about your artistic future?"

Maggie beamed back at him, "Actually, Pascal, I have. I have given it a great deal of thought. You see, I am not independently wealthy. I need to support myself and my counseling practice does that very nicely. As you might imagine, it is intimidating to consider giving it up. Yet, last summer I was feeling burned out to the point that I wondered if I could continue doing it. So, the art came at a serendipitous time for me. But still, there is fear. Like jumping from one lifeboat to another."

She glanced to see if he was following this long speech. Pascal nodded slowly, "Ah yes, fear. I do understand it well."

"Yet, I have found the work I did for the show truly enjoyable. I can't explain it. But it has nourished me in so many ways. And so, taking all these things into consideration, I've decided to continue counseling two days a week and to devote the rest of the time to art!" Maggie finished with a flourish and watched for Pascal's reaction.

He did not disappoint her, "Oh, Maggie, I am so happy to hear you say that. I know you have only started your art career and I know you have many great things inside you still."

Maggie shook her head slightly, "I don't know about that, but I know that I really enjoy doing it."

"I'm so glad to hear that. One item of the current business: After lunch we can put the unsold ones in your car. We could keep them and hang them, but there are very few left, not really enough for a show. They deserve to be shown to their best advantage. At some point we very well may want to exhibit them again. Often in the late Spring we hang a potpourri collection. I would love to hang the remaining works from this group at that time, but until then they will be better stored at your house. If you will just bring your car to the rear of the gallery, I'll help you load them."

"Hurrah, Mom! Not only an artist, but also a well-paid one! Congratulations again!"

Maggie smiled at her daughter as they exited the bank. "Yes. I wonder what ever happened to the concept of starving artists.

Depositing that check really did feel good."

As they carried the five unsold paintings into her condo, Maggie said, "Whatever am I going to do with these? I don't have that much storage room here."

Allie set her load down in a chair. Looking around, she said, "They are so great, Mom. It would be a shame to put them in a closet. Why don't you hang three of them over the sofa and put the remaining two in the hall? I think they'd be really good that way."

"Mmmm, Allie. I hadn't thought of hanging them here. I certainly am not too fond of those prints I have over the sofa. Let's see which ones have the best colors for the room."

An hour later they stood back to consider the new arrangements. "Perfect, Mom. I love them. They really add life to your room. You know what? I think we should find a couple of new sofa pillows to pick up some of the colors. What do you think?"

"Absolutely the best idea. Let's go shopping!"

After choosing new pillows, Maggie and Allie stopped by a marine outfitter and bought replacement boat shoes and jackets for the ones they had used on the boat. At the marina they found Bert at work on the *More Fun*. He grinned at them from the deck, "Hello, Miz McGill. Good t'see you. She's comin' along real good. You can see, nothin' too major. Actually, most of the sails are okay. We'll need to replace the jib, but that's all. Come on aboard. Take a look at the cabins. See what you think."

In the main cabin, Maggie said, "Goodness, Bert. You've just worked wonders! It looks good as new. How did you get so much done so quickly?"

Bert beamed, "Oh, it weren't no problem. T'weren't that much to do. Just regular maintenence stuff mostly." But, it was clear that he was pleased at the praise.

"Well, I can see that you've been hard at work. Just let me know what I owe you."

Again Bert beamed at her, "Sure. Sure, I will. But t'won't be that much. I was so glad to see her comin' back, that was almost payment enough." He paused, looked down, "Er, that is, there will be the cost of the jib and gettin' the radio fixed and having the fuel gauges checked. But, prob'ly the insurance'd cover that."

Maggie thought that Bert considered the marina boats almost like his children, "You know, Bert, I'd rather not have the Whitmores place a claim with their insurance. Really, I feel this whole thing is my responsibility. Just let me know. I'd like her to be back in shape before the Whitmores return."

Bert nodded his agreement.

Pascal hurried to the front of the gallery at the sound of the door-opening chime. It still was painful to realize that Veronique would not be there ever again to greet customers. But, this time, it was not a customer who met him.

"But, how wonderful to see you, Pascal. I was not sure you would be here. I had heard rumors . . . " Lazlo Leigh rushed forward to give Pascal a limp Gallic embrace.

"Hello, Lazlo. Yes, of course I am here. I am just fine and, as you see, the gallery is almost ready to open for business."

"Yes, I see. How fortunate for you that you are able to get it running so quickly." He smiled at Pascal, "But, I am sooo sorry to hear about Veronique. Do you have any news about the apprehension of the . . . er, the culprit?"

"No, nothing." Pascal returned rather curtly.

Lazlo's eyes wandered about the gallery. He seemed about to follow them when Pascal intervened, "It was nice of you to stop by, Lazlo. I appreciate your condolences. Is there anything I can do for you? I was just in the middle of something."

"Oh, no. Thank you. I wanted to express my sympathy."

Gently, Pascal edged his visitor toward the door. "In that case, thank you for your sentiments. Goodbye."

As the door closed behind Lazlo, Pascal turned to the back with a soft, "Whew."

"What're you 'whewing' about, Pascal?" Duane Simpson came from the back workroom.

"Oh, Duane. Hello. How are you? That Lazlo Leigh was here. I don't want to be uncharitable, but he really can be annoying."

"Yes, he can." Duane became all business, "I see you gave the check to Maggie McGill. Was she happy?"

"Oh, yes, very."

"Well, she should be. I can't remember when we've had such a quick turn around with a new artist. Let's hope she gets busy and turns out another bunch as good as this last."

"I believe she intends to continue working so that is a good sign."

"Pascal, what are we going to do about the imported art? The police still haven't released what they impounded. We need to put stuff on the walls. Do you think we should ask Mrs. McGill if we could hang her last five works? You know, the time we were closed, and now, with so little to hang . . . well, it's just not good." Duane's plump face was serious.

Pascal sighed, "I know, Duane. I know. But, no. I don't want to hang her stuff mixed in with other works. Her work is unique and really doesn't blend in with anything else we have. I'd like to save those remaining five works for the potpourri sale in May. I'll call that DEA man, Carrera. Maybe he can help us."

Pascal tiptoed into Marc's hospital room. He felt strangely timid approaching this person whom he'd known for so many years. Marc lay quietly with his eyes closed. Perhaps he was still sleeping. As Pascal eased himself into the visitor's chair it gave a little creak and Marc's eyes opened, "Ah, old man. So. It is you. Did you come to gloat?"

"Oh, no, Marc. Certainly not. I came to visit and to see how you are feeling."

"Well, I can tell you that I would feel better if I could get out of this bed. *Merde!* Hospitals! They always make one feel worse!"

Pascal smiled, cheered at this rebellious statement. Marc was sounding like his old self, "Ah good, Marc. You are sounding full of energy. Do you feel energetic as well?"

"I'll feel better when I'm out of here, I can tell you." Marc was silent for a moment, then, "Ah, er, Pascal. Can you tell me how I came to be here? They tell me nothing. What happened to me?"

"You do not remember?"

"No, I've been trying. I remember coming in the back door of the gallery the night of that opening. I remember wanting to talk to Veronique. She was being stubborn. Where is she, by the way? Why hasn't she come to see me? Can it be that she is still angry with me? One would think she would visit her only brother."

Pascal took a deep breath. He was unsure about how to proceed. Should he tell Marc about the murder? How could Marc not remember if he did it? But then, perhaps that would be a good reason for this amnesia of his. Perhaps he is unable to face the dreadful thing he had done. Pascal cleared his throat, "Ah, Marc. You had an accident and they brought you here. You were badly injured. They have done wonders to bring you to this level of functioning. It was serious."

"Then why do I not remember? I remember nothing of an accident."

"Perhaps it is your body's way of dealing with what happened and giving you a chance to heal."

"Well, old man, perhaps you are right. In any event, I'll be happy to be out of here."

"I am sure you will be. But, for now, it is good for you to rest and let your body heal. It has been good to see you, Marc. If you like, I will visit again." With that, Pascal left the room breathing a sigh of relief. He felt as if he had dodged a bullet. Marc would have to be told about Veronique and about that dreadful trip on the boat. But when? And who should tell him?

In the hall he met Dr. Johnson, "Ah, Dr. Johnson. I am happy to see you. I just visited Marc Duval."

"Mr. DuMonchet. Thank you for visiting Marc. How did you find him?"

"He seemed much his old self except that he seems to be unable to remember the details of his accident and that his sister was murdered. I told him nothing. But, if I visit again, I am not sure I will be able to avoid those questions."

"Yes. I see. It is a problem. I would like to wait another day or two and see how he gets along before we tell him those details. I am continuing to put the police off. He was very badly injured. I just want to be sure that his body has a chance to heal. Truly, I am happily surprised that he is doing as well as he is. Let's see if his memory can come back on its own."

"Hello."

"Ah, hello, Mr. Carrera? This is Pascal DuMonchet. I am calling about the art you removed from my gallery. When do you think you can return it?"

"Mr. DuMonchet. You understand that smuggling drugs is a serious crime. Not to mention the murder. Whether or not they're connected, that art is evidence. It may be some time before we can release it."

"I do understand. But, that art is crucial to the functioning of my gallery. Without it, I have nothing to display. It will take several weeks to get the next artist lined up. I won't be able to keep the gallery open. What am I to do?"

"I understand that it is a hardship, but those frames were specially constructed to hold the drugs. We need them as evidence."

Pascal paused for a moment then proceeded slowly, "You need the frames. I understand. But, do you need the art itself?" Pascal held his breath.

"Well, no. I guess not. But, how would we take it out? I mean, I'm not sure how that works. Can the pictures be removed without damaging the frames? Do you need a specialized workman to do it?"

"No. Not really. The frames and the art are quite separate. I could do it myself. Or, I could instruct your men on how to do it. It really is not difficult. One just needs to use care not to injure the art."

"Maybe we can work something out. The art is still here in town. Let's get together and see what we can do."

"That would be wonderful. Can I bring my partner, Duane Simpson?"

"Yes, I suppose so."

Duane came in the gallery back door. "Oh, hello Pascal. You still here?"

"Yes, Duane. And guess what! I think we may be able to get that art back. But we will need to get it reframed. Can we do that quickly?"

"Dunno. But, I'll find out. How'd you do it?"

He told Duane about the conversation with Arthur Carrera. "We meet with him tomorrow. Do you think you can help remove the art from those frames?"

Duane brightened, "Me? Sure. That's no problem. We'll pull this thing out of the fire after all."

Pascal and Duane worked quickly to remove the imported canvases from their frames with the help and the close supervision of the DEA men. It was accomplished in only a few hours and the two friends drove back to the gallery with the canvases in the back of the gallery van.

"What a relief, Duane. I am so happy that we'll soon be able to get these into the showroom."

"Yeah, me too. I've been really worried about the whole thing. I mean, our situation is sort of scary. We can't afford to go very long without something coming it. How long do you think it will take to get these reframed."

"I'm not sure, Duane, but we'll get it started this afternoon. I contacted the framer and he said he'd do it as quickly as possible.

"Well, I sure am glad we had money coming in from that McGill woman. We'd be in a fine pickle without it!" He paused for a minute, "You know, we run a pretty good gallery here. Good stuff. I manage the business pretty good. Sometimes I wonder how some of these other galleries manage."

"Yes, I do too. But then, some of them are only hobbies financed by other sources of income. For instance, the Objets gallery is a hobby for Stephanie Lancaster. Mr. Lancaster supports it for her. I guess he thinks it keeps her busy."

"Yeah, I see what you mean. Oh well. We can be proud that we make it on our own. And, most of the time we do just fine."

Marc Duval woke from a dream-filled sleep, "What are you doing here?"

"I just came to see you, Marc. I wanted to see for myself that you are okay."

"Okay? Well, as okay as I can be here in this bed!"

"Where did you go? You know, after . . . "

"After? After what?"

"You mean you don't remember?"

"Remember what? I remember the night of the art show. I remember coming in the gallery back door and waiting for Veronique. But, I can't remember anything else. Do you know what happened between then and now? How long has it been, anyway? A day or two?"

"Are you sure you don't remember anything else?"

Marc snorted, "Do you think I'd be asking if I did? Come on, tell me."

"When do you think they'll let you out of here? You know, we have some unfinished business . . . "

Ginny Randall entered her patient's room, "Well, Mr. Duval . . ." She stopped in mid-sentence. Hands on hips, "What are you doing here? Who are you anyway? This patient is not permitted any visitors. I'm afraid you will have to leave immediately." She frowned her strongest disapproving frown.

"Oh, I am sorry. I didn't know. I just wanted to visit my old friend."

"Well, you must leave NOW. You must speak to Dr. Johnson to obtain permission to visit."

"Yes, I will." The visitor backed out of the room.

"Well, Mr. Duval. How are you feeling this afternoon?" Ginny took his pulse. A little rapid. Probably that visitor. Why didn't people obey the rules? There was a notice on the door plainly stating that this patient was not allowed visitors. Really!

"Hello Pascal. This is Maggie McGill."

"Hello Maggie. How nice to hear your voice. How are you?"

"Oh, I'm well. I've been wondering about Marc. Do you have any news?"

"I spoke to his doctor this morning. He says that Marc is getting better, but that it is very slow. Physically he is recovering quite nicely. But, Marc still has no memory of kidnapping us or of the boat, or even, for that matter, of Veronique's death. The doctor is not sure when he can be released."

"It is good that his body is recovering. In truth, I can't imagine that remembering all those dreadful events could be good for him. What a mess it is!"

"Yes, that is so."

"Allie and I had wondered about visiting him, but it sounds like it would be better if we wait a few days."

"That may be so. I, myself, do not know whether or not I should pay him another visit. It is awkward when he begins to ask questions."

Chapter Thirteen

Arthur Carrera entered Dr. Johnson's office, "Thank you for seeing me, Doctor. I'm wondering how Marc Duval is coming along. When do you think we can question him?"

Dr. Johnson leaned back in his chair, "Well, Mr. Carrera, that is the question. I understand that you need information from him, and physically he is mending better than we had expected. He continues to be weak physically, but considering what he went through, we are pleased with his progress. However, there is a serious issue with his memory and I don't want to jolt that right now. You know, when he came in I really feared there was nothing we could do to help him. His body and apparently his psyche suffered serious trauma. I'm not a psychiatrist, but I fear that a sudden influx of information about the missing time could be disastrous. In that area he remains quite fragile."

"I see. Can you predict when he might regain some memory or when we might be able to talk to him?"

"These matters have their own time table and we need to continue to shelter him and watch for developments. No, I really can't predict when."

Carter Blake leaned back in his chair, "Well, Anderson? Where are you in the Duval murder? Anything new?"

Lt. Anderson shifted uncomfortably in his chair, "Er, no. That is, we are waiting to talk to Marc Duval. The doctor won't let us at him. Says he's still not strong enough for questioning."

"I see. Did he tell you when you'd be able to talk to Duval?"

"No. He says he can't predict when, says Duval's memory is gone. If you ask me, I'd bet Duval is faking it. After all, if you'd done murder, wouldn't it be convenient to lose your memory about it?"

"Yes, I suppose so. Well, stay on top of it and let me know if anything changes."

"Yes, sir."

Marc sat up in bed. It seemed he'd spent too much time in this bed. Why hadn't Veronique come to see him? Was she still angry about the argument they'd had? And old DuMonchet. Where was he? Really! Marc was feeling unhappy and neglected.

"Hello?"

"Hello, Maggie. Pascal calling. How are you?"

"Very well. And you?"

"Just fine. Maggie, I have a huge favor to ask you."

"You know I'm happy to do anything I can."

"Veronique rented a small house not far from the gallery. The lease will be up for renewal next month. The landlord contacted me about it. Well, the thing is, I need to clear out her house so we can vacate it. I'm wondering if you and Allie could help me just sort through things. I'm not so good with feminine items."

Maggie smiled and suppressed a chuckle, "Of course, Pascal. We'd be happy to help. When do you plan to go over there?"

"I was thinking tomorrow morning. Would that be convenient for you?"

"Yes, of course. We'll be there."

Maggie put down the phone and grinned at Allie, "That was Pascal."

Allie raised questioning eyebrows, "And?"

"He needs to clear out Veronique's house and would like us to help with the 'feminine items'."

"You mean he is shy about her underwear?"

"Apparently."

"Well, that is rather sweet, don't you think? When are we going?"

"Tomorrow morning."

"Mom, what about tonight? Do you want to do something?"

"Like what?"

"Well, it's Friday and I was thinking about Millie's fish fry. It might be fun. What do you think?"

"I think that would be perfect. Certainly a break from what we've been doing. It would be a taste of the old Florida. Let's go."

They donned jeans and sweaters and carried jackets in case the night became too cool. By eight o'clock Millie's was crowded. Millie, herself, greated them at the door and led them to a tiny outdoor table on the back deck where they could see both the bandstand and the dance floor. Tall gas heaters took the chill off the night air. Bright paper lanterns were strung from orange tree to orange tree giving the old orange juice stand a festive air.

"Hey, Mom, they have an open mike, remember? Should we sing?"

Maggie, remembering that Allie had inherited her singing voice from herself, said, "Sure. You first!"

Digging into her basket of fish and fries, Allie said, "Mom, I had forgotten how really good Florida fish can be. This is marvelous. Even better than the sandwiches!"

"Yes, it certainly is. Probably cholesterol ladden, but heavenly. I think the secret must be that it is freshly caught. Or maybe that Millie just has the right touch with it. Do you think this is grouper?"

"Don't know, but it is really delicious." Allie paused, then, "And, you know, the band is pretty good. These oldies are great. Being here at Millie's with this music is like being transported back to another era."

"Well yes. I guess so. I love the old music too. But then, I remember when it was in!" Maggie looked around at the silver-haired crowd and said ruefully, "Apparently I'm not the only one."

"I think Millie has a going thing here. Good for her. Let's stay a while longer. Okay?"

"Sure. Sounds great. But remember we're working tomorrow morning."

"Oh, yeah. Okay. How about one more set?"

"Perfect."

Allie and Maggie parked on the street in front of the modest bungalow that had been Veronique's home. Wicker chairs sat on the tiny front porch that was shaded by an ancient banyan tree. "This is a charming neighborhood. I didn't realize it was here," Maggie smiled at her daughter.

"It really is great. So close to the beach and the gallery. She chose a good spot."

"Yes, she did. You know, I still feel guilty that we made fun of her at that first meeting."

"Yeah, me too."

"Well, let's go in and see if we can make some sort of cosmic amends."

At the door they were greeted by a slightly disheveled Pascal, "Ah, Maggie, Allie. Thank you so much for coming. I really am having a difficult time with this. Everything reminds me of poor Veronique. So sad."

"Yes, it is," Maggie agreed, "but let's get started and see what we can do to make it better. Where would you like us to begin?"

Maggie and Allie worked in Veronique's bedroom for an hour, breaking their silence only to ask for advice from the other. Finally, they had cleared the closet and drawers and had boxes filled with the things they thought would be appropriate to donate to a thrift store. The few things that were not suitable were in trash bags to be set out next week.

"Whew! That's done. What next?"

"We'll have to ask Pascal." Allie paused and look around the small bedroom, "You know, for someone who had such an exotic appearance, her home is decorated quite conservatively."

"Yes, I was thinking the very same thing."

In the kitchen they found Pascal putting kitchen items in boxes for donation. "Ah, Maggie and Allie. I cannot thank you enough for your help. It begins to feel like not quite such a huge undertaking now."

"Well, the bedroom is completed. What about the living room? Do we need to do anything in there?"

"No. I don't think so. I will go through her desk and then just let the thrift shop people come and take everything else."

"How about the second bedroom?"

"Oh, I had forgotten about it. Let me take a look."

The guest room closet contained a few more clothes and

personal items. Pascal sighed, "If you wouldn't mind going through these, it would be a huge help."

"Of course, we'd be happy to do so. It won't take us long. Come on, Mom."

Pascal left them to start working on Veronique's desk.

"Mom?"

"Yes?"

Allie whispered, "You know, I think the main reason he wanted us here is not so much that he needed help with her belongings as that he just couldn't face the house and memories on his own."

Maggie nodded, "Yes, I think you're right."

They worked quietly for a while and then Pascal returned to the guest room and glanced at his watch, "Oh dear, it is past lunch time. Let's go out for some food first."

"Great plan."

Lunch was at a small cafe in the old section of Costa Mira. Checkered tablecloth-covered tables both inside and in a small courtyard lent a festive air. While they waited for their sandwiches, Pascal cleared his throat, "Ah, Maggie, I have some concerns about the condition of the boat. It is my intention to pay for any repairs that need to be made."

Maggie smiled at him, "Thank you, Pascal. That is very generous. I have spoken to Bert at the marina and he is hard at work putting the *More Fun* back into condition. He assures me that, other than the replacement of the jib sail and the radio repair, the costs will be modest. To tell the truth, I feel responsible and I plan to cover the costs, whatever they may be."

Pascal raised his hands, "Oh no, Maggie. Certainly not! If not for me and your effort to help me, nothing would have happened. This is my responsibility. I insist."

"Thank you, Pascal. However, I, too, feel responsible. I am fine with covering it."

Allie watched this exchange with a small grin, "You two! Each of you is so intent on taking responsibility. I can't believe it. Why don't you just split the cost? Then each of you will be happy."

Maggie and Pascal turned to her with words of protest.

"Wait. Wait. This is a very reasonable approach. If either of you wins this, the other will hold either resentment or guilt. You have a great business arrangement going. You don't want that blemished by this small issue. By splitting this cost, that may not be all that much anyway, each of you will feel he or she has done their part. It will not be a burden on either one of you."

Maggie and Pascal looked at one another with rueful grins. Somewhat reluctantly, they agreed that Allie's idea had merit.

After a more than satisfying lunch the workers returned to Veronique's house. Maggie pushed up her sleeves, "Let's get at this. We should finish it up in no time."

Once again they worked quietly for a while. Allie straightened her back and stretched, "Whew! We're out of boxes." She wandered into the living room where Pascal was sorting through the desk, "Pascal, do we have any more boxes?"

He stood, "I do think there are some in the back. Let's see." Together they walked through the kitchen into the tiny back yard.

Maggie stood up and stretched her back. A voice startled her, "Well, just who are you?"

She twirled to see a shaky Marc Duval standing in the doorway.

"Oh, hello, Marc. I'm surprised to see you. When did you get out of the hospital?"

"When did I . . . ? Wait a minute. Who are you and what are you doing in my sister's house? Where is she, anyway?" His voice was tremulous and irritated.

Maggie backed up and nearly fell over a box of clothing. Realizing that he still had not regained his memory of Veronique's death, she said, "Marc, I am just helping to clear out some things."

Just then Allie and Pascal walked in, their arms loaded with boxes. Pascal dropped his boxes, "Why, hello, Marc. How are you feeling?"

Marc wheeled and stumbled. Regaining his footing he croaked, "Hello, old man. I didn't expect to see you here. Where's Veronique? I came to see her."

Pascal drew a long breath, "Marc, Veronique is not here. She . . . ah, er, Marc, sit down. We need to talk."

Marc reeled backward and regained his footing, "Talk! Is that all you can do? I want to see my sister. Just where is she? And what are you doing here?" His voice rose and trembled at this last.

The doorbell interrupted the exchange. Relieved, Maggie went into the living room to admit Lt. Anderson. She led him into the bedroom where Marc teetered on his heels, "Lt. Anderson, meet Marc Duval."

Anderson stopped in surprise, "Marc Duval! What are you doing here?"

"Doing here? I'm here to see my sister. You need to ask these people why they are here. And ask what they have done with my sister."

"Sit down, Marc. How did you get out of the hospital?" Anderson's voice raised.

"I don't want to sit down. As to what I'm doing . . . " Marc's voice faltered and he plopped into a chair. He seemed startled to find himself there, but then he leaned against the chair cushions and closed his eyes.

Quietly, Pascal reached over and took Marc's hand, "We need to call an ambulance."

Lt. Anderson left with Marc in the ambulance. The workers looked at one another in stunned silence.

Allie broke the silence, "Wow! That was a bit of drama. I almost feel sorry for Marc. He really was out of it! What was Anderson doing here anyway?"

Pascal cleared his throat, "Oh, I told him I'd be working here. They released this house only a few days ago. I guess it's a good thing he came by."

Maggie, who found her knees a little weak, slumped into a chair, "Yes, poor Marc."

"Poor Marc, indeed," Pascal said. Concern on his face, "But, you, Maggie, and you, too, Allie. You have done too much. We are finished here. I'll just put these last boxes by the door for the pick-up tomorrow. Then let's go."

Maggie sighed, "Thank you, Pascal. Yes, I think we've had quite a day . . . again!"

"Indeed."

Maggie and Allie kicked off their shoes and sprawled on the sofa with their feet resting on Maggie's coffee table as they sipped tall sweaty glasses of iced tea.

"You know, Mom, I'm beginning to think Marc really didn't do it. He certainly isn't a very nice person, but he sincerely was looking for Veronique."

"That's true, but it might just be the amnesia. You know. He didn't know either of us. Even without amnesia, selective memory can be insidious. In this case, maybe that's all his amnesia is."

"Yes. Maybe. Still . . . " doubt clouded Allie's face.

"Well, if he didn't do it, who did?"

"That, of course, is the big question."

"The idea of any civilized human being killing another is hard for me to understand, anyway." Maggie's brow knitted in concentration.

"But, Mom, it happens all the time. You know that."

"I do, but still, I have a hard time understanding it."

"But in your work, you must come across all sorts of weirdness, you know, people doing bizarre behaviors."

"Yes, I do. Maybe that's the answer. Maybe all violence is a sort of pathology."

"Maybe. I guess we're lucky that we've never had to make the choice about whether or not to use violence."

"True. We've had sort of charmed lives." After a long silence, Maggie continued, "I know I'd do violence to anyone or anything that threatened you. So I guess we can't judge too harshly until we've been put to the test."

"I agree. But, you know, we've had a few adventures ourselves. Maybe what we did to those guys in California last year was violence. You know, when we were escaping."

Maggie nodded, "Yes, we were feeling desperate. Maybe that's the answer to why violence happens?"

"Anyway, I'm beginning to reconsider Marc's role in all this. For all his faults, he may not have been the one who did her in!"

"Yes, it was kind of eerie how he kept asking for Veronique. But I guess with amnesia, even if he did it, he wouldn't remember. I mean, that's the definition of amnesia. No?"

They were interrupted by a call from Pascal who reported that Marc was back in the hospital and that, in spite of his outing, Marc's condition remained much the same.

"So, Mom, we seem to be back in the same place. The mystery is as deep as ever."

"Hello, Pascal?"

"Hello Duane."

"Oh, Pascal. I'm at the gallery. I think you should get over here!"

"Yes, I can come. What's going on?"

"Have you been over here since last night?"

"No. Why?"

"Well, someone has been here. Come on over. You'll see."

Duane met Pascal at the back door of the gallery, "See, look around."

Pascal hurriedly paced around the gallery. A few newly framed paintings had been pulled out of their racks, the dust covers ripped from their backs. He frowned, "Oh yes. Someone definitely has been here. Have you called the police?"

"No, Pascal. I wanted you to see it first."

"Obviously someone is looking for the stuff that was in the frames. Someone who didn't know it had been discovered. Now I understand why Carrera wanted the smuggling kept so quiet."

"Yeah. I guess it's good that we don't have most of the paintings back from the framers yet. It's a mess!"

"Yes, it is. But Duane. It's only the dust covers. It'll be fairly simple to put them back on. I can do that myself."

"Pascal. What'll happen when we report this? D'you think they'll take these as evidence?"

Pascal sighed, "Probably. But what else can we do?"

"I don't know. But, we really can't afford to wait a lot longer before we get something back on the walls."

"Is our situation that precarious?"

"It isn't good. It's been almost two weeks. And we really don't know how the murder and all will affect our traffic. I'm worried, Pascal. Worried. It's not so much that we don't have a cushion. We have a little bit. But more that we don't want to lose clientele."

Pascal smiled bleakly at his old friend, "I'm inclined to think that it should be reported. On the other hand, I can't see that it gives us, or would give them, any new information. I mean, I'm sure there are no fingerprints. There haven't been up to now. It is such a small thing. Let's look over the rest of the gallery. If nothing has been taken, maybe we won't need to report it. Do you know how they got in?"

"Not sure. Nothing seems to be disturbed. Nothing broken. Nothing forced. I mean, it almost looks as if they had a key!"

"A key? How would that be possible?"

"Well, I sure don't know. But take a look around. See if you can spot something I missed."

The two men searched the gallery and examined the front and

back doors. Sitting in Duane's office they decided there had been no obvious break-in and that nothing had been taken.

"Ah, Duane, I think you are right. Whoever it was must have had a key."

"But who could that have been? I mean, there are only three keys, yours, mine and Veronique's. None of us would have given out a key."

"No, of course not."

"But, what happened to Veronique's keys?"

"I found them in her desk drawer after the . . . after she was gone, after the police had been here. I don't even remember if her gallery key was with them. They're back at my house now. You know, we cleared her stuff out of her house earlier today."

"Let's go take a look."

"Yes, of course. Let's."

Pascal and Duane found Veronique's keys on his entry table, where he had dropped them earlier. The gallery key was there, just as it should have been.

"I dunno, Pascal. Could she have given it to someone, maybe Marc?"

"Oh, I don't think so. She was very careful about things like that. And, even if he was her brother, I don't think she actually trusted him that much."

"Do you think he might have found a way to make a copy without her knowing about it?"

Pascal's brows came together in concentration, "That, I suppose, could have been possible. He was around the gallery a great deal and he knew where she kept her things. Yes, I suppose that is possible. But, I don't think Marc could have been our culprit. I mean he can hardly walk."

"Well, Pascal, we need to make a decision about the police. I'll do whatever you think we should. But, whatever, I'm going to have those locks changed today!"

"Yes. Yes, we should do that. I still think we should call Carrera. And, you know, Duane, there were only a few paintings affected. Thankfully most of them still are at the framers."

Arthur Carrera met Duane and Pascal at the gallery that same evening. He agreed that the break-in was connected with the drug smuggling. He also supported the idea that a key must have been used for access to the gallery.

"I encourage you two to keep both the drug smuggling and this latest break-in to yourselves. Apparently our culprit does not realize that the drugs have been discovered. I expect that he or she will continue to look for them. If this is so, then sooner or later that person will make a mistake and we will be able to apprehend him, er, or her, as the case may be."

Pascal cleared his throat, "Ah, Mr. Carrera? That is, what about these paintings? Will you need them? We still need to make our gallery operational as soon as possible. Would it be possible for us to use these?"

Carrera looked at the two anxious men, "Nothing was taken. If you reported this to the local police, I'm sure they would view it as a simple act of vandalism. Let me get someone in here to check for fingerprints. I really don't expect to find any, but we need to check. If nothing shows up, then I don't see why we should need these particular paintings."

The relief on Pascal's face was matched by that on Duane's, "Thank you, Mr. Carrera. That will help us a lot."

Carrera paused for a moment, "But, M. DuMonchet, do you realize that whoever did this continues to look for the drugs. They may try again. It is possible that he or she is feeling some pressure to deliver those drugs, to pass them on. This does put the gallery and you two, also, in a certain amount of danger."

"Do you really think so? I mean, the gallery was entered and searched, but it happened when we were safely away. It seems to me that whoever did it took pains not to encounter us."

"Perhaps. But, just the same, you could be in jeopardy."

Duane spoke, "I suppose so, but we will be in great financial jeopardy if we don't open soon."

"Okay. I'll get those guys in here as soon as possible. How about first thing tomorrow morning, say nine o'clock?"

"Perfect. We'll be here."

Chapter Fourteen

Maggie was asleep on the *More Fun*. The sea was quiet and the boat rocked gently on the waves. She thought perhaps she should get up and help with the boat. Was it time for her watch on deck? But, she wanted just a few more minutes of sleep. It seemed she could hear Hadi calling to her, "Wake up, my Maggie. Wake up."

Maggie gave a little groan, rolled over and sat up in bed. Who had called her? What was it about? "Rats." A dream. It was a dream about Hadi. What had happened to him? Where had he disappeared to? Why did he have to be so mysterious?

She glanced at the bedside clock. Its green numerals, larger now that she needed glasses for reading, read 4:17. "Rats." She lay back on the pillows, closed her eyes and tried to get back to sleep.

"Yeow!!! Yeow!!!" From somewhere in the condo came a loud blood-curdling yell followed by a thud and muttering.

"Mom? Mom? Is that you? Are you okay?" A frightened voice from Allie's room.

More scuffling.

Maggie jumped from bed and ran into the hall. "Allie?" Just then Allie ran out from her room.

"Mom? What happened?"

"I don't know. Let's get some light on the subject." Maggie

flipped light switches. Her terrified cat, Tilly, with her fur standing on end, ran from the room.

"Mom? Are you all right?" Allie threw her arms around her mother.

"Me? Of course. You?"

"Fine. I get scared when I think about something happening to you. Gee, what happened?"

"I can't imagine. Something really frightened Tilly. Let's look around." Slowly and cautiously, holding hands at first, they circuited the condo. The only thing they could find amiss was a French door to the balcony. It was ajar.

"Did we lock that door last night?"

"I'm not sure. I thought so, but who knows. I'm not too careful about it. After all, we're on the second floor."

"Do you think someone was here?"

"I don't know, but something got to Tilly. She sounded like something both hurt and frightened her. Allie, were you up?"

"Me? No. I was sound asleep. You?"

"I was awake, but definitely in bed. You know, as strange as it sounds, I do think someone was in here. I am almost sure I heard a voice when Tilly yowled."

"Really? Well, that is scary. Has anything been disturbed? Is anything missing?"

"Not at first glance. I can't think what someone would want from here. My television is old. The computer is where it should be." She checked the sideboard in the dining area. "The silver is here. Why would anyone want to break in here?"

"Well, I don't know, Mom. But, you know, Tilly is black and it would be easy to step on her in the dark. I've almost done it myself once or twice."

"That would fit with the way she yowled. Let's see if she is okay."

They found Tilly cowering under Maggie's bed. Finally, they were able to coax her out. Maggie felt her legs and checked her as best she could. "I think she's okay, but she's definitely been frightened."

"Me too."

"Wow! What a scare!"

"It's really early," glancing at the clock, "not even five yet. Do you want to get some more sleep?"

"Wish I could, but I don't think I could sleep after this."

"Yeah, me neither. Let's have some tea."

"Mom, what do you think is going on? Do you think our break-in is connected to the trouble at the gallery?" Allie frowned at her mother over the brim of her teacup. Once again the two women were lounging on Maggie's sofa, their feet on the coffee table. Most of the morning had been spent with the police who came to investigate the break-in. The police concluded that it was a robbery attempt. They cautioned Maggie about locking the balcony door in the future.

Maggie sighed, "I just don't know. It seems clear that Marc was involved with some drug smuggling at Pascal's gallery. But, for the life of me, I can't imagine how we could be connected to that in any way. Maybe it was just a simple robbery attempt."

"On the other hand, I think we need to be very careful about this condo and ourselves. You know, there could be some connection to all that's happened and, well . . . I mean, after all, Veronique was murdered!"

Maggie drew her brows into a frown, "Oh yes. I know that is so. It's just that I don't like to think of being involved in something like that."

"Yes. But, let's see what we know about this mystery. First, Veronique's murder. What do we know about that?"

"I guess we'd have to begin with what we know about Veronique. We know she was an orphan and that Pascal sort of rescued her."

Allie leaned forward and set her teacup on the coffee table, "Yes, that's true. And we know from Pascal something about her parents and, more importantly, we know a little bit about Marc. Marc was a problem child, always getting into trouble. Right?"

"That's what Pascal said. He also said that Marc had always been jealous of Veronique."

"So, that would give him a sort of motive for murdering Veronique, right?"

"I guess so. Do you think he did it?"

"I don't know. What do you think?"

Maggie sighed, "I always come back to his amnesia. One could make a case for his forgetting that he had done such a dreadful thing, a sort of defense mechanism. But, if so, and his memory has reverted to before the murder, we are left with his attitude toward Veronique as it would have been then. He doesn't seem to be holding deep hateful feelings toward her. In fact, he seems to be more or less emotionally dependent on her. Like his needing to find her yesterday at her house. That concern for Veronique leads me to doubt that his apparent antisocial behavior, in spite of his history, is deep seated."

Allie nodded her head, "Well, you're the shrink, Mom. What you say makes sense. But if Marc didn't do it, who did?"

"That, of course, is the question. First of all, the psyche is a mysterious thing and my thoughts are pretty much an educated guess. I could be wrong about him. But, if I'm not, then I think it must be connected to the drug thing."

"Well, if it is, the first question is, did Veronique know what was going on?"

"There's no way to know really. I keep going back to that first day and our impression of her. I believe she was under some sort of stress that first day we met her. My experience of her later was that she was very pleasant and easy to communicate with. She really seemed like a nice person. I hate to think that she could have been involved in something so ugly as drug smuggling."

"I know, Mom. But then, you always try to see the best in everyone. I think your initial thing with Veronique came out of your being so nervous about showing your art."

"Allie, have you ever thought you might have been a really good therapist?"

"Mom!"

"No, I'm serious. You have great insight into people. You certainly see more than the surface."

"Well, maybe. But let's get back to solving this mystery, or mysteries, as the case may be."

Maggie frowned in concentration, "The drug thing? It seems likely that Marc was involved in that. His past history certainly would lead us to believe that he could be."

"And, it would seem that Veronique's death is connected to the drug smuggling at the gallery. If we assume Marc didn't kill Veronique, who did?"

Maggie sighed, "Well, we've come full circle. Who indeed?"

Now Allie's brow wrinkled in concentration, "Let's list the likely suspects." She reached for a note pad and pencil.

"Okay. First?"

"I guess we can eliminate Pascal?"

"Oh yes, I think so. I can't see Pascal doing anything so violent."

"Then?"

"I guess by elimination we come to Duane Simpson as the only other person closely connected to the gallery." Maggie shook her head, "I have a hard time with the thought that he could have done it, but he is a logical choice."

"Yes, he is. Maybe he has been dealing in drugs to supplement the gallery's income."

"Well, yes, I guess. But then Pascal might have known about it also. I mean, how could Duane account for the extra income?"

"Maybe he did it just for himself."

Allie placed the notepad on the coffee table and wrote:

1. Duane Simpson

"Okay, Mom. Let's list motive and opportunity."

"Well, Duane is connected to the gallery. If he is in on the smuggling and if Veronique also was in on the smuggling, they could have had an argument about it. A sort of falling out among thieves."

"What if Veronique didn't know about the smuggling?"

"Then, I guess that, itself, might have been a motive. If she found out about it, she might have been killed to keep her from talking."

"That's motive. How about opportunity?"

"Opportunity? Well, I can't think of anyone we could eliminate, except you, Hadi, and me. There were a lot of people at the opening. In the crowd, anyone could have slipped back into the office at almost any time. For that matter, someone could have come in through the backroom. They might not even have attended the opening."

"Right. A wide-open field! Well, you know, even though it seems very unlikely, if we are going to do this scientifically, we need to put Pascal on the suspect list. I mean, he was there when the murder occurred. If he knew about the smuggling, he could have had a motive."

Maggie frowned, "I guess you are right. I would have a hard time believing he could do it, but by rights, his name belongs on the list. Who else?"

"Marc, of course."

"Okay. Marc." She added his name to the list.

"Same thing for motive and opportunity. Right?"

"Right. Anyone else?"

"Well, anyone at the opening. Anyone who might have been in on the drug smuggling might have had a motive. There might even have been someone who disliked Veronique for some other reason. I suppose her murder might not have been connected to the drugs."

Maggie sighed and stood up, "That could be. Oh my, Allie! We're right back where we started. Anyone might have done it. Anyone in the whole world could have slipped in that back door. Anyone."

Allie stretched and got to her feet, "Right, anyone. Are you hungry? Let's go out for lunch. What about Cuban?"

True to his word, Carrera sent the fingerprint team to the gallery at nine. They worked quickly and efficiently and were finished, leaving only traces of white powder, by ten.

Duane swept and Pascal followed with a cloth and mop. They had all traces of the investigation cleaned up before noon.

Duane leaned on his broom, "Pascal, when will the framers be done with the other stuff?"

"They promised Tuesday. Usually they are prompt. Why?"

"Let's get the word out and open up soon. Could we get the reopening scheduled by Saturday? I will feel better when we can get back to some kind of normal and have some money coming in."

Pascal knitted his brow, "That's pretty fast, but maybe we could do it. I could put the ads in the paper and on TV tomorrow. I can get those dust covers back on today. I'd like to have the gallery open without any fanfare a day or so before the official opening. You know, a sort of practice run, if possible."

"That'd be good. Could we open the doors by Thursday afternoon? We might even get a little foot traffic. Anything would be good. We need to get ourselves out there as a gallery again. It wouldn't be good if folks forgot us or if our artists lost faith in us."

"That's so. Okay. Let's do it."

"Hello, Maggie?"

"Hello Pascal. How are you today?"

"I'm very well. I have some news. I'd like to invite you and Allie to the gallery reopening. We're planning an opening reception this Saturday night. We will be displaying some South American art. It would be nice if you could come."

Maggie smiled into the phone, "Of course we'll come. It is great that you are able to reopen so soon. You must have been working really hard."

"Ah, yes. That is so. But it is good work."

"Good. Do you need any help? Is there anything we can do?"

"I can't think of anything. Thank you for the offer. Just come."

The telephone's persistent ring brought Maggie inside from the balcony where she and Allie had been sipping late afternoon tea and watching the shadows lengthen over the landscaped lawn. "Hello, is that you Miz McGill?"

"Yes, Bert. It is. How are you? How is the boat coming along?"

"Oh, I'm okay, I mean, just fine. And the *More Fun*, she's good. I'm just callin' to let you know I finished with her. She's all done and shipshape again. How 'bout you come down and take a look?"

"Oh, Bert. Thank you. Yes, I'll be there tomorrow morning."

Maggie called the Whitmores and left a message welcoming them back and saying that she would need to visit with them when they returned.

The next morning she and Allie inspected the *More Fun*. Everything seemed to be in order. Even the radio had been repaired. Bert, rightly, was proud as a peacock of his work.

"Miz McGill, don't she look good? Can't even tell what she went through."

"Yes, Bert, she looks absolutely wonderful. I can't tell you how much I appreciate your hard work. I wouldn't have known where to begin to fix her."

Bert seemed to grow an inch taller, "Well, really t'weren't nothin'. I'm glad you're happy."

"Well, I am. Let's see now. How much do I owe you."

Bert named a figure that Maggie had a hard time believing. Even with Bert's modest estimate, she had expected it to be more. She wrote a check and added an extra hundred out of gratitude for his extra hard work.

"Allie, I need to get back to work. That run-in with Madeline Fortescue certainly made me realize that. I need to at least bring her to closure and place her with another therapist. I mean, this has been going on too long. Don't you agree?"

"Yes, Mom. It has. And I, too, need to pay attention to photography or I will start losing clients."

"Yes, me too. It's not such a big deal for me. I intend to decrease my practice anyway. But, I can't just drop clients. I need to bring each one to some closure so that they can be referred out. What about you? How long can you stay away?"

"I've been thinking about it. I believe I can reschedule most of the shoots that were pending and maybe I can find some here in Florida. I've had some inquiries from Florida and this could be a serendipitous time to do them. It's just that I don't want to leave until I feel comfortable about this situation. You know, I can't bear the thought of your being in danger."

"I know. It sort of puts you in an difficult position, doesn't it?"

"Not so much difficult. Just frustrating."

"Well, you know I'd love it if you could stay for months. But, I don't want you to sacrifice what you've worked so hard to build up."

"No, me neither. Let me see what I can arrange."

"Perfect."

Maggie returned to her counseling practice, seeing only the most urgent cases. She was beginning to pare down her practice to the promised two days per week. She contacted a few other therapists who she thought might be interested in sharing her office as her clientele dwindled. One therapist, Martha Clement, expressed interest. They met and made an agreement that Martha would use the office three days per week starting April first. This arrangement made it even more imperative that Maggie decrease her number of clients. Martha, who was just building her practice was happy to accept some referrals from Maggie.

Allie was able to reschedule many of her photographic shoots. She remained reluctant to leave Maggie until she felt sure the unsolved murder presented no danger to her mother. She was able to schedule some shoots in Florida, in Tampa and in Sarasota. These were one-day trips and she was back in Costa Mira each day in time for a late dinner.

Marc sat up in bed. It seemed he had been there for weeks. He longed to be out of the hospital and, perhaps, out of the country. But he remembered his abortive attempt to leave. How long ago was that? He really had been very weak. Maybe he should stay where he was for a few more days. It all was very frustrating. Where was Veronique?

Saturday night was balmy and pleasant, the sort of evening that caused the snowbirds to flock to south Florida. The old section of Costa Mira had a festive air, busy with people out strolling, visiting galleries and restaurants. Maggie parked a few blocks from the gallery. The air was soft and warm. Maggie had chosen a dark green silk pants suit and Allie wore a slim floor length dark blue sheath. As they walked, Maggie gazed up through the palm fronds at the starlit sky, "Oh, Allie, isn't this just a perfect evening? Look at those stars!"

"It is beautiful, Mom. Very romantic!"

"Romance! Oh, Allie, I think I'm beyond romance. I fear those days are gone."

"Mom!" Allie's voice was outraged and she stopped walking and stood with her hands on her hips, "I can't believe you said that! You are a vibrant and lovely woman. All you have to do is open your eyes and be open to a romance. I know there must be many opportunities."

"Perhaps. But I just can't recall one."

"One? How about Harry Cavanaugh?" Allie was referring to the CIA operative who had helped them through last year's adventure in California.

"Harry? Oh, you know. You were there. Harry was just a good friend to both of us."

"Sure, a good friend. He would have been more if you had given him even half a chance!"

"But, long distance? I don't think so."

"Okay. Long distance relationships are tough. How about Pascal? I see the way he looks at you."

Maggie's voice rose slightly, "Pascal really is just a business acquaintance."

"Mom!"

"Well, okay. He's a friend, too."

Allie sighed, "He'd like to deepen that friendship. I can tell."

Now it was Maggie's turn to sigh, "Oh, I don't know, Allie. Relationships are such hard work. I just don't know."

"Well, here we are." As Allie reached out to open the door for her mother, she whispered, "Smile. Give him a chance."

The gallery was brightly lit and already had a crowd of some forty art fanciers. They found Pascal, in his opening black tie and dinner jacket, chatting with a well-dressed couple. He smiled as they approached and introduced Maggie as one of his artists. Maggie found this introduction both flattering and daunting. Pascal encouraged the couple to find the champagne and hors d'oeurve table. As they walked away, he took both Maggie's and Allie's hands, "It is good to see you both. Thank you so much for coming."

Remembering Allie's injunction, Maggie smiled broadly and said, "Oh, Pascal, we wouldn't have missed it for the world. What a nice crowd! Aren't you pleased?"

He smiled back and said, "Well, of course I am. But truthfully, I'm not sure how much of the interest is in the art and how much is a rather morbid desire to see the scene of the recent crime. Does that sound cynical?"

Allie answered, "Perhaps a bit, but you know, people are bound to be curious. It's just human nature."

"I suppose so. And, in any event, I am pleased to have such a good crowd so early in the evening. We will see how many sales we have and that will tell the story. Duane has been quite nervous about our situation. This crowd, even if they buy little, should reassure him." Changing the subject, "Do you know this artist? Federico Chavez? He's one of several we represent from Latin America. What do you think?"

Maggie looked around, "They look quite nice. Let us take a closer look. You'll need to continue to greet your guests." She and Allie headed for the nearest display. Most of the art was representational, jungle scenes from which peered assorted wild animals.

"They're very tropical, Mom. They should sell well, especially here in south Florida."

"Yes, that's so. You know, I really like them." She peered closely at the discreet card that announced the price, "Oh my! Well, I guess I won't be buying one right now!"

A rather dapper young man caught Allie's eye and engaged her in conversation about the relative merits of imported and domestic artists.

Maggie wandered to the bar where she ordered her usual mineral water. Her drink in hand, she turned to watch the crowd. It had grown considerably larger as the evening progressed. Maggie noticed some familiar faces from her own opening three weeks ago. Had it only been that short a time? It seemed to Maggie that her opening had been months ago. She imagined that she saw Veronique working through the crowd, looking elegant, slightly exotic, but always friendly and welcoming. Pascal would miss her.

As the evening progressed and the crowd began to thin, Maggie wondered if she and Allie should leave. Just then, Pascal appeared, "Ah, Maggie, it has gone well, no?"

"Why yes, Pascal, I do believe it has. Good for you. But, were you really concerned that it wouldn't?" She smiled at him.

"Not so much, really. But Duane was quite concerned. He feared that our customers would forget us if we remained closed for too long." Pascal shrugged and smiled, "But you know, Duane has a tendency to fret about finances. It is good that he does, because I sometimes don't remember to think about them."

"Oh, yes. I can see that he might have been worried, but, you know, your gallery has an excellent reputation and I think it would take a lot to make people forget it and you."

"Perhaps. But, at any rate, here we are and we even sold some paintings. I am pleased and I am sure Duane will be also." He paused for a moment, "Ah, Maggie. Veronique and I had the habit of going out for a supper after an opening. I was wondering if you and Allie would like to accompany me for a late supper once the last patrons have left. We were not able to do it after your very successful show and I would like to do so now."

Maggie, remembering Allie's advice, smiled, "That sounds really nice, Pascal. We could do it in remembrance of Veronique. Let me check with Allie."

Chapter Fifteen

Duane Simpson joined the supper party at a casually elegant old town bistro. At this hour it was a dark cave of a room with cranberry red tablecloths, candles and chunky stemmed glassware. In spite of the hour, there were several tables of late diners and the air was festive. Maggie did not remember seeing Duane at the opening. Perhaps he had been in one of the back offices. Certainly he had not dressed for a formal event. His rumpled suit fit him badly and was in sharp contrast to Pascal's attire. His close cropped red hair was reminiscent of an earlier era. Once again, he seemed a poor match for Pascal's natural elegance. Even so, his welcoming smile was warm. After Pascal ordered champagne for the party, Duane leaned back in his chair and grinned, "Well, Pascal, that was just great! Aren't you glad we went ahead and did it?"

Pascal nodded his head, "Oh, yes, Duane. I certainly am glad. You were exactly right that we needed to get ourselves back in business. It was a good opening." He included Allie and Maggie in his wide smile, "Duane is the business end of the gallery. I thank all that is for his business expertise. I'd be lost without it!"

Duane turned a bright shade of pink and mumbled, "Oh, Pascal. You know you would have come to it on your own." He averted his eyes and looked completely embarrassed.

Pascal took pity on his friend, "Ah, Duane, please do not feel embarrassed. I only wanted to say what a wonderful business partner you are and how much you have added to the success of the gallery."

Duane smiled, but continued to look uncomfortable at the praise. Pascal then led the conversation to the art opening. They chatted for a while about the opening, the size and makeup of the crowd, the quality of the art, and how many paintings had been sold.

During a lull in the conversation, Pascal said, "Maggie, I have been thinking about having a memorial service for Veronique. She did not have many close friends, but this, after all, has been her home for many years. She was a great asset to the gallery and, other than Marc, I am the closest she had to family. She came here as a young girl, really almost a teenager. Her family was gone, and I was it." He shrugged, "So, I think it only fitting that we have a service for her."

Maggie smiled at him, "Of course. That is a wonderful idea."

"I haven't thought much further than that. But, I have been hoping to wait until Marc has recovered his memory. I would like for him to be able to be there."

Allie said, "But Pascal, do you have any idea when he might be able to come?"

"No. That is the problem. I don't want to wait too long. And the doctors don't give me any good news. Truly, I think they are as mystified as anyone about his condition."

Maggie took a sip of her conch chowder, perfect for so late at night, warm, creamy, and rich. "So, what do you plan to do, Pascal?"

"I'm not sure. What do you think? Should we go ahead with it or should we wait for Marc's recovery?" He looked around the table.

Duane sat back in his chair, "Well, Pascal. You know that I cared for Veronique as if she had been my daughter. But, Marc? What will happen to him when he is ready to leave the hospital? Would he even be free to come to a service?"

"That, of course, is an issue. I'm not sure about the answer."

Allie sipped her champagne, "What would have pleased Veronique? What would she want you to do?"

Pascal's brow wrinkled in concentration, "Veronique? I hadn't thought of it that way. Marc was her brother and she felt a certain, er, I believe, a certain obligation to him for that reason, perhaps even some affection for him. They never were close. He had caused her a lot of pain during her life. But still, he was her brother." He turned to Duane, "What do you think, Duane?"

Duane blew a big breath of air out through puffed cheeks, "Oh,

I agree with you, Pascal. It seemed to me that she was happier when he was not around. I often noticed how tense she seemed when he was at the gallery. Almost like she was waiting for something bad to happen. Yet, I think we should respect the family connection if we can."

Pascal remained thoughtful for a while, "Well yes. Thank you, my friends. You have been very helpful. Let me give it some more thought." He paused for a moment and then, the perfect host, asked, "Would anyone like dessert?"

They all agreed that dessert would put them over the top, food-wise.

"Hello, Dr. Johnson? This is Pascal DuMonchet. I am wondering how Marc Duval is doing. Is there any improvement in his condition?"

"Hello, Mr. DuMonchet. Well, yes. There is improvement in his physical condition. He seems to be on the mend physically. Actually, I am thinking of having him moved to a recovery facility. He really has progressed so well that I do not believe he needs any further hospitalization. And we certainly could use the bed."

"Ah, that is very good news. How about his memory? Do you see any signs of its improving?"

Dr. Johnson replied, "That is another issue. I haven't seen any improvement there. He was seen last week by Dr. Chambers, our staff psychiatrist, who says that Mr. Duval's memory may return at any time or it could even be months or years before it comes back, if ever. We just don't know."

"I see. Do you think I should visit him again? I mean, is he ready to hear about his sister's death and the other issues he will have to deal with?"

"I'm not sure, Mr. DuMonchet. At this point it is more of a question for the psychiatrist than me. Once he leaves the hospital I no longer will be able to protect him from the police and their questions."

"Ah. Do I understand that at that point they probably will question him about the murder, the drugs, and our kidnapping?"

Dr. Johnson answered, "Yes. I guess that is it, unless, of course, Dr. Chambers is able to forestall it. I am sorry, but physically, in spite of that excursion away from the hospital, he is regaining his strength. There is little more I can do."

159

Now Pascal sighed, "Yes. I see. Well, thank you, Dr. Johnson."

Pascal learned that Marc was scheduled to be released from the hospital on Tuesday morning and transferred to a recovery center adjacent to the hospital. Because he was concerned about Marc's ability to cope with the coming police interrogation he set an appointment to see Dr. Chambers.

"Come in, Mr. DuMonchet. What can I do for you?" Dr. Chambers ushered Pascal into a roomy consultation office equipped with a heavy walnut desk and chair and several commodious chairs set in a semi-circle facing the desk. The theme of the office decor was subdued elegance. Pascal thought that Dr. Chambers must have a successful practice.

Dr. Chambers, himself, was a tall, portly man with thinning silver hair. He was dressed casually in khaki slacks and a long sleeved blue shirt.

"Thank you for seeing me, Dr. Chambers. I have come to discuss the condition of Marc Duval. Marc has no family here in the States. I was a close friend of his family and I have known him since he was an infant. So, I feel a certain responsibility for him."

"I see. And what do you wish from me?"

Pascal found this question off-putting, but continued, "Ah, it is that Marc has always been difficult and has been in some kind of trouble for most of his life. Now, he has this memory loss and soon he will be questioned by the police unless you protect him from it."

Dr. Chambers raised his hand.

Pascal continued before he could speak, "I am not asking you to do that unless, of course, you feel it is necessary to do so for his well-being. I am just wondering if there is something I can do to be a help."

"Dr. Johnson filled me in on Mr. Duval's situation and he did mention that you are the nearest he has to family. In what way do you think you could be helpful?"

Pascal thought that this man was not being particularly helpful, himself, but he continued, "If you do not think it wise or necessary to protect him from the knowledge of what has happened during his memory loss, would it be a help or could it do damage if I were the one who informed him about those events?"

Dr. Chambers leaned back in his chair and blew out a deep breath, "Oh, I see. These amnesia cases often are a puzzle. It is difficult to know whether this one is a result of the blow he took to his head or if it comes from a psychological trauma related to something he simply refuses to remember. The most recent MRI indicates that the head wound has healed and that there is no discernable damage to his brain. So I am inclined to believe that, at this point, his psyche simply is not willing to remember. We refer to that as hysterical post-traumatic amnesia."

"I see?" Pascal's face showed a degree of not seeing.

Dr. Chambers smiled, "That is often just the way I feel. As I said, amnesia can be a puzzle for us. But, now that Mr. Duval seems to be regaining his physical strength, I believe that he could benefit from some psychotherapy. There are drug therapies that we might try that sometimes are beneficial. We might even attempt some hypnotherapy. I believe that it is important to help him regain these lost memories sooner rather than later. And, I tend to believe that, in spite of the other options, psychotherapy often is the most effective one. So, in answer to your question, yes. I do think it might be helpful if you, as an old friend, were to inform him about those missing memories. It would be a sort of shock therapy."

Pascal drew a long breath, "I see. I do not look forward to doing this; however, I believe it would less of a shock to him if he hears it from me than if the police inform him. After all, he has lost his only family, his sister."

"Yes. I agree. What would you think of the two of us talking to him together? This might provide some reassurance for you and your presence might make it easier for him to accept me."

Pascal remained thoughtful for a moment, "Yes. Yes, I think that could be the very best. If I should blunder in some way in my telling him, you would be there so help me. As I said, I certainly do not want to do him any harm."

"No. Nor do I. Let's see, you say he's to be moved to the recovery center tomorrow morning?"

Pascal nodded.

Dr. Chambers consulted his book, "Let's give him a day to acclimate, and then, how about we meet there at 10:30 Wednesday morning. I have a cancellation and no other appointments until after lunch. That would give us plenty of time."

Pascal agreed.

"Hello, Maggie."

"Hello, Pascal. How are you today?"

"Very well, thank you. Ah, Maggie, I have decided to hold the memorial service for Veronique Sunday afternoon. I thought we could have it on the beach. She loved it and often took long walks there. Then we might have a few refreshments at the gallery. You know that we are closed on Sundays. I believe that the gallery and her work there were a sort of haven for Veronique and I think that would please her."

"Why Pascal, I think that is a perfect plan."

"It will be a very simple service. She was not particularly religious, but she did have her Roman Catholic background and perhaps I can find a priest who would say a few words. I plan to put a notice in the paper so that her friends will know."

"That sounds just right."

"Good."

Wednesday dawned bright and clear with a soft breeze off the Gulf. But Pascal walked slowly into the recovery center. He was not looking forward to this interview with Marc. He found Marc sitting in the recliner in his room, wearing faded slacks and a rumpled terry bathrobe.

"Hello, old man. What brings you here?" Marc's greeting was as challenging as ever.

"Hello, Marc. I came to visit you, of course. How are you feeling? You look much improved from the last time I saw you."

"Yeah. I am getting stronger by the day. They told me I no longer need to be in the hospital so I must be getting better," Marc's voice still held a challenge, but it softened a little.

"Ah, it certainly is good to see you looking so well. And you do seem much stronger."

"Yes. Yes, I am."

Pascal drew up a straight chair and sat down near Marc, "Ah, Marc. I came to visit with you and to see how your memory is coming along. I know you have been missing some memories and I am wondering if any of those have come back."

"Well, old man. Not really. Everyone keeps asking me about that. But, so far, it's a blank," he glared a Pascal.

Just then, Dr. Chambers entered the room, "Hello Mr. Duval. How are you today?"

Marc mumbled, "Okay, I guess. What are you doing here?"

Dr. Chambers replied, "Well, Marc, I am here because I have some concerns about your memory loss and Mr. DuMonchet and I would like to help you with its recovery." He peered intensely at Marc, "You do want to remember, don't you?"

Again Marc glared, "Yeah. I do. That's a stupid question."

Pascal spoke softly, "Marc, we have known each other for a very long time. You know that I wish you well. One of the ways I may be able to help you is to tell you all that I can about what has happened to you. You know, I guess, that you were very seriously injured in an accident, and that accident may have contributed to your amnesia?"

"Yeah, I guess so."

"Are you curious about those missing memories?"

"Sure. Sure, I am. I'd like to know how I ended up in that hospital. That was a real bummer! I know there are things I should be doing."

Dr. Chambers sat back in his straight chair and let Pascal continue, "What things, Marc? Do you have any memories of things you should be doing?"

"Er, no. I guess not. But still, it feels like there is something."

Pascal sighed, "Yes, I am sure it feels that way." He cleared his throat, "With your permission I want to tell you what I know about that missing time."

Marc nodded his agreement.

"*Bien.* Do you remember the art opening at the gallery where Mrs. McGill's work was shown?"

"That old broad? Sure. I remember."

"What do you remember after that?"

"Not a damned thing. That's the frustrating part."

"Okay. I will tell you what I remember. There are some pieces of that evening that I learned about only later. It was fairly late in the evening, the guests were beginning to leave. I couldn't find Veronique so I went back to my office to look for her. She was sitting at my desk. She seemed to be arguing with someone who was behind the door. I started to turn to see who that person was and, for me, the lights went out! I must have been hit on the head."

Marc remained impassive and said nothing.

"When I awoke, I was tied up in a shack out on the edge of the everglades. I had a dreadful headache. I was not able to move. The shack was dirty. I was dirty. It was very uncomfortable."

He paused to look at Marc. No response.

Then, I heard voices, young voices. Two young boys broke into the shack and freed me. My cell phone was missing. But I was able to walk to a crossroads where there was a telephone booth. I called friends who came and rescued me. That was nearly forty-eight hours after the opening reception."

Again Pascal paused. He was having trouble finding the words to continue and to tell Marc about his sister's death. He glanced at Dr. Chambers who gave him a nearly imperceptible nod.

Marc remained silent, but his belligerent expression had changed to one of mild interest.

Pascal drew a deep breath, "Marc, when my friends picked me up, they gave me some very sad news." Again he paused to look at Marc.

"My friends told me that there had been a crime at the gallery, that Veronique had been killed."

Marc's face went white and he reeled, almost as if he had been struck a blow. He mumbled, "Veronique? Veronique, my sister?"

"Yes, Marc. I am so sorry to have to tell you. But you need to know. We all loved Veronique and it is a great tragedy. But, Marc. You need to know."

Pascal waited in silence as Marc adjusted to this new information.

In a very quiet voice, "How? How did it happen? Was it an accident?"

"No, Marc. Someone did it."

"Oh, no. No. It can't be."

"Again, I am so very sorry. But that is the way it is."

"Who did it? Who would do such a thing to little Veronique?"

"The police are working on it, but we still do not know who is responsible."

"Responsible? Responsible? My little Veronique gone?" Marc continued to mumble, seemingly unaware of the two men.

Pascal looked at Dr. Chambers, a question in his eyes. Dr. Chambers raised his hand slightly as if to say, wait.

Pascal reached over and took Marc's hand. He held it firmly in his two hands, hoping to give the younger man some encouragement. Marc seemed completely unaware of the contact and continued to stare unbelievingly into space.

After what seemed like hours instead of a few minutes, Marc

raised his head and took back his hand, "Thank you, old man. I know you mean well." He shook his head and some of the old defiance came back to his eyes, "I *will* find out who did this and that person *will* pay. You may be sure of that."

Pascal answered him, "Marc, I do understand how you feel. I, too, wish to find whoever would do such a dreadful thing. But, really, Marc, we must let the authorities find that person. There is a rule of law and we must abide by it."

"Maybe, old man, maybe."

"Does any of this bring back any memories for you?"

Marc shook his head, "No. Not really. As you described it, it seemed as if I could see Veronique in your chair, but you know, that could be a memory from any time, any time at all."

"Yes, I understand. That is true."

Dr. Chambers interjected, "Marc, let this sit inside you for a while. Don't try to force any memories, just let your mind work with what it has now. Would you like us to meet again. More information may help you to fill in some of those blank spaces."

Uncharacteristically, Marc responded, "Yes. Yes, I think that could be a good idea. I will fight to bring back the memories. Maybe they can help me find who did this. When can you come again?"

Pascal answered, "I can come at any time, any time at all."

Dr. Chambers said, "Let me get back to the office. I will come as soon as there is an opening in my schedule."

"Good. I want to get on with it." Marc sat back in the recliner with his jaw set.

Pascal followed Dr. Chambers out to the parking lot, "What do you think? Did we help or cause harm?"

"It is not easy to say. It seemed to me that we may have jogged his memory a little. Clearly the news of his sister's death was a shock. I'm going to try to free up an hour or so for tomorrow. I don't want this to drag on."

"That sounds good to me. Will you let me know, please? I'd like to be there to help."

Dr. Chambers nodded, "Of course. It is important that you are there. You have the information to fill in more details of his missing memory."

"Ah, Dr. Chambers? I am planning a memorial service for his sister on Sunday. Do you think Marc could attend?"

"I don't see why not. He seems to be strong enough physically. And now that he knows about her, it might even be a positive thing."

"Ah, the other issue is the police. They suspect him of the murder and of drug dealing. They have been very persistent in wanting to question him. I am not sure that they would permit him to go."

Dr. Chambers nodded, "I will do what I can to forestall their questioning until we have had a day or so to work with him. I'll do what I can."

Pascal sighed his relief, "That is good of you. I'll wait to hear about tomorrow."

Pascal arrived at the recovery center a few moments before Dr. Chambers. He found Marc once again sitting in his recliner in his room. But, today, Marc was dressed in faded jeans, an old button down shirt and an equally old sweater. For the first time Pascal wondered about the origin of these clothes. Perhaps they were from donations to the recovery center. In any event, Marc was clean-shaven and his normally unruly hair looked as if he had made an attempt to groom it.

"Hello Marc. How are you today?"

Marc response was subdued, "Hello old man. I guess I'm okay. At least, I'm not as weak as I was a week ago."

"You look stronger each time I see you, Marc. That is good news. No?

"Yeah, I suppose so," from a glum Marc.

Just then Dr. Chambers entered the room, "Good afternoon, Marc."

"Oh, hello. Are you guys here to go through more stuff?"

"That depends on you, Marc. Do you still want to work on your memory issues?" Dr. Chambers peered closely at Marc.

Marc straightened in his chair, "Yes. Yes, I do. I want to remember so I can do something about whoever it was that hurt Veronique. Yes. I sure do." His voice was stronger and held some of its old defiance.

Dr. Chambers smiled, "Good. That is good. Well, let's get started." He turned to Pascal, "Mr. DuMonchet, is there more you can tell us that might help Marc's memory?"

Pascal cleared his throat, "Ah yes. Marc, yesterday I told you about how I was kidnapped and about poor Veronique. I am not especially proud of what came next. It turned out that the police had a warrant for my arrest. I believe now that I should have surrendered myself to them at that moment. However, I chose to allow my friends hide me on a boat. That was okay for the first day. I was pretty exhausted by the kidnapping and the rest was good. But then, something else happened that wasn't so good.

Pascal paused and looked at Marc, "Marc, I don't want you to think that I bear you any ill will for this. Please do not take umbrage at what I am going to say. I say it not as an accusation or even to place blame, but rather to inform you about the facts as I know them."

Again he paused and looked Marc in the eyes. Then Pascal related the details of the kidnapping aboard the *More Fun* and of Marc's injury and being swept into the sea.

"You were badly injured, Marc. We were fearful that you might not survive until we could get you to medical help. Indeed, even the doctors did not at first give you much of a chance. Truly, you are lucky to be alive."

Marc sat in silence for a while digesting this new information. Then he sighed, "Thank you, old man, for telling me what happened. I wish I could say that I actually remember any of these things that you say, but I don't. For some reason, I do believe you are telling me the truth. What you say agrees with the way my body has felt." Marc stared into space, "You say I almost died?"

Pascal nodded, "It would appear so. You were in the water for a long time. I gave you mouth-to-mouth resuscitation and you certainly spit up a lot of water."

Again Marc was silent, his face showing some consternation. Finally, with a look at Dr. Chambers, "Ah, doc?"

"Yes?"

"Ah, is it possible . . .? I mean, it seems maybe I AM remembering something." Again, a long silence and then, looking at Pascal, "Who was that guy with the turban?"

Pascal stared at Marc, "Turban?"

"Yes. Wasn't there a guy with a turban there with you?"

"There was. His name is Hadi. But, what do you remember about him?"

"Did he fix the radio?"

Now it was Pascal's turn to looked puzzled, "Marc, he did fix the GPS and the radio. But, Marc, that was after your accident. You were out cold. How could you have any knowledge of that?" Pascal turned to Dr. Chambers.

Dr. Chambers sighed, "Well, gentlemen. This is very interesting. I understand from the medical records that Marc was in a coma from the time of the accident until well after he was in the hospital."

Pascal nodded his agreement.

"This Hadi person? Had Marc seen him before he was injured?"

Pascal answered, "Yes. Of course. Hadi was among the persons that were kidnapped."

Dr. Chambers said, "I see. Perhaps Marc remembers Hadi from the time before the accident. That would explain the memory."

"But how did he know that Hadi repaired the radio and GPS?"

Dr. Chambers cleared his throat, "There is, er, that is, there might be any number of explanations for this." He cleared his throat and looked uncomfortable, "What I am about to say is controversial. I am not saying one way or the other that this is so. I will just tell you a theory. There is a theory that sometimes persons who are in a coma have an awareness of all that is happening around them. I am sure you have heard of near death experiences. There are theories that persons who have had near death experiences also have awarenesses of events occurring during them. It is possible that Marc did have an awareness of what was happening during the time he was unconscious. It is equally possible that Marc's memory is beginning to return and that without a conscious awareness of it, he is beginning to piece together the events that occurred during his memory loss."

At this Marc sat quite still. He did not meet anyone's eye. He seemed to be far away.

Pascal spoke, "That is an interesting theory, doctor. It would explain a lot. But, you say it is only a theory?"

"The study of consciousness is relatively new. Although there is a lot of new research into how the brain functions, there still is much we do not know. After many years working with people, I seem to be coming to the idea that the brain and the mind are not synonynous." Dr. Chambers paused and sighed, "I am sorry. I tend to run on at times." He turned to Marc, "Marc, I really don't know for sure why you have this . . . what shall I call it? Memory? But, I do believe this is a helpful sign. It may be that you are just on the brink of having recall of the missing time. We shall see."

Dr. Chambers rose and bid Marc and Pascal goodbye. Pascal followed him into the hall, "Dr. Chambers, do you still agree that it would be advisable for Marc to attend his sister's memorial service?"

"Why, yes. I don't see why not."

"Yes, well, thank you."

Pascal returned to Marc's room where he found Marc quiet and subdued, "Ah, Marc. I just wanted to tell you that I have planned a small memorial service for Veronique for this Sunday afternoon. It is to be on the beach down from my house. Afterward we will have a gathering at the gallery. Would you like to come?"

Marc shifted in the chair and raised his head, "Yes, old man, yes, I would. Do you think they will let me out of here?"

"Dr. Chambers has given his approval. There may be some issues with the police, but we will see what can be worked out. If it can be arranged, I'll pick you up and take you there."

In a quiet voice, "Thank you, old man. I think it would please Veronique to be remembered. Her life was not always easy, but you helped her a lot. I am grateful to you for that."

"I did what I could for her, Marc, that is true. But she was very good at her job. She really helped the gallery be successful. She also was a good friend. I will miss her very much."

"Yes, I, too, will miss her. Poor little Veronique."

"Yes, poor Veronique."

"Hello, Maggie? It is Pascal calling. How are you today?"

"Hello, Pascal. How nice to hear from you. I am well. And you?"

"Oh, I am well also. I have just spent some time with Marc and now I have another great favor to ask you."

"You know I will do anything I can."

"I'm wondering if you and Allie could help me choose some clothes for Marc. He wants to attend the memorial service and apparently he is being dressed by cast-offs from some charity. You know, I don't know where he was living, or even if he had a place. I just thought it might be nice if he had something new."

"Of course it would. We'll be glad to help."

"Ah, good. How good of you. I will pick you up and then we can go to the store. Once we've made our choices, let's have lunch and I'll fill you in on what has been happening."

"Perfect."

Their foray into the men's store was a success. Clearly this was a store where Pascal purchased his own clothing. The clerk greeted him warmly and made several helpful suggestions. They purchased dark gray trousers, a crisp button-down shirt and a dark gray sweater jacket that added a dressy accent and, at the same time, would provide some warmth against the sea breezes. In addition, Pascal chose two more outfits that would give Marc some relief from the donated clothing.

Over lunch, Pascal inquired about the status of the *More Fun*. Maggie reported that the repairs had been completed and that she was satisfied with the results. Pascal immediately wrote a check for half the amount Maggie had paid Bert.

Then Pascal related the meetings with Dr. Chambers, "You know, it was very strange. Marc wanted to know about the guy in the turban who repaired the radio."

Allie stopped, her fork in mid air, "But, Pascal. Marc was unconscious when that happened. How could he have known?"

Pascal gave a Gallic shrug, "Ah, I do not know, Allie. I just don't know. It is very strange."

Maggie agreed, "Very strange. What did Dr. Chambers say?"

Another Gallic shrug, "Ah, he talked some, but didn't say much."

"Oh."

Chapter Sixteen

Sunday was a warm cool day, warm sun and cool breezes. Maggie and Allie dressed warmly, knowing that, in spite of the sun, the beach would be cool. It was late afternoon when a crowd of some thirty mourners gathered on the beach. Allie commented, "Mom, look how nice Marc looks. The clothes are perfect."

Maggie agreed, "Yes, they are, but he does seem very serious and quiet. I suppose we can expect him to be subdued. He's had such an ordeal and now he's lost his sister."

Pascal met them and reported that Dr. Chambers had been able to arrange Marc's attendance without police escort. He confided that the police had insisted that Marc wear an ankle monitor that would prevent his escaping.

The priest gave a short eulogy that ended with a prayer for Veronique's soul. Some of her friends spoke a few words about their fond memories of Veronique. Pascal spoke, saying that he had known her all her life. He related how she had come to Florida following the death of her parents, and how much he valued both her friendship and her expertise in the gallery.

Just at the end, when Maggie thought the service was over, Marc faced the mourners. The sea breeze ruffled his hair as he spoke, "Veronique was my sister. I remember her as a little child in France. She always seemed to be a happy child. But, I left home early and I did not see her for many years. Yet, here in Costa Mira, she made me welcome. I shall miss her greatly. She was a good person and she did not deserve to die as I am told she did." Marc's face was pale and lined. But it was fierce and he stared into the group, first at one face and then another. As he looked, his expression slowly changed to one of comprehension.

Watching closely, Pascal wished that Dr. Chambers were present.

Following Marc's short speech there was an unnatural hush in the group. Then, almost as one, the mourners started to murmur among themselves. It was as if they felt somehow embarrassed at this show of emotion.

Allie whispered, "I wouldn't want to be the culprit if Marc knew who it was!"

Maggie noticed the change in Marc's expression and she scanned the crowd. Exactly who had he been looking at when his facial expression had changed? She whispered, "Oh, Allie, I am not sure, but something just changed. It may be that he does know. I'm not so sure. Allie, if he does, then that person is here right now! Who was he looking at? What did he just see?"

Allie's brows raised, "You think? That's pretty scary!"

Twenty or so people gathered at the gallery for refreshments. The bar served only wine and a few canapés. It was a quiet gathering. Allie said, "Some of those people at the beach might have been curiosity seekers, but here, I think are the true mourners."

Maggie agreed, "Yes, I suppose so. Did you notice that Mr. Carrera and Lt. Anderson were there? They stood at the back, just watching."

"No, I didn't see them. Do you think they were hoping to find the culprit at the service?"

"I don't know, but maybe so." She waved at Duane Simpson as he walked toward the back of the gallery and the offices.

Soon the gathering started to disperse. When the last of the mourners had gone through the heavy glass door, Maggie was surprised that only she and Allie were left in the gallery. Where were Pascal and Duane? Most of all, where was Marc?

Allie said, "Where is everyone? This has a sort of weird *deja vu* feel. Don't you agree?"

Maggie nodded, "I don't like it. It isn't like Pascal not to see the last of the guests out. Weird is right. And spooky too."

Allie caught her mother's hand and in a quiet voice, "Let's see if they're in the back."

Together the two women tiptoed cautiously into the office area. No one. Each office was empty. Allie breathed a sigh of relief, "I didn't really expect to find a body with a knife in it, but still, it does sort of have that 'been here, done that' feel!"

The heavy door to the workroom loomed ominously. With unspoken agreement, they turned around and headed back to the gallery.

Maggie shivered her agreement and whispered, "Oh, Allie, do be careful. Do you think we should call someone?"

Still whispering, "Who would we call? What would we say?"

"I don't know. But this is too weird! It makes my hair stand on end." With that she ran a nervous hand over her tousled head. "Wait a minute! I have Mr. Carrera's card somewhere. Let's see if he still is in the neighborhood. There may be nothing to it, but I'd feel better if I could call him before we look further." Maggie sat on a bentwood chair and searched her purse, "Ah, yes. Here it is and here's my cell phone."

She dialed and was happy to hear Carrera's deep voice pick up on the second ring.

"Mr. Carrera, Maggie McGill here."

"Yes, Mrs. McGill. What can I do for you?"

Still whispering, Maggie related the details of the empty gallery, "I don't know. Maybe it's nothing, but it seems very strange to us. We haven't looked in the backroom yet. We feel a little afraid." She mumbled the last, feeling chagrin to have to admit it.

"Well, Mrs. McGill. Thank you for calling. I agree that it may be nothing or it may be something very important. You two should leave through the front of the gallery and wait for me outside. I'm on the north side of town right now, but I'll be there as soon as possible."

Maggie dropped the card and her phone back in her purse, "Allie, he wants us to wait outside until he gets here."

"That's probably the best idea. Come on." Allie headed for the door.

Maggie started to follow, but stopped and caught at her arm, "Oh, Allie, oh! Wait a minute. Just wait." Maggie's whispered voice was breathless, "Wait, let me think just a moment!" Maggie stood very still and her brows were scrunched in a fierce frown.

"Mom?" Allie whispered, "Mom, let's just go outside and wait for help."

"But Allie! Allie, I think I know who it was, who did it!" was the fierce whispered reply. "Don't you see? I know who he was looking at when he was talking. I know who it is and it all fits. It all fits. Don't you see?"

Now it was Allie's turn to frown, "No, Mom. No, I don't see. But I do think we should wait outside like Carrera said. Come on! Let's get out the door and you can tell me what you think."

Maggie sighed, "Yes, of course. That is the best thing. Why don't you go out and wait. I think I'll just poke my head into the backroom for a peek. If there's no one there we can call Mr. Carrera back and he won't have to come all the way back down here."

"Mom! Absolutely not. Too dangerous. Come on." Allie felt the hair on the back of her neck prickle.

Maggie started for the backroom. Allie grabbed for her arm, but Maggie now was nearly halfway across the gallery.

"Oh, Mom! Please come back," Allie's whisper was louder as she hurried after her delinquent mother.

Allie caught her mother's arm just as Maggie pushed open the heavy door to the backroom, only a crack. Then, slowly she inched it open a bit more, poking her head into the opening. Allie stood behind her mother, still holding onto her arm. She could see over her mother's head into the room. What met their eyes was daunting. Marc was standing beside Pascal, their backs against a worktable, facing the area behind the door. Duane lay crmpled on the floor at their feet. The two men stood stiffly, almost as if at attention. Clearly they were uncomfortable. When he noticed the two women Pascal frowned and shook his head slightly. He made a small motion with his hand as if to shoo them away. But, it was too late. From behind the door, "Do come in. Let me see who is here."

Maggie tried to push Allie back into the gallery, but again, it was too late. An arm holding a handgun appeared around the door, followed by the arm's owner.

"Hello, Mr. Leigh. How nice to see you," Maggie could think of nothing else to say. Her heart sank. It was just as she had thought. Lazlo Leigh, as well as being persistent, was the guy, the one who had murdered Veronique! Maggie thought she should have known it before.

"Oh, Mom!" was Allie's dispirited quiet response in her mother's ear.

Lazlo Leigh, his hair disheveled, looked at them with eyes that were both wild and cold, "You two! Come in here and stand beside your friends."

Maggie found her tongue, "I didn't realize you were here, Mr. Leigh."

Allie took her mother's hand and squeezed it, "Mr. Leigh, how nice to see you again. Were you able to come to the memorial service?" It seemed to Allie that time was slowing down and that things were happening in slow motion. Even though this was not the first time she and her mother had been threatened with a gun, this seemed very dangerous. It wasn't that Lazlo Leigh appeared to be deranged, but rather that he seemed somehow to be more evil. Nasty was the word that came to her mind. Just nasty!

Lazlo Leigh's French accent was slipping. His speech was beginning to sound more like New Jersey than France. He waved the revolver in their direction, "You stand over there all together while I decide what to do with you."

Pascal spoke, "Now, Lazlo, what do you want from us? I'm sure we can work something out. Please put that gun down and we can talk about it. It doesn't have to be this way. Whatever it is, we can resolve it."

"Oh, you, DuMonchet. Just be quiet. You are always so correct! So proper! Just shut up!" Lazlo's veneer of artistic refinement had slipped away completely.

"I will be happy to shut up, Lazlo, if only you will put that thing down and talk to us like a civilized human being. Duane has been injured and Marc here is ill. He has been dangerously ill. Clearly both of them belong in the hospital. Can't you see that?"

Lazlo Leigh, ignoring Pascal, turned to Marc, "Marc, you and I need to go somewhere and talk. We have some business to discuss."

Marc shifted uncomfortably, "Now, Lazlo. Why are you so upset? Sure, we can talk about things. Let's go in the office and sit down."

"We'll sit down when I say so. Don't you know what has happened?"

"What has happened?" Marc mumbled, "No. I don't. That is just what I want you to tell me." Marc brushed the hair away from his pale face.

Lazlo stared at Marc, "You really don't remember? I thought you were faking just to fool the cops."

Pascal turned to stare at Marc. He was sure Marc was remembering something. After the sessions with Dr. Chambers, he had become more aware of the nuances in Marc's face. And, Pascal was remembering the look on Marc's face at the beach.

Maggie, in turn, stared at Marc. It seemed to her that Marc did, indeed, remember something. She felt sure that now he was faking his memory loss. She hoped Lazlo didn't realize this also. "Mr. Leigh, why don't you tell us exactly what has you so upset. We'd all like to help if we can."

Lazlo turned to Maggie, the gun still steady in his hand, "Oh, you! Are you in on it, too? Do you know where the stuff is?"

"Er, what stuff?" Maggie suspected he was referring to the drugs. She remembered that Carrera had insisted that they keep quiet about the discovery of the drugs in the art frames. But, better to play dumb right now. "I'd be happy to help you, Mr. Leigh. But I don't know what you're talking about."

To Maggie the whole scene seemed surreal. She looked around the workspace with its racks of art lining the walls and the worktables down the center of the room. This ordinary space now was like something out of a horrid movie. Worse still, she could see no place where one could manage an escape. The back door to the alley seemed miles away. And Lazlo now stood between them and the gallery door. What could she do to get them out of this situation? Oh, why hadn't she listened to Allie? Her beautiful, smart Allie. Allie knew that this could be dangerous. Why, oh why, hadn't she listened? Now she had put Allie in danger. Maggie was feeling too impetuous and very stupid. She had been so intent on proving that she was right and really had figured out who had killed Veronique that she threw caution to wind. Pride, indeed, had preceded this disaster. I am a very bad mother, she thought. That thought was almost more daunting than this nasty man with his ugly gun.

The ugly gun waved at her, "Oh yes, you want to help. How about that cat of yours? Nearly scared me to death! You didn't help then!"

Allie's eyes met her mother's. The break-in at the condo. But why?

Maggie smiled sweetly, her voice trembled, "Was that you, Mr. Leigh? You should have told us. Tilly is not exactly a watch cat. If we had known you wanted to look at our apartment, we would have shown it to you."

Leigh's eyes rolled, "Oh you! So proper! Sure!" Sarcasm did not fit his former artistic facade. "You know you would've just brushed me off the way you did every time we met. I had no choice but to take a look-see on my own. So, where is it? Where's my stuff?"

"Stuff?"

"You know what I'm talking about. Did they put it in the frames of your art? I can't find it anywhere!"

Now the gun waved at Marc, "Okay Marc, do you know where it is? It disappeared completely. I looked for it here and it's not here. Did you take it? Did you give it to someone? Did you give it to DuMonchet? It had to go somewhere. Where? Tell me. I have expenses. There are people who want it. I need it. It is mine!"

Marc shook his head dumbly.

Allie entered the conversation. She wanted to prolong this interchange, hoping that Carrera would arrive and save them. But, how would he arrive? If he stormed into the room, Leigh might be panicked and hurt someone else, "Mr. Leigh, I can assure you that we have nothing that belongs to you. Why don't you put down that gun and let's sort this out."

"Yes, Lazlo. We don't want to deprive you of whatever it is that you are missing. I'm sure we can sort it out," Pascal's voice was soft and soothing, but it seemed only to enrage Leigh more.

"You, you! Oh, no, Pascal. Oh, no! You and your perfect gallery! You and your perfect artists! You and your perfect everything! You think you are so very smart! The way you got all the best artists." Lazlo sneered and spoke through clenched teeth, "Who do you think you are? You always thought you were better than me! What makes you think you can tell me what to do? Oh, no! I am not going to listen to you. Not this time. This time, I win!"

Marc stepped forward, voice calm and placating, "Now, Lazlo. I don't know what happened to it, but I'll help you look. If the art was sold, maybe it was just passed along with the art. Those buyers wouldn't have any idea that it was there. Maybe we can save it somehow. Let's see if we can find a way.

"If it was sold . . .? But, he never showed it. He never hung it. How could he have sold it? What happened to it? Something's fishy somewhere!"

"I don't know, but I'll find out. You know that Pascal and these women know nothing. Pascal never knew that the stuff was in the art.

Only you and I knew. You know that."

"Yes. That might be so. But what about these people?" Leigh waved the gun in the direction of Maggie, Allie and Pascal, "What should I do with them? They know too much. I can't let them go."

Marc smiled and spoke softly, "Lazlo, of course not. I can do it. Just let me deal with them. I know how. I'll take care of them!"

"Sure, sure you will. Just like you took care of DuMonchet. He came back and now everything is lost!" Leigh's sneer was even more ugly than before and his voice rose.

"I know. I know. But this time I'll really get rid of them. I know how. You don't want to know what I'll do. You'll never know. They will just disappear. No one will know what happened. We'll find the stuff. You can go back to your regular life. Everything will work out the way you want it to."

Allie held her breath. Should she say something? What could she say? "Mr. Leigh, tell us exactly what you want. If we can we will help you. There has to be a way that we can help."

But Leigh was not to be diverted. Again he waved the gun, "I can do it right now. I'll just take care of them now. They've caused me too much trouble! If they don't know where the stuff is, they're useless to me!"

"No, Lazlo. Not here. Too many questions if it happens here. Let me take care of it. I know how to make it all go away. I'll find a better way this time. I can take them out through the back here. I'll lose thm in the glades. No problem. No one will see. No one will ever know. Then we can track down the stuff. We'll find it."

Lazlo wavered, "Maybe. But, you know, it would make me feel really good to do away with this one." He smiled and pointed the gun at Pascal. "This one has been a thorn in my side for a long time, taking my business, stealing the best artists, trying to be so perfect. Yes, I think I'll take care of this one myself. It would make me very happy to do it. You can handle the women." With that he pointed the gun directly at Pascal.

Maggie could see his finger tightening on the trigger. She held her breath, afraid to make a sound. She wasn't aware of it, but she must have squeezed her eyes closed. Because, just then many things happened at once. The gun fired. Maggie's eyes shot open. What she saw caused her heart to stop. Marc had thrown himself in front of Pascal and now Marc lay on the floor, blood oozing from his body. The door from the gallery flew open and suddenly Carrera was there holding Lazlo's arms behind his back. The ugly gun lay on the floor.

Pascal knelt beside Marc. Marc's eyes fluttered open and he smiled and, through clenched teeth, said, "Well, old man. It looks like my memory did come back, just like the doc said. I couldn't let Lazlo do you in, you know. You're one of the good guys." Marc paused, closed his eyes, grimaced, and passed out.

Both Pascal and Maggie knelt beside Duane. Only then did Maggie notice a wound on his head that was oozing blood, "Oh, Duane!" Turning to Pascal, "Will he be okay?"

Pascal felt Duane's pulse and said, "I hope so. Lazlo hit him when he came into the room."

Allie took a breath, reached in her purse for her cell phone and dialed 911 for an ambulance.

Carrera slipped cuffs on Lazlo and pushed him onto a chair.

Then, suddenly, the gallery was filled with police and DEA officers.

The Costa Mira police and the DEA investigators took charge of the gallery yet one more time. Questions were asked and answered. The ambulance arrived and Marc, who had saved Pascal's life, was transported to the hospital along with Duane who was just beginning to wake up. Finally, after what seemed hours of questioning, Pascal, Maggie and Allie stepped out of the gallery into the cool night air.

Maggie's eyes turned toward the velvety night sky, "Oh, my! I am so very happy to see this sky and this beautiful night."

Allie clutched her hand, "Yeah, Mom. Me, too. Isn't it good to be alive and to be free!"

Pascal echoed their sentiments and then, after a long pause, "Ah, er, Maggie, ah, there is so much I'd like to say. I mean, why did you come into the workroom? Ah, I think we need to talk."

Maggie stood quite still. Then, still clutching Allie's hand, "Yes, Pascal, perhaps we all need to talk. I mean, we've had even one more scary time together. I think it deserves to be talked out. Don't you?"

Now it was Pascal's turn to stand still, "Ah, yes. I guess that is so. But not on the street. Shall we go to my house?"

Maggie spoke slowly and quietly, "You know, I think we should go to my house. I'd feel better there. Is that okay with you?"

"Of course."

Chapter Seventeen

When they arrived at Maggie's condo, Pascal called the hospital to inquire about Duane and Marc. He was told that Duane was being treated in the Emergency Room for a head injury and that he would be released that same night. They said that Marc had sustained a bullet wound to his shoulder and that while it was serious, he was expected to recover.

Lounging on Maggie's deep, comfy white sofa, with Pascal equally at ease in her easy chair, they reviewed the events of the evening. Then Allie rose and excused herself, "It's late and none of us has had any dinner. I don't know about you, but my tummy is growling. I'm going to put something together. Would you like wine?"

Even Pascal shook his head no and she left for the kitchen. Maggie started to rise to help her and Allie motioned her to sit still. Gratefully Maggie sank back into the sofa. Would her knees ever stop shaking?

Pascal and Maggie continued their conversation. Before they knew it, Allie reappeared with a pretty tray of sandwiches, fruit and cookies from Maggie's larder. She poured tea for everyone.

Finally, the knot in Maggie's stomach began to loosen up, "I cannot tell you how very happy I am to be here with you both. I wasn't sure we'd make it this time. But, thanks to Marc, Pascal, you are here with us, uninjured."

Pascal nodded, "Yes, thanks to Marc. He did regain his memory, didn't he?"

Now Maggie nodded, "I saw it happen there on the beach. Now I know he was looking at Lazlo, but then I couldn't be sure who it was. I just knew that he had remembered something about Veronique's death. I could see it in his face."

"Yes, I think you are correct. I, too, saw something happen to him there. From that moment I don't think Lazlo had a chance. And, I think he must have suspected it."

Allie asked, "How do you think Marc is? Will he be okay? I mean, he really saved us all. Don't you think he intended to let us go, to rescue us from Lazlo?"

Pascal answered, "Oh, yes. I'm sure of it. He stepped right in front of that bullet. I'll check on him tomorrow. The hospital doesn't seem to be terribly upset about his condition. But, he has been through quite a lot." After a long silence, Pascal continued, "Of course, I am not a doctor, but, I believe that something happened to Marc during his ordeal on the boat. Didn't you think he seemed different? I mean, there in the workroom. It seemed to me that he must have been trying to shield us from danger, to save us from Lazlo."

Allie nodded, "Absolutely! I believe he intended to get us out of there and then release us. He threw himself in front of you, Pascal. He took that bullet for you. I have no doubt that he intended to save us. I'm sure of it."

Maggie agreed, "Yes, I think so, too. But what a transformation from that guy who kidnapped us onto the boat! Really, it is quite amazing."

They chatted on into the night. Finally, Pascal rose, expressed his thanks and left.

They returned to the sofa and Maggie turned to Allie, "Sweetie, I need to ask your forgiveness."

Allie's brow rose in question.

"I was rash and impetuous leading us into that backroom. I put you in danger and I'll never be able to forgive myself for doing that. It was a thoughtless and stupid thing to do. It was arrogance on my part. I can't believe I did it. Can you forgive me?"

Allie reached for her mother's hand, "Oh, Mom. Of course.

There is nothing to forgive. You were just caught up in the moment. You had figured it out and you were concerned about Pascal. You made me think of the elephant's child who was filled with 'satiable curiosity." Allie squeezed her mother's hand and gave her a reassuring smile.

Maggie smiled ruefully, "Well, 'satiable curiosity got the elephant in trouble and I'm afraid it did us, too."

Allie continued, "Who knows? If we hadn't gone back there, it might have turned out more tragically. Lazlo was ready to kill Pascal. He really seemed to hate him. He must have been jealous of Pascal for a long time. If we hadn't gone in there when we did, he might have done so right then. Maybe you bought Pascal a little time. If the timing had been even a little different, there could have been a very different outcome. It is possible that you saved Pascal's life. I love you, Mom. I was concerned about you, you know. I didn't want you to get hurt. I think we were just lucky. Anyway, there's nothing to forgive. We're okay now." She smiled at her mother.

Although she wasn't completely reassured, Maggie hugged this daughter whom she loved so much.

This time there was an armed uniformed guard sitting outside of Marc's room. Pascal was told that Marc was expected to make a full recovery. He learned that Duane had been treated in the emergency room for the blow to his head and sent home well after midnight.

"Hello, Marc. How are you feeling this morning?"

"Hello, old man. Not too bad considering someone put a hole in my shoulder. They tell me I should be up and about before long."

"Ah, that is good news, no?"

"Yes, I suppose so. How are you, old man?"

"I am well, Marc. This has not been an easy time for us, has it?"

"No. Not easy. But, maybe it has been necessary."

"Necessary?"

"Yes, old man. I do not understand it. But it seems that I have come out of a sort of fog that I was in for a long time. I don't understand it. But, there it is."

Pascal nodded, "In what way, a fog?"

"It is not easy to talk about. It seems as if it was an old fog of anger and resentment. I can remember my life before, my life filled with anger. I can remember making bad decisions and doing some pretty dastardly things. But, it almost is as if it wasn't me. I mean, I remember making the choices I did. I know I made a lot of serious mistakes. I remember that I was angry, angry about a lot of things. But, somehow now, I can't relate to myself as I was then. I don't know. It seems very strange. It is almost as if my life before was a dream and I finally woke up." Mark stopped, looked Pascal in the eye and shook his head.

Pascal cleared his throat, "Ah, Marc. I don't know what to make of it either. But, it does sound as if you have had a sort of breakthrough." He turned his head and wiped tears from his eyes.

Marc's voice became hoarse, "Old man, I am sorry for all the grief I have caused you. I regret the grief I caused many people, but especially my parents, Veronique and you. It is true, old man, you are one of the good ones."

"That is kind of you to say, Marc."

"I say it because it is so. You know, I saw him murder little Veronique. She overheard us talking about the drugs and she was very angry. It was during that argument that you came into the office and that Lazlo hit you over the head. You cannot imagine how much more upset Veronique became. She had her hand on the phone to call the police and Lazlo just walked around the desk, grabbed the letter opener and stabbed her. Ah, old man! I cannot tell you how sad it made me. It made me sad, but somehow I turned that into more anger. It was a generalized anger, not directed at Lazlo, as it should have been, but just anger. I promised him I would dispose of you and that is how you came to be locked up in that shed."

Marc paused and took a deep breath that caused him to grimace and ease his shoulder, "Lazlo needed money. I guess his gallery was not doing well and he had a big fancy house. He thought dealing the drugs would be the answer. You know, he was not very good as an art dealer. I think he always was jealous of you."

"When I came here it was because I needed a place to hide from Immigration. Veronique was kind to me, but I could tell that she had reservations about me. No wonder. I had caused her a lot of trouble in the past. Anyway, I met Lazlo on my second day here. Why he thought I would help with the drug deal, I don't know, but he offered me a cut of the proceeds if I would field it out of your gallery. I guess he was afraid to do it from his own. So, that is how it started. It made me some money, enough for me to rent a room and eat. I think it made Lazlo a lot."

"You see, I remember these things. I remember the things I did all my life. But, I cannot now relate to the person I was, the person who did all those things. As I said, it is like a bad dream." Marc paused for a moment, "You know, old man, it almost is as if I have had a second birth day."

The conversation continued for a while with Marc filling in missing details for Pascal.

The sun had burned off the early morning mist by the time Allie and Maggie were up. Allie gave a sigh of pure pleasure as she took the first sip of her morning tea, "Now, this is the life. Warm sun, cool air, no worries, no threats, and, most of all, no mystery! Life is good."

Maggie set her teacup on the table and stretched her arms above her head, "So true. I am glad that we are here now and that there is nothing else to worry about."

"With Lazlo Leigh safely behind bars, I think we are as safe as we can be." Allie sighed, "Well, Mom, I should make arrangements to get back home and start working again."

Maggie's brow furrowed, "I wish you could stay a little longer. Maybe we could just hang out for a while with no stress." She grinned a wicked little grin, "We could go back to Millie's and sing!"

"Sounds like fun! But you go first!" Allie's grin matched her mother's. "I really do need to get back to it. Gabe probably won't even know me."

"Oh, I understand. Even with all the stress, it has been great having you here. Truly, I couldn't have gotten through all this without you. I'll miss you when you're gone."

"Me, too. But that is life."

After a long silence, Allie said, "Mom? What about Pascal? Did you two have a good conversation while I was making snacks last night?"

"Er, no. I mean, yes. We talked about what had happened. You know, just as we did when you were there."

"Oh. I got the impression that Pascal wanted to say something more. You know, about the two of you."

"I don't think so. And if he had, I wouldn't have known what to say."

"But, Mom, aren't you fond of him?"

"Sure, as a friend. But, I'm really not looking for anything else right now. I'm too busy with life to seek anything more."

"But, Mom. Do you want to be alone all your life?"

"Oh, Allie, honey. No, I guess not. I would need to find someone really, really special."

Allie sighed, "And Pascal is not special enough?"

"I don't know. Probably not. He's very nice and I like him a lot. But, I like him as a friend." Maggie sat in thought for a long while, "I guess it may be that I've worked very hard to put my life together and to be independent. Not just financially self-sufficient, but also emotionally self-sufficient. I've learned how to do 'alone' and it has not been an easy lesson. I think it would take someone extraordinary to make me want to give that up."

Their conversation was interrupted by the telephone.

"Hello. Oh, hello, Pascal." Maggie listened for a minute, "Of course, do come right over." Maggie hung up and turned to Allie, "He's coming over. Said he just visited Marc and he wants to tell us about it."

Pascal arrived at lunch time with carryout Thai food. They made a picnic on Maggie's coffee table. He told them that he had talked to Duane who had a sore head, but who was feeling his old self and was ready to get back to work.

During the meal, Pascal related to them what he had learned from Marc, "Marc cleared up one small mystery. He had taken Veronique's gallery key and had copies made. He gave a copy to Lazlo, so that is how Lazlo was able to break into the gallery."

Allie finished a mouthful of Panang curry and asked, "How is Marc physically? Will he be in the hospital long? I don't know anything about gunshot wounds, but they have to be pretty serious. I mean, they can kill someone!"

Pascal smiled, "Yes, they can, Allie. But Marc was lucky. This one entered his shoulder and passed through without doing much damage. They say there are no complications. He will have pain for some time, but basically, it is not considered serious and he should be able to leave the hospital in a few days."

"Then what?" Allie asked.

"Then what, indeed! I imagine he will be returned to the recovery center for a while, and then, probably jail."

"Oh, poor Marc. Not something for him to look forward to,"

Maggie said.

"No, it's not. It's not a pretty picture, is it?"

"Not in the least."

Allie commented, "That Lazlo Leigh! What a nasty man! Mom and I thought he was unpleasant from the beginning. But, we just didn't know how nasty he was!"

"Yes. I guess there can be no doubt now that Leigh was behind everything. With Marc's eye witness account of all that happened, Lazlo probably will be put away for life."

"What exactly are the charges against Marc?"

Pascal sighed, "Ah, there are the drug dealing charges, and then there's kidnapping, first me, and then all of us, stealing the boat, and, oh, illegal entry into the country. I'm not sure what all that adds up to legally, but it's a lot. The thing is, Marc understands things are not good. But he's resigned to whatever comes. It is almost as if he feels he needs to pay his dues."

Maggie questioned, "It sounds as if Marc has made a huge change inside himself?"

"Ah, yes, Maggie. I do believe he has. In all his life I never have seen him so genuinely contrite. It is amazing to me that his attitude, no, not just his attitude, more his whole being, seems dramatically changed. It is almost as if he is a different person. It is not easy to describe. The anger that he carried throughout his life seems to have evaporated. He appears to be truly transformed. There is an aura of, I'm not sure what, of peace, I guess."

Maggie commented, "Transformation can happen. People can change. I wouldn't have become a therapist if I didn't believe that, but this is a pretty dramatic change. Almost like a miracle."

Allie spoke thoughtfully, "Of all the charges against him, if he truly has changed, if he truly is remorseful, is there punishment that is less severe? Is there any way he could be charged with fewer things?"

"I'm not sure, Allie. Maybe. Maybe, if we didn't press charges, maybe the kidnapping could be avoided. The boat is back and has been repaired. So, if the owners are satisfied, maybe the theft of the boat could be avoided. But, even so, at the very least, there's illegal immigration and drug dealing. Not small charges. With only those two charges, I'm not sure if he would be prosecuted here or if they would extradite him. Or both. Poor Marc!"

"Yes. Poor Marc," Maggie agreed. "Do you think he could get

a reduced sentence by testifying against Lazlo? He was an eye-witness, after all. And, he did save your life. That should count for something." She raised her eyebrows toward Pascal.

"That is possible perhaps. I'm not a lawyer. I'll ask Eliot Grayson to recommend someone good."

The three friends concluded their discussion with coconut ice cream.

After Pascal left, Maggie and Allie sat on the condo balcony looking out over the landscaped lawn with its grove of tall coconut palms. In the distance the sky dissolved into a soft blue that portended the ocean. Tilly circled and settled herself on Maggie's lap. "Mom?"

"Yes?"

"Mom, I've been wondering. I mean, what happened to Hadi? We haven't heard anything from him for a long time."

Maggie's brow furrowed, "I've been wondering the same thing. He is such a mystery to me. Somehow I'm surprised he didn't show up during this last scary thing."

"Me, too. Do you think we've seen the last of him?"

Maggie sighed, "I don't know. He has been a big part of our adventures, but I never thought he would be there always. I don't know."

Allie said thoughtfully, "Perhaps he has been with us just to help us learn some things and perhaps when he thinks he has done that, he will go. I mean, he has always said that we cannot be separated. Why do you suppose he's always said that?"

Maggie smiled and shrugged, "Oh, darling, I just don't know."

"It seems as if we spend a lot of time in airports," Maggie complained, looking around at the crowded waiting room.

Allie shifted her tote bag to another shoulder, "Yes, that's so. Mom, even with all the things that happened, it has been great. We have had quite an adventure. Something to tell our grandchildren!" Allie changed the subject, "You know, we are invited out to Sally Livingston's ranch. Want to go?"

Maggie grinned, "Of course. When do you think we should do it?"

"I'm not sure. Let me talk to her. I had the idea that the ranch wasn't quite ready yet for guests. I'm guessing not before fall. In any event we don't want to be there in the summer heat. I think we'd be sort of shakedown guests for her when the ranch is ready. So, while it would be a nice vacation for us, it could help them as well. Shall we plan for it?"

"Let's. Dry land sounds great after this last adventure!"

"Oh, Mom. I do love you!"

"Me too. Love you, sweetie."